a mother's

KISSES

Also by Bruce Jay Friedman

Novels
STERN
A MOTHER'S KISSES
THE DICK
ABOUT HARRY TOWNS
TOKYO WOES
THE CURRENT CLIMATE
A FATHER'S KISSES

Collections
FAR FROM THE CITY OF CLASS
BLACK ANGELS
LET'S HEAR IT FOR A BEAUTIFUL GUY
BLACK HUMOR
THE COLLECTED SHORT FICTION
EVEN THE RHINOS WERE NYMPHOS

Plays
SCUBA DUBA
STEAMBATH

Nonfiction
THE LONELY GUY'S BOOK OF LIFE
THE SLIGHTLY OLDER GUY

a mother's

KISSES

*a novel by
Bruce Jay Friedman*

THE UNIVERSITY OF CHICAGO PRESS
CHICAGO AND LONDON

For Josh, Drew, and Kipp

The University of Chicago Press, Chicago 60637
The University of Chicago Press, Ltd., London
Copyright © 1964 by Bruce Jay Friedman
Introduction Copyright © 1985 by Stanley Kauffmann
All rights reserved. Originally published 1964
University of Chicago Press edition 2000
Printed in the United States of America
05 04 03 02 01 00   6 5 4 3 2 1

Library of Congress Cataloging-in-Publication Data

Friedman, Bruce Jay, 1930–
    A mother's kisses : a novel / by Bruce Jay Friedman.—University of Chicago Press ed.
        p.   cm.
    ISBN 0-226-26416-5 (pbk. : acid-free paper)
    1. Brooklyn (New York, N.Y.)—Fiction. 2. Mothers and sons—Fiction. 3. College
students—Fiction. 4. Jewish families—Fiction. 5. Teenage boys—Fiction. 6.
Kansas—Fiction. I. Title

PS3556.R5 M6   2000
813´.54—dc21   00-033772

♾ The paper used in this publication meets the minimum requirements of the American
National Standard for Information Sciences–Permanence of Paper for Printed Library
Materials, ANSI Z39.48-1992.

introduction

There is an ironic relation between the history of the novel and the fate of modern novelists. The novel grew with the growth of the middle class; now the middle class has become the world and, in its size, weight, self-satisfaction and spiritual torpor, is settling back comfily on its own invention, the novel, squashing it. Under that broad rump, the young novelist is jabbing away desperately with every pin at his disposal.

Two years ago Bruce Jay Friedman, a New Yorker, produced a novel called *Stern*, which explored—at a comic-pathetic sideways angle—the plight of a man who has all the psychic equipment and needs of the contemporary non-hero and is also a Jew. This slyly truthful book established, from its first page, that Friedman, whatever his faults, had what authors want and readers long for: a tonality, a voice of his own—disturbing, live, endearing. One could not read *Stern* without remembering it tenderly and also being a bit apprehensive of what the author would next treat with merciless compassion. Last year Friedman's *Far from the City of Class* appeared. It was a collection of stories, written over the preceding ten years, of mixed quality but generally of appetizing perception. Now he has developed themes of three of those stories in his second novel, *A Mother's Kisses*, and he has plentifully justified readers' somewhat nervous anticipation. This is a horror comedy of an ambivalent mother-son relationship in which possessiveness, embarrassment, dependence create a story so resonant with sexual depths that to cite the Oedipus complex as its base is like observing that there are tides in the ocean.

It takes place shortly after World War II and deals with the seventeenth summer of Joseph, a Brooklyn boy just graduated from high school, as he looks for a college that will accept him, works as a camp waiter, finally goes to a small cow-college in Kansas. These much-used materials of adolescent travail are jounced out of familiarity and into continual uproar by Joseph's mother, who has browbeaten the camp into taking him as a waiter, browbeats the director into quasi-apology when Joseph steals some money, uses her ample wiles on a goatish old man to get her son accepted in the Kansas college, accompanies Joseph to college for his first weeks, brings him sweaters in class, picks up men in the hotel bar. When Joseph finally persuades her to leave, he shouts after the departed train, "You're not great at all. I never enjoyed one second with you." But we know that she is like a mortifyingly aggressive, loud-mouthed goddess who has relentlessly taken care of him.

Her diction is a furious mixture of Molly Goldberg, boardwalk auctioneer and backseat tease. ". . . You're such a child. . . . Did your mother ever let you down? . . . Will you please learn to put your last buck down on this baby? . . . What happened, darling? Girls didn't devour you? . . . Go downstairs right this second in the lobby that I just arrived here and nobody's supposed to know I'm alive." She is the mother bred by centuries of closeted Jewish tradition, now released into an America of conning and cunning, still fiercely protective of her child in a cagily wanton yet almost masculine way.

Friedman, not content to tip over Whistler's mother's chair, uses his book like a steel whip on some cozy acceptances of family and social life. He has no use for the tremulous novel of adolescence that celebrates an aspirant young soul bruised by the world's crassness. He interests us in Joseph by two means: the boy's negative actions and the book's prose. Joseph's tyro-connoisseur procedures with willing girls, restrained by a secret fastidiousness; his despair at being rejected by Columbia University that finds an outlet in irrational pilfering; his impatience with his shadowy, stupid father; his behavior toward his mother, compounded of flesh-crawling shame and fearful respect for a Titan who governs the stars in their courses—these are some of the elements that create a protagonist who, without enouncing an ideal or yearning for much more than popularity and acceptance, becomes a human being for whom we wish the best.

Friedman's style may be described as wry Salinger without (in Koestler's epithet) the stink of Zen. His dialogue is precise without being phonographic; in fact, he is especially skillful at implication, at indicating movement, pause, facial expression by words omitted, by phrase curved neatly into place. Friedman does not merely narrate or describe. Everything is converted into vernacular images that try to stun us.

The risk in this method (as with Salinger, to some extent) is that we read each sentence as if we were watching a performer, applauding when he does the trick, wincing when he doesn't. The book is sprinkled with many small sparklers: a runner's stitching pain "like loose glass in his ribs," a grandmother whose "sole activities were knitting and slumping over into dozes," a girl at a dance who is "fragrantly clammy." But there are also strains and excesses like "his voice took leave of him, broke into a faded crackle like sandwiches being wrapped behind a far-off door."

Friedman's writing belongs to the new school of vaudeville Americana. He spins figures of speech like Indian clubs. He is a show-off who makes his truth precisely by showing off, who achieves poignancy by the very indirection of his bravura. When this method succeeds—as, by and large, it does here—it is insidiously moving because of its transparent hip pretense that it is not concerned to move us. By pushing forward with every iota of egotism, taking the center of the stage with all his talents awhirl, Friedman creates a flashy, sad art that finally belongs to the characters and the reader, with the author shyly hidden behind his own glitter.

—Stanley Kauffmann
From *Life*, August 21, 1964

book one

Once, when he was five, a Negro woman had been assigned to watch him through the summer, allowing him to wander only twenty paces in each direction. Each time he reached the edge of a building and tried to go around it she would rein him back to her side. He spent the summer a lidless city pavement animal, tied to a chain, wheeling drugged and lazy in the sun. Now, twelve years later, it seemed to Joseph that he was chained again and that there was nothing to do but stand in front of his apartment house and stretch and try to breathe and wait for the days to pass. There did not seem to be any way for him to get off by himself around some corner. He had finished high school and sent out applications to two colleges for the fall, Columbia and Bates, the latter because he liked the name. Once, at a summer resort, he had watched a short scrappy fellow with heavy thighs play basketball, staying all over his man, hollering out catcalls, giving his opponent no quarter. The fellow said he went to Bates and Joseph had come to think of the school as a scrappy little heavy-thighed college full of fast little fellows who pressed their opponents. He chose Columbia in case the out-of-town school rejected him for not being scrappy enough.

Although Joseph did very well in high school, he did not get very much in the way of college guidance. All such assistance came under the direction of a folksy old hygiene teacher named Pop Frebble who walked with a cane; when Joseph approached him in the hall one day about colleges, he winced and held his side as though the question had slashed at his hip. It was understood that each term Pop Frebble took only two boys under his wing for guidance, the one with the best grades in the eight-hundred-man graduating class and the fellow with the keenest sense of union arbitration problems, since Frebble had excellent connections with an upstate labor school and could slip any man he wanted to into its freshman ranks. It was generally felt that two careers were about as many as you could expect a folksy old man with a hip condition to oversee; all other graduates knew that they were to fend for themselves. When Joseph asked his mother about college, she said, "The money will be there."

"I don't mean that. I don't know which ones to send off to."

"Don't worry about the money," she said. "We'll get it somehow. It'll be there."

And so Joseph stood pat with his original two college ideas. One day a letter arrived from Bates, slightly astonished that he should want to go to it and informing him that the freshman quota was full. Joseph consoled himself with the thought that there was nothing really substantial behind all those scrappy hollering fellows out at Bates and that scrappiness would be of little use off the basketball court, in a room, for example, when you were trying to read or talk. He settled back, waiting to hear from Columbia. Of his ten neighborhood friends, eight or nine had already been accepted by various out-of-town schools and had lit out for summer resorts to work as waiters and earn money for their tuitions; only two people he knew remained behind in the city, one a boy named Himber who was going to be a doctor and had decided to get a head start by putting in a summer learning facts.

"I'll have you a contest on names of Cabinet members, Wilson to Roosevelt's second term," he said to Joseph in the street. "Up in my room this afternoon."

"What good are they going to do you?" asked Joseph.

"I just want to know them, as many as I can learn. What's the capital of Ecuador? Southern Rhodesia?"

Joseph brushed off Himber, but had a premonition one day that the boy might be right and spent an evening memorizing names of hydroelectric projects.

The other neighborhood person remaining in the city was a girl named Eileen Fastner who had matured early and was nicknamed "Fasty"; in junior high school she was always being brought home drooling by hygiene teachers after having been violated by rowdies in the school clothing closet. In recent years, however, she had straightened out and was now a comely brunette with shiny hair and a sophisticated manner, one semester of Syracuse already tucked beneath her belt. Joseph whiled away some of his days sunbathing on the roof of his apartment building; she would take a chair next to him, lowering her halter straps sophisticatedly and giving him leads on what to expect in the way of freshman Beowulf lectures. But she was still "Fasty" to him and he could not erase the picture of those post-clothing-closet marches at the side of hygiene teachers.

Joseph was a tall and scattered-looking boy with an Indian nose; sometimes, as he sat on the burning tar of the apartment building roof, he wondered whether he should be sending off applications to other colleges, ones whose catalogue names had a good ring to them. Wouldn't Duke, for example, be a fine-sounding, masculine kind of place to tell people you were going to. And Bowdoin, which was right next to Bates in the catalogue and might turn out to be just as scrappy, only in a quiet, more scholarly way. Why not get one off to Colgate, a scrubbed and beaming, crew-cut place, and Bucknell, too, brash, white-sneak-ered and cocky as a pup. How about more contemplative-sounding ones, Brown, for example, a leafy poetic place, good for taking nostalgic walks through low-hanging leaf arbors. It seemed to him that almost any of those fine-sounding places would do very nicely; but since he had told Bates that he had wanted to go to it ever since he was a child ("Why do you want to go to Bates?"), he could not bring himself to inform Ithaca and Carnegie Tech he had been thirsting to attend them, too. Besides, his one turndown had been wounding; he felt certain that something in the tone of his applications would tip off Kent State and Oberlin that he was a Bates reject. Perhaps Bates had gotten out a circular on all its castoffs, mailing it to the other scrappy schools in its hustling little conference.

And so he waited for Columbia, bored and stifled, unable to find a place to put himself, the Bensonhurst sun gnawing a warm circle on top of his head. Sometimes, when the hot roof cinders filled his nose, he would take long oppressive walks to a track inside an abandoned stadium and jog around it until a stitching pain, like loose glass in his ribs, forced him to stop and sit alone in the ruined box seats. Or he would stroll for miles in the patched shade of an el, trains screaming above his head, hoping to wind up somewhere lovely, perhaps on the rolling scented lawns of Rollins College or in Hamilton's cool tradi-tion-haunted halls. Other days he would stand opposite an end-less railroad yard, listening to the squawk and clatter of nearby power generators, feeling a little bad he did not really know what all the machinery was for; people who did were ushered warmly into Bates and Antioch and Purdue. All he seemed to be good at was feeling flat and lonely standing next to such things; he knew how to smell them and get their carbon flakes in his mouth. Sometimes he would wind up the afternoons sitting on a giant stone courthouse lion; when he was a child, leaps from its neck to the pavement had seemed courageous death-defying plunges, but now his feet dangled over, almost touching the concrete paws. The lion, the railroad yard, the abandoned track—all were boyhood relics; he seemed to have them laid out like infield bases, running around them, stepping on them one last time as though he could then gather up the lot in a bag and present them as an admission ticket to the gates of one of those wondrous, faraway places such as Tufts or Coe or S.M.U.

Often he tried to stretch his sleep so that he could perhaps skip a day; once his mother put her head into the covers and said, "Why not a date with the Fastner girl? She turned out nice and there's money."

"I remember things about her and I've got to have a college before girls."

"I'm having some time with you," she said. "They tell me daughters are hard. They never heard of boys."

When there seemed no way to sleep through the whole summer, he would walk out of the apartment, often meeting the fact-gathering Himber's mother in the elevator. Her son had been accepted by Rochester University, one of the few catalogue names that sounded unappetizing to Joseph, a slatelike and industrial place of little mystery. But in her mind, all other boys in the Western world were frustrated Rochester applicants.

"Dickie's set for Rochester," she said once. "What about you?"

"I don't know yet."

"They can't take everybody. It's one of those things. I wouldn't brood about it. There are plenty of other good colleges, and you can't always get what you want. Have you heard Dickie on dates of great battles?"

"Not yet," Joseph answered.

The drugstore was a good place to slouch and languish and trace pictures on the counter in the wet overflow of sodas. But Shep Varnes, the proprietor, had a son who was to start Southern Cal in the fall. Varnes's brother, a man who made rims on panties, had gotten him in for engineering, using West Coast political influence. In the drugstore, knowing Joseph's plight, he would run his hand through the boy's hair and chuck him under the chin, cheering him along by saying "C'mon" and "Awwww" and "Hey, boy." But Joseph knew he hadn't chin-chucked and hey-boyed his own son. What he'd done for *him* was to go on his knees to his panty-rim brother and plead him into college; that's what he'd done.

"Get close to your father," Joseph's mother said to him. "This is a good time for it."

The father was a quiet man who worked on sectional couches. One morning Joseph awakened early to accompany him to his plant, crusty-eyed, dressing glumly in the dusk, feeling he was going to a hospital. His father stopped at the corner to buy a newspaper and said, "I buy a paper here." In the subway car he said, "I usually stand at this end and hold on to a strap."

He took Joseph up to a great gray loft full of couch skeletons, steering him directly over to a machine. "This cuts couches," he said to Joseph. He flipped it on, letting it slice a piece of couch in half.

"It's plenty sharp, isn't it? I use that machine a lot. If you go over and fool around with it, I'll smack you."

When they had taken off their coats, Joseph's father went right to work, spreading a large piece of paper on a table and writing on it. "I draw up my couch on this and then I do the couch right next to the table here."

His father's boss came over then and put his hand on Joseph's shoulder, his eyes at the ceiling.

"What do you want to be when you're ready?" he asked, looking past Joseph to the end of the loft.

"I don't think I want to be in couch work," said Joseph.

The boss seemed greatly relieved. He began to dart about excitedly, finally picking up a piece of leather and handing it to Joseph. "Here, kid," he said. "Keep it. Take it home with you." Then he said to Joseph's father, "You got a nice son there. Smart boy."

Joseph's father worked a while on his paper, then said, "The fellow I'm going to bring over now, I'm the boss of him."

A terribly round-shouldered Greek man approached. "This is Freddy," Joseph's father said. "He works for me."

The man gave Joseph a wringing-wet hand. "Hi, kid. I work for your dad."

When the man walked away, Joseph's father whispered, "He only makes ninety-eight a week. Imagine that."

At lunchtime, Joseph and his father had a sandwich at a crowded counter nearby. The older man tossed down his last few bites, then began to walk briskly back toward his office, finally breaking into a trot. "I only take a fast bite," he said to Joseph, who was trotting by his side. When he got back to the loft, the father flung off his coat, looking warily about him, then buried his head in his planning paper. At the end of the day, closing up the loft, Joseph's father locked the front door and said, "I've been in the couch game for twenty-seven years." Then on the subway, he said to Joseph, "Now is when I read my paper."

That night, after dinner, Joseph and his father walked silently across the park, finally ducking into a neighborhood movie to break the tension. Inside the theater, Joseph saw the fact-gathering Himber and Fasty together on a side aisle; he slid down in his seat, not wanting them to know he went to movies with a father and no girl.

Sitting next to his silent couch-making dad that night, it seemed to Joseph that outside the streets rocked and thundered with news of children who had smashed down the barriers of proud Villanova, been welcomed warmly into snowy Colorado U. Great armies of proud-breasted aunts patrolled the city, all abuzz with stories of nephews who were "going up to Maine," nieces "heading down to Miami." As he walked home later with his father, one such woman stopped them, told of a grandson who'd be "on his way to Lehigh" in September, then asked, "Where is your boy going out to in the fall?"

"I don't know," Joseph's father chuckled. "He hasn't said a word to me about it yet. Where are you going, kid?"

"To some college," Joseph said.

How he yearned to be one of those nephews and nieces going up to, down to and out to some golden, fragrant knowledge-heavy institution. How he longed even to be "burrowing underground to," "working his way overland toward," or even "sailing across the damned ocean in the direction of" one of those fine proud catalogue places.

To duck people, Joseph spent the next three days indoors wearing a bathrobe. It was a tradition in his family to get right into one during periods of crisis. Once, during the only extended quarrel Joseph could remember his parents' having, his mother had stayed in one for a month. It broke up a romance of his. He had been standing on the sidewalk about to kiss a twig-thin dark-haired girl who lived in the next building and whose father had recently been snatched off to prison as a forger; out of the corner of his eye he spotted his mother making her way up the hill wearing the bathrobe. He hadn't counted on her making a street appearance in the robe and hoped she would cross to the other side. But she moved forward, irrevocably, until the thin girl spotted her.

"Why does your mother wear bathrobes downstairs?"

17

"She just wears them," he said, knowing the romance had been snapped off right there.

Those three bathrobed days, Joseph dreamed that in some miraculous way wonderful catalogue colleges would learn of people such as himself, leftover boys with special qualities, hailing them forward grandly under a special no-application-needed quota. Each morning, with bathrobe tightly furled about him, he would go downstairs to the family mailbox slot to peer inside for Columbia letters; but he kept one tense and lonely eye out, too, for the friendly, outgoing letterhead of Nevada Southern, the prim ascetic seal of Claremont Men's.

On one such morning Joseph's mother followed him to the mail slot in a robe of her own and said, "All right, that settles it. No more having a crazy son. I'm taking a place in the country and getting you into a camp across the lake. There'll be health and getting your mind off colleges. I've had enough of you in that bathrobe."

"I'm not budging until I've got Columbia straightened out. How can I go to the country when I'm not going anywhere yet?"

"Instead of fainting here you'll faint at the camp. I'm going to go upstairs and start getting into my girdle."

In the apartment Joseph's mother asked, "Have you seen my girdle around?"

"No," said Joseph. "And I don't want to know about it either. Why do I have to be brought in on your girdle-wearing?"

"Watch your mouth. Get dressed. I'm taking you over to see Doc Salamandro about the camp. He's tough, but I can handle that kind."

Joseph had heard about Doc Salamandro, the director of Camp Fleetwind, had once seen a picture of him handing over a bag of charity in a local newspaper. He was a short gray-haired man with great bulging legs, who was known to jump up on people's fenders. Once some men had knocked him down and robbed the camp, fleeing in a car. Doc Salamandro had chased them, leaped up on their fender and pummeled the driver through the car window. He did the same thing to some parents who had tried to escape without paying.

On the way to his office, Joseph said, "The only way I'll go to this camp is if I can work there and get some money. It would be nice to have a good hunk in case a miracle happens and I get to go to college somewhere."

"You're always worried about money," she said to Joseph. "You know what money's always meant to me?"

"What's that?"

"Crap."

She took that approach often. But other times, giving Joseph some money, she would say, "Be careful how you spend it. Your father's labor is in every dollar." And she kept her bills crumpled up in sorrowful little black change purses. Whenever she tried to buy Joseph a suit, he would say, "I don't need it," knowing it would have to be paid for with tear-soaked dollars from the little black jobs.

They found Doc Salamandro seated behind a desk in his study, his great trunklike legs up on a console, waving a pencil in time to a Chopin mazurka. He was smiling slightly, but Joseph had the idea that if a movement were to be misinterpreted, he would race out the door, down to the record company and leap right up on the conductor's fenders.

"My son's going crazy over colleges, Doc," said Joseph's mother, "and I'd like to get him into your camp. I've known your wife for years from the neighborhood."

"I'd like to make some money, though," said Joseph, sorry immediately that he had spoken, wondering whether Salamandro would leap up at him.

"You look like a sensible boy," said Salamandro. "I'm making you a professional waiter. They wait on the guests and make a thousand a season. But we'll have to ship you up there as a camper waiter. They're young kids and only make around forty dollars a season. That's so the four professional waiters don't get sore. They've got their deal all set and wouldn't want another boy horning in. But as soon as you get up there I'll tell them and that'll be that. One hundred and forty dollars for uniforms and sweaters and camp equipment. My brother Harley will give you your size in the next room." He picked up the mazurka beat again with the pencil, gesturing with his head toward a box in which Joseph's mother was to put the money.

When she took out one of her purses Joseph called her aside. "I don't want to be out a hundred and forty dollars even before I start," he said. "How do I know I'll even want to stay there?"

"He's worried about money," Joseph's mother shouted over to Doc Salamandro. "I told him money to me has always been crap."

Salamandro smiled, not missing a beat. Joseph said, "What was the sense of my calling you over here if you were going to tell him everything I said?"

"You're at some age."

She counted out the money and put it in the box. Switching the pencil to his other hand, Doc Salamandro took the money out of the box and put it in his pocket. When the record was over he said, "I've got the greatest food of any camp. It'll melt in your mouth, I don't care what camps you've been to. Another thing. Be a sugar boy and we'll get along. Fling horseturds at me and I'll jump right up on your back."

"He's some brilliant guy," Joseph's mother said as they walked to the supply room.

"I didn't see that," said Joseph. "Not brilliance."

"We should all have his head."

Salamandro's brother was a stooped-over man with a sagging, rope-lipped, rabbinical face. "Did you pay the hundred and forty?" he asked. "You look like a thirty-six long. Christ, we're losing a fortune this year."

"How do you know you're losing a fortune when the season hasn't begun?" asked Joseph.

"I just know," he said. "We're getting killed."

Joseph's mother pinched the man's cheek. "I'll bet you'd like to try one of those T shirts on me."

He stooped over, reddening. "There's no money in camps."

On the way out Joseph asked, "Was he brilliant, too?"

"Don't sell him short. He has a head on his shoulders."

"Why did you have to get sexy with him? I didn't see any reason for that."

"You never know," she said. "If you're nice to people you never know when it's going to pay dividends."

That night Joseph sat in his room, hating the Fleetwind clothing, estimating it was worth around twelve dollars. His room was actually part of the apartment kitchen, a small dinette that Joseph's mother had fixed up to look "just like a real room." There was no door separating the dinette and the kitchen, so that when Joseph's mother did some cooking, she would face straight ahead and holler out, "I don't even see you in there. I just came in to boil something. I'll be out of here in two seconds and I don't even know you're alive. You've got your own room." There were other tricky effects in the small one-bedroom apartment. Joseph's older sister slept in a living-room bed that turned into a bookcase, so that all that was visible by day was three shelves of Balzac. Whenever people visited, they would ask, "But where do you all sleep in this little place?" Joseph, whose room had been switched back into a dinette, would gesture off in the direction of the one bedroom, pretending it connected onto many others and praying there would be no inspection. For those who guessed right off there was only one bedroom and insisted they know the sleeping arrangements, Joseph would put on a demonstration, breaking the Balzacs

21

down into his sister Claire's bed and showing them how one of the dinette end tables turned into his. He did it all gleefully as though it were a triumph of ingenuity and actually great fun to do your sleeping in such a tricky way.

Now Joseph put the Fleetwind terribles into a suitcase, placing them at the bottom and sealing them over with his own pure-white T shirts so that he would not have to look at the greens; then he began to do some of his mouth sounds. He had elastic lips and cheeks and by putting a finger in one cheek and snapping it he could produce a variety of funny noises, the main one being a loud *thworrp* affair that could be heard for blocks around. That was the kind of thing he was good at, but he knew it would not slip him past the admissions dean of alert and peppy Indiana, nor fling wide the gates of philosophical, Orient-facing Pomona U.

"I'm not sure you're in there," his mother said, putting on a stew. "But you're some nervous boy. You'll pull your face off with those noises."

"You're sending me to the right place for a nervousness cure," he said. "That's just where I want to be. With those green sweaters."

"There'll be good times."

Joseph went downstairs and stood beside his father in front of the darkened building, watching old newspapers fly up against the brick walls; once ringed with neat shrubs, the building now wore a girdle of stray pages from the *Daily News*, Klein's shirt ads and earthy no-punches-pulled editorial sections. Evenings, Joseph's father talked death with the fact-gathering Himber's dad, a small man who wore a great spring coat and each year shriveled a little farther into it; now only his eyes, nose and cigar were visible, giving him a bobbing periscope effect.

"Still hanging on?" asked Himber's dad from his coat.

"Yes," said Joseph's father, "but it won't be long now."

"That's the way it goes," came a voice from the coat.

"*Poof* and you're out of business."

They passed now to a discussion of people in the building who had "gone" in recent days. Aside from Joseph, young Himber and the promiscuous "Fasty," it was a building of forlorn, leftover people who were dropping like flies.

"You know 3E went the other night, don't you?" said Himber's dad.

"No, but I'm not surprised. This is all some deal, isn't it?"

"You work your ass off and then there's the big payoff."

"And you got some chance to beat it, too, don't you," observed Joseph's father.

"Yeah," said Himber's dad. "Just tell them who you are and they send you back home. Haw."

When a plane flew overhead, Joseph said it was the nine o'clock Boston. He wasn't at all sure of his facts, but he said that about any plane that flew by at night, noticing that no one ever contradicted him. In any case, he imagined it to be full of glass-clinking, gentle chuckling and good-natured warmth; he wanted to leap right up on it, sure it was speeding to a rich, green suburban cocktaily place where hardly anyone ever "went." And if they had to "go," it would all come off in a much more convivial manner. It would never be a case of 3E being shuffled down the hall through the cooking smells to the elevator.

"Some setup, eh?" said Joseph's father.

"These kids don't know," said Mr. Himber, slinking deeper into his overcoat. "Wait till they grow up and find out about the payoff for the whole deal. They're going to love that."

The next day Joseph's father and mother drove him up to the New England camp. At the wheel Joseph's father squinted his eyes, giving himself quiet driving instructions. "You've got to be careful," he whispered. "You can't kid around and suddenly swing out. You've got to watch the guy in back of you."

23

"Why do you have to keep telling yourself things?" asked Joseph.

"Are you kidding?" said Joseph's father. "What do you think this is, a joke or something? This is a car."

Joseph sat in the back with his mother and her rascally, great-bosomed Irish friend who laughed uncontrollably at his mother's jokes, making wide, pinwheeling leg crossings every few minutes to get comfortable. Joseph was not sure whether he was supposed to look inside them and decided to take peeks at the alternate ones, staring out the window for the others. During the drive Joseph's mother would smash her friend on the shoulder and say, "Oh, this is some bitch I'm bringing along. I wouldn't trust her as far as you could throw ten pianos. She doesn't know what she's doing with those bitch legs either, does she? Not much. I've got news for you. That's for your father's benefit and I wouldn't put it past her it's for yours, too. This is some bargain I'm bringing along. I really needed her. I don't have enough with you and what you're going through with colleges."

She smashed her again, saying, "Bitcheroo. You know who I'd really trust you with when my back is turned? Him," she said, pointing to Joseph's father. "The one who's so busy with his important car. He hasn't seen those legs of yours once. Not much. I really needed those legs along on this trip. With what's facing me this summer."

"Jesus," the friend said, her powdered Irish face breaking into helpless laughter. "Your mother's the dickens, isn't she?" The woman made a giant, sweeping, fragrant leg cross, Joseph deciding to break his sequence and take it in.

"No more talking like that in front of the kid," said Joseph's father. "What's wrong with you back there?"

Fleetwind was a tangle of thick greenery, encircled by giant fir trees and now, at early evening, so closely resembled one of Joseph's catalogue imaginings he decided to pretend for a few minutes it really was one; he enclosed the idea in his mind, snapped it shut and had four minutes of feeling he was rolling up on the lawn to begin a semester at one of those grand places for other people. He changed to his Fleetwind greens inside the car; next to the camp gate his mother said, "I'll be right across the lake, darling. I know what's inside your head but don't worry about anything. Concentrate on health and forget money. It's crap. Say goodby to your father and to this bitch here." Joseph kissed his father, who said to him, "Remember, kid. Don't do any stupid things." He kissed his mother's friend, then opened the door and hesitated, hopefully. She came through with a final swift but deep crossing and he left the car gratefully, the bonus safely stored in his head.

Inside the camp he was greeted by a short blond boy, hustling and peppery in the Bates style; he seemed not so much to be welcoming Joseph as guarding him, afraid he might make a dash toward some quickly erected goal line.

"I didn't know they were going to have old guys as camper waiters," said the boy whose name was Ruffio. "I'm a professional waiter. We make around a thousand a season, maybe more. Why would you want to be a camper waiter when you only make forty dollars? The uniforms alone cost you around a hundred and forty. We don't have to wear any. I've been up here two weeks waiting on guests, making money. This is how much I've made already."

He took out a roll of bills and riffled them.

"Here, hold them if you like. It's more than five times as much as you'll make all season. Why'd you want to be a camper waiter?

That was stupid of you. You'll only bring home forty shitty dollars."

Joseph did not see any point in telling the boy he had been promised a professional waitership. He thought Doc Salamandro would announce it at the proper time and so he said, "Oh, I didn't want to knock myself out. I just want to fool around a little and then go to Columbia in the fall."

"Oh no, you've got it all wrong," said Ruffio, balanced lightly on his toes, making a few harassing gestures lest Joseph suddenly strike out downfield. "That's not the way it works at all. You work just as hard as we do. You really sweat your tail. The point I've been trying to drive home is that you come out of a long bitch of a season with forty dollars while we're carting home a thousand."

"I don't care that much about money," said Joseph. "My father's in couches."

He carried his bags to a cabin marked CAMPER WAITERS where he was met by a squat and powerful man in his middle twenties who said his name was Dick Kenzie, that he had been in the Marines and was in charge of the camper waiters. He had a rock-jawed, indomitable face, and it was easy to imagine him charging forward boldly to pin down beachheads. Yet he smiled easily, as though he felt a little silly inside such a face, and he did not seem particularly graceful. Joseph wondered whether he had not been a terrible Marine, forced always into yielding critical Pacific Island positions to lithe and graceful, however thin-chested, Japanese who had feinted him into blunders.

He invited Joseph back to the only partially enclosed cubicle in the cabin, then vaulted to the top of a double-decker bed, saying, "I hear you're going to Columbia in the fall, which gives us something in common. I'm back at college on the GI bill. Each night, after taps, I haul down the machine and slam out some slick stuff. I do about a pound a night, really stack it up. I want to do slick stuff for a living if I can get it polished to a high shine. I used to sit out in the trenches at Iwo and dream of becoming a rahter.

"Glom over some of this," he said, handing Joseph a sheaf of papers.

It read a little heavily to Joseph although it had a courageous and rock-jawed way of not giving up without a fight.

"Sound slick? I'm just going to keep at it, doing a pound a night. Maybe you'd like to sit up here with me some nights when I'm piling up reams of the stuff with great Wolfean energy."

"That's great," said Joseph. "Only even though I'm wearing this green uniform I'm going to wait on guests, not campers."

"I hadn't heard about that," said Kenzie. "But you've just given me an idea for a slickie. The way you just kind of wandered in here, biting your lip, sort of, a real nice kid, a little confused. I'll bet the slicks would eat up six thousand words of that situation, handled properly."

Outside the cubicle the camper waiters had come back from serving the evening meal and Joseph went out to meet them.

"Hey, here's the old guy," said one. "Boy, is it going to be great to have an old guy in the group this year."

"How old are you?" asked another.

"Seventeen," said Joseph.

"Jesus," said one of them, smacking his head and tumbling backward on the bed. "Is that old! What a break. Maybe he can help us get more than forty bucks this year."

There were about eight camper waiters; although they could not have been more than fourteen, they all had the faces of middle-aged manufacturers Joseph knew from his neighborhood who had somehow been lashed back through time and forced, embarrassingly, to be children. Looking at them was like coming across a group of old album pictures of relatives, taken on cobbled childhood streets in Lithuania and hidden away in attics.

They all congratulated Joseph once again on his age, then let him unpack. The one who had gone tumbling over backward sat on the next cot and said, "You'll meet Portugee tonight and is she hot. She's from Europe where they have some kind of special hotbone or something. Anyway, you'll be able to handle her because of your age. Wait till she finds out how old you are."

He was a plump boy named Hortz who most of the time panted happily and puppylike, letting his tongue hang free, but whose face every so often became sullen and petulant, a successful manufacturer embittered at finding himself trapped in layers of fourteen-year-old baby fat.

"I don't know about girls on the first night," said Joseph. "I've got a lot on my mind."

A little later Joseph walked along at Dick Kenzie's side as he took the camper waiters to the lake; the Marine led the group in hearty chants that seemed specially gotten up for people on their way to lakes for early evening swims. In the water Kenzie took surging, courageous Marinelike strokes. Each time he squatted on the raft for dives, he would bare his teeth, making indomitable hell-for-leather faces. But his forward motion in the water was sluggish and Joseph imagined he would be a sitting duck for the thin-shouldered well-oiled overtaking strokes of killer Jap sea commandos. On the way back to the cabin, Joseph did some of his thworrping mouth sounds for the young embittered manufacturers, who clapped him on the back, Hortz saying for all of them, "That's what you get when you have an old guy around."

At dark, Joseph accompanied Hortz to the social hall to meet the Fleetwind girls. Hortz had an unusual comedy style which Joseph could not quite get the hang of; he used the word "crazy" often, pronouncing it "cdazy." And he said "veddy" instead of "very." Now he said to Joseph, "You're a veddy,

veddy cdazy fellow. Veddy wild." Joseph was not sure whether it was hilarious, but it had a certain catchiness and later, deep inside his head, he heard his own voice whisper, "I'm a veddy, veddy cdazy fellow." Another thing Hortz did was to fall suddenly into an imitation of a thief being caught in a lie. He would throw his hands up in fright and then, as though cringing in a police spotlight, say, "But, but, but, I, I, I, but, but . . ." He also did a flustered girl, rejecting a hand on her knee with the words "I hardly know you." It was a mixed bag of comedy approaches, Joseph wondering whether each routine had not been learned separately in a different country.

Inside the social hall now, Joseph put on the special face he used for such occasions, gritting his teeth, tightening up his nose and peering through squinted eyes as though he had just detected a fire at the other end of the room. He had first made the face at a school dance, quickly attracting a heavy-chested girl who had run over to say he looked sinister. But he had been unable to follow up that night, fading into a kind of jocularity which did not go with the face at all; the girl vanished after a single fox-trot. One trouble with the expression was that it hurt his face when he held it too long, forcing him to put his head in his hands for occasional rests.

He had just emerged from his palms when Hortz danced over with a young girl, holding her as far from him as possible. He made the fat, petulant face as though here he was with a girl who would be a sitting duck for his sly after-hours manufacturing love tricks and it was his luck to be doing a thirty-year stretch in an airtight babyfat prison.

"This is Portugee," he said, then whispered, "the one with the hotbone. Veddy, veddy cdazy. I can't handle her, she's too hot, but I've told her how old you are."

He sprang back now, fingers flicking, and said, "But, but, but, I, I, I, I, I," spilling the beans to invisible police squadrons.

She was a willowy girl with historical-novel ringlets in her hair and teeth set nakedly in a nut-brown face; her lips were wet and sly, her eyes startled as though invisible Cyril Ritchards were fawning alongside of her whispering delicious courtroom gossip in her ear. Hortz had said she was from Europe and Joseph saw her as having an aging, widowed Louis Jourdan of a dad, nursing him along through a web of affairs with a drawing room wisdom beyond her years, the two of them kicking words like "indiscreet" around a lot.

Joseph got up to dance with her, relaxing his face a little when it was out of her view. She was fragrantly clammy as though she had just finished several sets of tennis off in a glade somewhere, played by an illicit little foursome. Each time the ball rolled off in the bushes, two of the players would scamper in for it and come out giggling after a whispered, indiscreet little exchange. Joseph could not get the hang of her breasts; their size and shape seemed to have been left deliberately up in the air by some remarkable silken French contraption. Her tennis fragrance got to him though, and before they had circled the dance floor, he felt he was in love with her.

"This is my second summer here," she said, her voice coming from a small French music box, in the guest room of a château in Nancy. "I'm a French girl, but when I got here they had a nurse named Frenchie so they made up the name Portugee. I went to a party just before I left, where a famous celebrity got me in a corner and stripped me down with his eyes. Once I had an operation and woke up to find my breasts numbered 'one' and 'two' over my hospital nightgown. Things are always happening to me. The floor waxer at home once asked me if I could lift my skirt a little while he sat on the couch and did a little something with himself. He said he'd gotten that way by hanging around with racetrack women."

She began to kiss his ear, to strain against him as they danced, Joseph holding her in an astonished manner, as though she were a pan of water he was carrying to wash the blackboards. He

31

was delighted at how well he was doing; when he had first seen her, she seemed so much more complicated, and he had gotten the feeling only swarthy fellows named Hernando would be able to arouse her. He wondered if in some accidental way he had not brushed against her European hotbone, whatever that was.

"I've been watching you," she said. "You're gentle and yet you're not a fellow trying to be gentle. Your body tells me things. And I heard how old you are. You make those mad faces, too. Oh Jesus, you got me going. Once I get rolling, there's no stopping me. Oh my darling, this is evil. We mustn't. Why do you have to make those slightly angry faces?"

She licked his ear as they danced; he felt he had put his head in a grove of rained-on frangipani. After a long shiver, she made a series of hopeless little noises, as though valuables of hers were being dropped from a speeding train. Then she sighed and said, "Oh my darling, isn't release glorious. The only trouble is I'm off again. You and your stern faces . . ."

Salamandro's mournful, rabbinical brother flicked on a microphone at the end of the hall and announced, "Sleepy-peepy for camper waiters. Professionals to stay up a full two hours extra as per arrangement." Dick Kenzie herded the yawning manufacturers toward the door, then tapped Joseph on the shoulder. His face was indomitable, but kindly, too, a Marine at war's end, mopping up a group of Jap stragglers with deep stomach wounds, having no appetite for the job.

"C'mon, kid, when the others are sleeping I get out the word machine and we pound out a batch together."

"I'm not in this," said Joseph. He released the French girl, first scanning the room to see if there wasn't some sort of post he could hitch her up to; then he dashed up to Salamandro's brother, stooped, Biblical, a rabbi snatched in mid-prayer from a synagogue and thrown into softball sneakers.

"Your brother said professional waiter. You were there."

"What do I know? Ask me about a laundry increase we got this morning that could choke a horse. Anyone ever tells you to get into the camping business, give him his walking papers."

"All right then, I'm seeing your brother," said Joseph. He hollered out to the girl across the hall, "I'm not finished staying up yet," but she was facing Ruffio and another professional waiter, both of whom took turns doing Joseph's mouth sounds.

"How do they know about those?" he asked Dick Kenzie. "I just got here."

"You showed them to the kids. They got around."

"Does she know they're mine?"

"I'm not sure. But I'll send somebody back to tell her if you like."

Hortz came over to warn Joseph about the second professional waiter, a tall, black-haired, poetic-looking boy. "He's sentimental and he gives girls presents."

Outside, the air was wet, campusy, romantic. "I've never been to bed this early in my life," Joseph said to Dick Kenzie. "It would take me twelve hours to fall asleep."

The camp director opened the door of his cabin, bare-chested, great legs thundering out of his BVDs. Behind him stood a pretty middle-aged woman in a tragic-looking girdle, thin, defeated, as though she were anticipating one of Salamandro's powerful-legged leaps onto her sexual fenders and knew they could not hold out much longer.

"They want me to go to bed now with the camper waiters. You said I would be a professional waiter in your office to my mother."

He avoided Salamandro's eyes as he spoke, looking instead at the girdled wife and wondering why he never got to see middle-aged women unless they were in foundation garments. He wondered, too, whether he ought to scoop up her bluish girdled form and make a dash with her across the lake to safety at his mother's place.

33

"You come up here now," said Salamandro, his words thin, strangled as though so much power had been poured into his legs there was none left for his voice. "At this kind of an hour. I tell you to be a sugar boy and yet you come up here and start flinging it at me. Get out of my way, troublemonger. Get out of here or I'll jump all over your face."

He slammed the door of the cabin and Joseph asked Dick Kenzie if he could make a phone call. Kenzie said it was all right, that he would wait for Joseph back at the camper waiter cabin. The phone was outside the social hall. Joseph looked in through the window and saw the French girl standing in the center of the dance floor with the poetic professional waiter. He had taken out a slender box with two glistening things inside. They seemed to be girls' cuff links. Joseph called his mother across the lake.

"Hello, Mother, this is your son, Joseph. They really slipped it to me. Remember that thing about how I was supposed to be a professional waiter? No deal. They never meant it and I'm in there with a bunch of fourteen-year-old bed-wetters. I have to go to sleep the second the sun goes down. They want me to work myself into a skeleton and at the end of the season I get forty dollars. Take off the hundred and forty for those green lovelies they made me buy and I've made minus one hundred dollars for the whole season. So I'm pulling out tonight, all right? I'm coming over there to your place."

"You know who I'm talking to now?" asked his mother.

"Who's that?"

"An excited boy. I can always tell that when you start talking about money."

"I called you and told you how I feel and this is the line you want the conversation to take."

"Look, darling, I'm a few years older than you and I think I know my own son. You have food to eat. You have sun on your body. You have a place to get your mind off things. Stay there and you'll see that tomorrow you'll wish you'd never made this call. You want tips, I'll come over and give them to you. More than you can spend. You know how your mother's always felt about money. Your mother spits on it."

"So I can't come over to your place, then?"

"You could come over to a thousand places if I thought it would do you any good. But I think I know a little bit about my own son. Do you want to start giving me a few lessons in my own child at this stage of the game?"

Back at the cabin the only light came from Dick Kenzie's cubicle. He was on the upper tier of the two-decker bed, typing away, his hairy, chipper, combat-toughened legs dangling over the side. The dance music from the social hall seemed to steal into Joseph's green Fleetwind pants, fan out along his body and form a tight circle around his throat.

"Hey, I'm really flying," said Dick Kenzie. "Watch me go. I don't think I've ever been this hot. Wait till you read a potload of this. Say, listen, you got any thoughts you want worked in, just let me have them and I'll get them in there. I can do that kind of thing when I'm sizzling. And listen, for crying out loud, keep up a line of chatter. That kind of thing sparks me. I get character ideas from it."

"All I know," said Joseph, "is that after all this is over, there isn't even anything good coming up. I don't even have a college to go to."

The next morning Joseph reported to the kitchen where Salamandro's brother met him. "I hear you called your mother last night. All right, we're giving you a guest table the way we promised. I'm going to be the guest there, and also the hygiene inspector from the capital who'll be here two weeks. You bring me my meals and at the end of the season I give you a tip just like I'm a real guest. The way we've worked it out, you've got yourself a couple of guests and the professional waiters don't feel we're spoiling their arrangement."

Before Joseph was allowed to tackle his tiny guest table each day, there were two massive camper tables that had to be gotten out of the way; at the first, the counselor in charge was a short, sunbaked boy who was at least two years younger than Joseph but earned many thousands of dollars as the camp golfing pro. Before Joseph began his first meal, the boy shook hands with him and said it was a pleasure to get an old guy for a waiter, that maybe they could get some good service for a change. Joseph was in awe of the young fairway king; during the meal he ran furiously all over the kitchen digging up extra platters of peas, anxious to show that he, too, was a pro, in the game he had chosen, waiting on tables. Joseph tried to carry his tray stylishly, doing a little swooping maneuver with it when he approached the golfer's table. Each time he served up a vegetable platter, the young pro would pat him on the shoulder as though congratulating him on a well-executed birdie four.

Joseph's other table was headed up by an elderly counselor whose two little boys were among the seated campers. Instead of a salary he was paid in the form of free camp vacations for his two thin little sons. He was cautious about not showing favoritism to his own boys; during the meal Joseph would have to certify that the old counselor was not shelling out extra food to them. "All right, you're a witness. I'm passing out the chicken, but no extra goes to my kids, right?" Or he would say to Joseph, "Pour us out some milk, the same amount for the two skinny ones at the end as everybody else. If for some reason you're a little short on milk today, pass my kids right by." At the end of the meal the two hollow-cheeked children would run up to their father with arms outstretched. He would wave them aside, saying, "During camp you're not my kids." On his day off, Joseph heard, he would stretch his arms out to them and say, "Today you're my kids."

At the end of the first camper meal, Joseph stood by streaming with sweat while the golfing pro arose, slapped him on the back and said, "It certainly is a pleasure to get served by someone who knows what he's doing."

The elderly counselor filed by. "How much did I serve each child, no matter who he was?"

"The same amount," said Joseph.

After the dining room had been emptied of the campers and camper waiters, Joseph walked to another section of the floor and began to serve his tiny guest table. Salamandro's brother gave his breakfast order, saying, "I'm just like any other guest." The hygiene inspector was pale and thin-lipped, Joseph guessing he would be good at best for only thin, hygienic tips. The other professional waiters had either four or five tables apiece, each of them crammed with people. When Joseph finished serving his two sparse-eating guests, he walked over to Ruffio's area and began to help pile some dishes. The short scrappy boy made a few poking gestures, then ran over to Salamandro's brother, saying, "I thought we had our deal all set."

"You do, you do," he chanted, shouting at Joseph, "Back over here to your group, kid."

At the end of the meal the hygiene inspector rose prissily and wiped his mouth, telling Joseph the meal was very good. Salamandro's brother got up, jabbed Joseph in the ribs, winked and said, "Take it easy, *professional* waiter." The other guests rose in scattered groups, many of them reaching into their pockets to pull out bills for the professionals.

A slender blond woman, whose body seemed all pressed out beneath her slacks, came over and said she was Mrs. Hortz. She had a whimpering look to her face as though a young, handsome rogue had just run out of her starved and loveless mansion; it was a whipped Barbara Stanwyck style Joseph knew he was going to find attractive later in life although he was in no hurry to get to that stage. She was with a stout man who picked his teeth.

"My son Hortzie told me about the crummy deal they're handing you," she said, "and we want to give you a tip."

"Here, kid," said her escort, flicking out a five-dollar bill.

"I don't want that," said Joseph. "You've missed the point."

After serving the second breakfast, Joseph went back into the kitchen to rest, standing next to a wizened, hollow-toothed old man whose job it was to scrape the whole camp's dishes clean with his hand, getting them ready for the dishwashing machine. He did each dish with a curving graceful little swipe; as terrible as the job seemed, Joseph had an urge to try a few, wondering if he could execute the swipes with equal grace. The man, whose name was Lemuel, spoke with a crooked, snaggletoothed wisdom, tilting his head a little and making learned old seaman's faces. But the things he said were surprisingly standard, Joseph deciding it was only the wise old face that lent them stature.

"You're a little older than them other kids, ain't ya?" he said, snaggling his face at Joseph.

"Yes, I am."

"That's what I thought," he said with a wise old cackle. "You look a little older. . . . You know where?" He fixed Joseph with a fishlike squint.

"Where's that?" asked Joseph.

"Around the face," he said.

He was a noseless man with a horizontal three in the center of his face. The nose might have been snatched away by pliers, the face then stamped in the manner of a ceramics crate. Joseph wondered in what faraway port the nose had been taken, in what manner of seaman's activity the old man had been engaged during the removal. He wondered whether the nose still existed, perhaps as a souvenir at the end of a sailor's chain—or had it merely been kicked off to the side in a Singapore alley to shrivel and blow away?

Doc Salamandro came in then, wearing little-boy shorts. Joseph heard he was very rough on the old derelicts of the dish crew; they respected him, however, for getting them out of the town jail after their day-off binges; he would post bail for the group and then herd them back to the camp kitchen in a truck. "I'm sore as a boil," he said now, "and I have to come in here and see all this." He glanced around the kitchen, then walked over to Lemuel, suddenly punching him in his three, the blow boneless and sloshy, sending the old man against the dish bins as though he were a part of the meal that had found its way into the saucers and would take more than the usual number of swipes to get rid of.

Some other hollow boneless types appeared. Legs pumped up, ready for leaps, Salamandro said, "Leave the place this way and I'm giving it to you every day the way I just did this man. Do your work and I'll soft-pedal."

"Your friends, eh?" he said to Joseph, then stormed off.

Joseph pulled Lemuel out of the bin. "What did he have to do that for?" he asked.

Lemuel tried to get his face into a wise and crotchety old squint. "Oh, he's all right. He just likes to come down here and raise a little fuss."

"He doesn't have to hit guys in the face though, does he?"

"He's not so bad," said Lemuel, scooping out a half-moon of oatmeal with all of his artistry. "I've worked for worse. . . . You know what," he said, Ahab now, craftily appraising a squall off the starboard bow.

"What's that?"

"A man sometimes will do a funny thing."

"What do you mean?"

"That's what I mean," he said. "That's just what I mean."

Joseph did not want to hurt his feelings and so he gave his head a little shake as though the thought hadn't quite penetrated just yet, but he was going to go off and do a lot of pondering about it.

Joseph passed the next several weeks slightly dazed and nauseated as though he had been dipped in a heavy syrup and forced to walk about with a layer of it still clinging to him. He prayed for a carnival man to appear with a gadget that would shove him along two years in time so that he could suddenly find himself doing what he would be doing then, probably working in a cannery somewhere, but at least away from the camp. He could not imagine his mother allowing him to be so humiliated and kept looking across the lake, wanting to set up a public address system and shout his troubles across the lake to her: *"I'm too old for these little guys. And don't forget I don't even have a college."*

His few triumphs were all of the wrong stripe, and it cheered him little that he appeared as a great hero to the swarm of young manufacturers. One day he led them in a basketball triumph against the professional waiters, a tall hook-shooting Golem come to liberate them from fast, slick ball-handling Mongol hordes.

The best player on the professional side had been a spindly fellow, all gotten up in padded knee guards, elbow clasps and elasticized groin defenders. Before the game Ruffio had brought him a steel-webbed glasses protector and helped him into an upper thigh support. It thrilled Joseph to be tossing in shots against a fellow with all these contraptions, although after the game he felt a little bad about his triumph. He shook hands with the boy in the locker room and felt that because of all his devices, the boy perhaps should be given credit for having won the game, that he really would have won if his machines had been functioning properly. Mrs. Hortz had watched the game along with a thin man whose hands were buried deep in his pockets as though he were trying to get at his socks in a new way. Young Hortz said the man was his father. "What about the other guy?" Joseph asked. Hortz said that was his father, too. Joseph thought he understood why Hortz's comedy style was so erratic. It went along with having a series of dads.

It was the custom of the professional waiters, after each meal, to stack their tips in a pile atop their trunks, then parade about, comparing pile thicknesses. The camper waiters had won two dollars each on the basketball game. After it was over, they congratulated Joseph and proudly stacked the twos atop their own trunks.

■ ■

He helped them, too, in their grievances against Doc Salamandro. One night the camp director stood before them in boyish shorts which only made his legs more fearful.

"I've met with you. I'm treating you like big fellows. Everything between us is sincere."

"Why do we have to make only forty?" asked Hortz, a courageous manufacturer bucking the industry with a daring new style. "We'd like to make sixty-five."

"I'm trying to do what I can," said Salamandro. "It didn't look as though there'd even be forty this season, but I'm going to stay in there and see that you get it."

"He's trying to run a camp," said Salamandro's mournful brother. "He's in a tough game."

"How about the food?" asked Hortz. "We get leftovers."

"We have a fellow here from other camps," said Salamandro. "Tell them how our food compares, Joseph."

"It's about the same."

"All right, I'm coming after you," said Salamandro. "Everybody mark my words, I'm getting this smart apple for that."

After the "sleepy-peepy" disgrace, Joseph was reluctant to go back to the social hall. But the following night young Hortz prodded him, saying, "The French kid's coming no-pants tonight. One of the other girls told me. You can get right through to her like a thief in the night." Joseph had never seen a no-pants girl before, and when Portugee came in she certainly looked like one, eyes wet and startled, her walk a little bouncy, as though defying convent governesses to make her slip into a pair. When Joseph approached her, she shoved his chest as though he were the swinging door of a frontier saloon. "You go to bed early," she said, walking toward the romantic guest waiter who was seated on the side with a small gift-wrapped package on his lap. Joseph continued in the direction of the shove, smiling confidently as though things were going exactly according to plan. Hortz ran over with clenched fist, saying, "I tell you she's bare-ass under there."

"Don't I *know* that," said Joseph, who then went back to the cabin, the dance music tied around his neck like a muffler, biting the pillow until he fell asleep.

He went to bed early for the following two weeks, venturing out only once, when the music had been too much for him. That night, he took a dazed, befuddled walk through the darkness until he came to a clearing behind the kitchen. A man he recognized as the camp baker was holding his wife's hair and dragging her along through the dust, her skirt flung back over giant flour-dipped thighs, as though he had yanked her squatting from a great vat of white batter, stirred by someone who was making cupcakes for the world. He would stop every few feet, curse at her in a Slavic tongue, then kick at her vast, flour-crushed baker's body. Joseph was not at all sure what he was supposed to do and wondered whether it was his role to charge out and say, "Stop kicking your wife" to the incensed baker, then snatch her heavy body and run off with it somewhere, perhaps to the same place he had planned to store the girdled Mrs. Salamandro. He seemed to be amassing a large group of people's wives to protect, all of them lined up against the wall of a distant auditorium with no scheduled activities. At the door of the kitchen, the woman grabbed at the wiry Slavic baker's thighs, begging forgiveness, after which he smacked her ear; they disappeared, Joseph guessed, for a nightlong session of hot, doughy oven-baked love.

At the end of two weeks, he summoned up his courage and ventured tentatively back into the social hall.

A small man wearing loose, meticulously embroidered Alpine

shorts squired his daughter over to Joseph; he had tiny, elegant fingers that glistened as though he had been licking them after elaborate Viennese dinners.

"Why don't you kids get together," he said. "She's as good a dancer as anyone."

Joseph had noticed the girl previously; she had a small frenzied behind and breasts that seemed a trifle too large to go with it; her skin was one shade paler than it should have been, her lips a fraction too cherrylike, as though she had gotten them that shade by running a month-long high fever; as she approached, her walk was loose-necked and puppety, her father staying a step or two behind as though he were paying her out on a line, ready to lunge forth with Viennese swiftness should her fever return. She reminded Joseph of a girl in his neighborhood who was always going off summers to have things done to her head, later to appear on the street tightly wedged between her parents, smiling sweetly. The neighborhood girl had always been gotten up in tricky, colorful Latin American festival hats as though to conceal scalp patches. He recalled her being so vigorously scrubbed you could smell her cleanliness halfway down the block. Whenever the girl had passed by, Joseph's mother would say, "There's plenty of money there, but what good is it when they've got their hands full like that." And Joseph would have fantasies about her. She had long, lovely springing legs, a hauntingly sculptured behind. He would imagine himself having to marry her, putting in short sessions at her clean, handsome body, somehow bypassing her head, then running out to spend the money that was "there" at great restaurants.

Now the social hall girl said to him, "Do you mind if girls ask you to dance?" her father adding, "I'll stack her dancing up against any girl here." When Joseph got up, the father asked, "What's your line?"

"What do you mean?" said Joseph. "I don't have any. I'm not even in a college yet. I'm just a young fellow."

"You don't need a college these days," said the man. "I've got a little something going in imported silks I'd like to talk to you about. You won't need any schools. Go ahead. Dance with my little girl. They're crazy. There's nothing wrong with her. Wouldn't I be the first to admit it?"

"Can you come to dinner?" the girl asked as they danced.

"When's that?"

"After camp. We'd like to have you on the first Tuesday after we get home and the Thursday after that."

"I'm just dancing with you for the first time," said Joseph. "I don't know about any dinners. There's going to be a lot about getting into colleges around that time and I don't know where I'll be."

She bit her lips and Joseph, who couldn't stand to see girls under any sort of pressure, held her close. "Maybe I can get over there for a quick bite. I'll see." Her hair was black and attractively piled up so that it was difficult to tell whether there had been any patchlike rearrangement beneath it; her style had been rather bright-eyed and alert, and as she kept her balance fairly well during dips, it occurred to Joseph that perhaps she *hadn't* gone on any mysterious summer trips with her father. He had been a little afraid of her breasts but now he saw no reason to shun them even if by some chance they did owe their size to a strange feverlike disorder; he let them settle against him, finding them large and shivering though completely out of balance with her slender, poignant little body.

At the end of the dance the father said, "Go ahead, kids, take a little stroll outside while I wait right here. It's working out fine. I've had her in the finest schools. Nothing stopped me." His eyes watered with bitterness.

Outside, in the darkness of a bridle path, she said, "There was a sickness. It was awful for a while but I'm all better now and want to have fun. We have time to do a few things."

She kissed him then, going at his lips as though word had just come in that a wave of world-ending enemy missiles was on the way and this was her last chance at someone. Her body shuddered, Joseph being reluctant to take credit for it since the tremor seemed a strange, malarial-type reaction that might have come on with equal force had he been a mosquito.

"There's time to do me on top, too," she said, then watched as Joseph lightly touched her breasts; she was calm now, wide-eyed, as though being introduced to the new interne and wondering about the funny colored instruments in his bag. Joseph glanced back toward the social hall, then kissed the center of one through her halter; she craned her neck widely, saying what sounded like "Nawwwrrrr," a sudden plumbing defect in a far-off house at midnight.

"What's up?" asked Joseph, leaving the breast.

"One of the things that happens," she said. "Don't pay any attention to it."

"What are some of the others?" he asked. "That threw me off. Let's get back."

Mincing forward on tiny feet, the father said, "Now, does my little Droshkula have an exquisite personality or not? I should have them shot for telling me things about her."

He took Joseph aside and told him about the fabrics; they were brought in from Turkey where nomads spun them for pennies and he was able to bring them across and "make a little something on them" in America.

"There'll be carpeting, too, and we're going into perfume."

The girl craned in on the other side of Joseph. There seemed no way to escape the pair. Once you had started in on a neck craner, given one hope, it was immoral to drop her. You would send her into one long defective-plumbing sound that all the mysterious summer vacations in the world would not cure. Unless his mother came over quickly and took the matter to court, it seemed to be all set for him to skip college, marry the craner all cloaked in finely spun nomadic wedding gowns, then be shipped off to sell carpets and Middle Eastern draperies in musty Turkish-owned lofts.

When Salamandro's brother played "Good night, Irene," as a hint to the camper waiters, the French girl slipped in through the bridle path door, the Verlainelike professional waiter at her heels. Her neck glistened with a faint clamminess, Joseph imagining her that night getting off a wire to her continental father in confession of her latest little indelicacy.

The new girl held Joseph's arm. "Did my throatie scare you?" she asked.

"Uh-uh," he said. "Just took me by surprise. What's he mean by Droshkula?"

"It's my nickname."

"I didn't know anything about that," said Joseph.

Later that night Dick Kenzie let the camper waiters play poker in the cabin by candlelight.

"It's my ass if they catch me," he said, "but I'll be a good Joe."

They were joined by Ruffio and the elasticized athlete. Midway through the game, Joseph caught Ruffio stacking the cards. He let the scrappy professional waiter deal himself a winning hand while he constructed a withering George Sanders line with which to expose the boy. When the cards were dealt, Joseph arose and said, "One would think that a thousand-dollar earner would not see fit to profiteer on those who are only earning forty."

It came out much wordier than he had planned, but then he flipped over Ruffio's cards, revealing four aces, and Hortz said, "All right, let's cut his balls off."

"Wait," said Ruffio. "I'll tell you why I cheat. How would some of you like to have a mother who's so strict that she makes you work in stores when you're a kid? And then if you don't bring home enough money, she makes you stand in a yard,

47

sometimes in the sun. Once she kicked my leg, and I never had a dad."

Joseph did not really see the tragedy of Ruffio's situation, but the speech seemed to work its purpose on the group. It was late, there seemed no appetite for ball-cutting and the game merely broke up at that point. Joseph went to bed, wondering what the Viennese father would do if he just ignored his daughter the following night, pretended he had never set off her plumbing sounds.

The next day, after serving two breakfasts, Joseph went back to the kitchen to see his cagey old friend Lemuel and spotted the elderly counselor stuffing leftover rolls into a bag.

"I'm just taking these," he said to Joseph. "You didn't think I was bringing them out to my kids, did you?"

"I didn't think of anything," said Joseph.

"If I was bringing anything out to anyone it would be to distribute them equally among all the little people," he said.

When he left, Lemuel stopped doing his rice-pudding half-moons to narrow his eyes and say, "Know what?"

"What?" asked Joseph.

"That man's up to something," he said. "I been all over the world, twice up to Canada, and I seen a lot of men. I been with the Merchants and started taking little booze nippies out on deck. After a while the whole day was just one long nippy and my water give out. In China I learned how to kabuke a man in the neck. I can give a man a kabuke tap in the neck so's he'll sleep the weekend. Someone corners me straight on in a bar and starts to work me around, I know how to slip away from that fellow out the sides. I been with women so big in Singapore you couldn't cut the corners. When I want my pleasure I just slip Madame a little of the old Polish sausage and she's not going anywhere. Anyway, I seen a lot of men and I know when one of them's got something in his head. He's going to do something with those rolls. You wait and see."

Joseph loved listening to the adventurous old fellow. As the dish scraper spoke of faraway lands, Joseph felt he was off in some of those places himself.

"How come you didn't slip away from Salamandro the other day?" he asked.

"He had me sides covered."

Later Joseph picked up Hortz, the two of them taking a long silent walk through wet grass in the fields beyond the camp until they came to a stable. Hortz said it half belonged to the camp and half to a nearby farmer, that not enough campers had been interested in riding to justify hiring an instructor, so the horses were just standing around unused. Inside the stable the stalls were filled with bad dumpy reject horses, all with terrible posture and little knobs coming out of their legs. But there was one in the corner that was taller than the others and caught Joseph's eye. He had a sulky, Robert Ryan look about him and seemed disdainful of his situation, closeted with a bunch of losers. He reminded Joseph of a ballplayer who had just pitched a perfect World Series game, then immediately come down with elbow trouble, having to be sent to the minors where it was hoped he would regain his stuff. Tall, proud, obviously a class horse, the glamour of major league cheers still ringing in

50

his ears, he was stuck among down-and-outers who could not carry his uniform when his fast ball was hopping. Joseph fell right in love with him. In a way, it was as though the horse, too, was an "old guy," doomed to a season among young bed-wetters. Hortz said he knew a little about horses since he had gone to a great many military schools while his mom was breaking in new dads. He led the horse out of his stall and said you measured horses' height in hands and that this one was fifteen hands, actually tall for a horse; it was just the kind of fact Joseph loved. A few of those on a subject and you could sound like an expert; he knew that whenever a horse was being talked about in future conversations, he would ask, "How many hands was he?"

Hortz said the horse's name was "The Blue," and that he was the only decent one in the stable, his slight nervousness notwithstanding. Joseph was certain that if he ever rode him he would be thrown to the ground for a smashed head, but decided to try and sneak up on him, ride him a few steps, then vault to the ground before the horse got wind he was up there. Hortz said he would saddle and bridle him if Joseph liked and Joseph said okay, loving the horse more and more, hoping he would regain his greatness, the way he always hoped old, retired fighters would suddenly go back into training and defeat the current champion. The horse made a pained, teeth-baring Ryan face, Joseph seeing him then as an ex-pro football player, now in the arms-running racket in Costa Rica, used to big money and glamour and having to take any quick-buck jobs he could get, surrounded by plenty of women who kept asking, "What are you running away from, American?"

Joseph got up on The Blue and felt very high, mostly because he knew the horse was fifteen hands and that it was probably better to start your riding on thirteens. The horse did not seem to mind a little workout, going easily into a light frisking trot around the stable. It was as though rumors had started in the locker room that he had completely lost his stuff and the other horses were complaining about his high salary; so now he was uncorking a few high hard ones while his teammates stared in disbelief, muttering they had never known such speed existed. Joseph had not done much riding, mainly because it was so expensive in his neighborhood; it always seemed that the second he got out of the stable he owed $11.80. Now he waved goodby to young Hortz and began to trot off on The Blue, certain someone would fly after him on a pinto with a bill for several hundred.

The first few dozen yards were through a confined and hunched-up path, but the horse then broke out into a vast meadow you could not see the end of and began to fly along, a crazy eccentric rookie now, getting a chance to show his talents beneath the open sky, far from the howling stadium crowds and reporters, the way it was when he was a high school athlete back in Iowa. Joseph sat back like a spectator, swallowing the meadow air like spoonfuls of health, pitying himself for being an apartment fellow and wondering how many swallows he would have to take to catch up with rural types who had been gulping it down since birth. Joseph had always felt that galloping was only for rich fellows, but The Blue broke into one before he had had a chance to tell him he was needy and that there had been no lessons. After sprinting for miles, the horse slowed down a little, breathing hard, but apparently pleased he still had his stuff. And with his kind of horse, it was how *he* felt that counted, not the press. Joseph pulled back on the reins, and on an impulse dismounted, certain the horse would break away and run off, Salamandro getting a call saying he had been found in Canada. But the horse stayed in one place until Joseph got back on, thrilled he had not had to use attendants and elaborate stable mounting apparatus.

Nearing the stable, Joseph felt that he had been off bumming around with Robert Ryan and that he had really gotten to know what made him tick—and yet there had been no embarrassment to the great actor since he had been traveling as a horse and was supposed to have riders. But when Hortz led The Blue back to his stall, the horse flashed Joseph a pained and sullen look as though he was not to get any idea about continuing the relationship. He had taken Joseph for a ride the way a great but temperamental hitter might step out of character and give a rookie some pointers, but that was as far as it was going to go.

The road they took back to the camp ran parallel to a lake; as they neared the gate, a canoe shot by, carrying the craner and several other girls. She was wearing a sailor hat, well back on her head, and Joseph wondered if it was there to conceal bare, freshly tampered-with scalp sections. Pushed to her feet on thinly whittled legs, she gave Joseph a pale wave.

"There's your doll, cdazy fellow," said Hortz.

"I know," said Joseph. "I'm waving back."

In the social hall that night Joseph pretended he was a new fellow, just arrived at camp, and grabbed a dance with a tough little girl who said she could not understand all the excitement over French kissing.

"It leaves me cold," she said, her face tough and grim.

Over her shoulder Joseph spotted the craner and her tiny-footed Viennese dad, sitting together, shifting positions, tapping their feet, refugee eyes burning holes in his shoulder blades. Expecting Federal marshals to seize him at any moment, he broke off at the end of the dance and joined them.

On the darkened bridle path he said to the craner, "Too bad you had to be sick that time you told me about. Real pity."

"Pity," she said. "Shitty pity, shitty shitty pity."

He had never heard a girl use that word before and he decided it had something to do with having logged time in institutions. It probably pulled all the stops out of a person so

53

that you could say "shitty" to a fellow you hardly knew. You could probably try wild things on institutionals; what secrets could they possibly conceal during lice baths, while being shaved down for head tamperings? It was like coming across an unconscious girl in an accident, not marked up too badly, and getting to examine her beneath her skirt all you wanted before medical assistance came, no one ever getting to know. A thieflike feeling stole across him and he decided to take advantage of her institutional background. He told himself that her body was too good to waste, that she was probably going back into one anyway and that would seal her lips forever, in case she ever decided to get back at him and spill everything to his folks. He approached her as though she were a wonderful store; he had four minutes to take anything he wanted before the owner came back from dinner. He made a furtive examination of her body, not so much enjoying the touches as collecting them like baseball cards, each breast a Bill Dickey, her behind a pair of Stan Musials. He asked her choked questions as he roamed her body, adding her answers to his pile. He saw her as a girl he had somehow gotten into a capsule with, all sealed off from the rest of the world; he was allowed five vacuum-packed minutes to do anything he wanted with her, however crazy, after which the capsule would burst, penalties flying in through the cracks for future infractions.

"What happens to you when you run real fast? On top?"

"They jiggle," she said.

"What places get you the craziest?"

"Right on the tips."

"Inside or outside?" he asked.

"Either," she said. "The tops of my legs are good, too.

He took her breasts out of her halter, fattening his card stack, and when she touched the length of him, he put that right on the pile, too. She said, "Do you like this?" putting her hand through his shorts so that it covered his behind. "I'm not sure," he said, taking it away, but fully aware that she had dealt him a Babe Ruth and that he would never own another like it. It was definitely an institutional thing to do and you would never get anything that great from a girl who had not been in one; right to the top of the pile it went, his collection nearly complete.

Girls' pants always fascinated him; he wondered God knows what they were going to spring on him and speculated often on whether certain girls would resemble their pants in any way. He went beneath the craner's shorts, finding hers defenseless, butterfly-soft, the finest of all nomadic cloth, obviously to compensate for her craning difficulties. They moved to the side almost in rhythm to Joseph's thoughts, but then he got the defective-plumbing sound and held off further exploration.

"I can't seem to get in the mood tonight," he said, feeling somehow that the store owner had returned, trapping him among the high-priced German binoculars. He felt stale and wondered if he could somehow retain the memory of the last few minutes, snipping the craner out of his dream and dummying up a young, fresh, confused ballet dancer in her place, much in the style of the old tabloid composographs.

"I'm glad we'll be seeing each other for dinners," she said.

Inside the social hall the father told Joseph about several trunkloads of gems he had been able to keep whipping on ahead of Hitler, finally getting them out of the country via the Netherlands. He said he thought he ought to mention them since they were part of the overall picture.

At the start of the third week, Salamandro's lugubrious brother told Joseph he was getting another guest table to wait on that Sunday, his own folks. It was a special visitors' day and they had called up to say they were coming. "I'm putting them at your table and at the end of the meal they'll give you the tip."

On the specified Sunday, Joseph's mother and father took a

large rowboat across the lake to the camp. Along were Joseph's sister and her boyfriend, also his mother's leg-crossing Irish friend.

At the dock Joseph's father took him aside and said, "You want to hear about the car?"

"All right."

"I gave it a 12,000-mile check. It was all right except the oil was dirty."

"Is that what you wanted me to hear?" asked Joseph.

"You've got to take care of a car," said the father. "You'll see when you get older. They did a nice job on it. I wish I had it here so I could show you."

Joseph's sister was several years older then he was, blond, round-bottomed, a piece of her behind always sticking out of her shorts. Joseph's mother called the sections "pulkas." As she stepped out of the rowboat, she tugged at her husband's shirt and said, "Tell her to get them in there."

"Why do I have to be the one?" asked Joseph's father. Then he whispered to the girl, "Stick them in," and she pulled down her shorts.

The sister's boyfriend was a small, unshaven man who wore a thin overcoat in midsummer and was known to be an outstanding college football scatback. He cornered Joseph at the edge of the dock, squatting down in lineman's position. "Come through me," he said.

"Not out here," said Joseph.

"A guy tries to come through you, you always do this to him," said the boyfriend, jabbing his elbow lightly into Joseph's groin. "Look the other way when you're doing it and be smiling." He glanced over at Joseph's sister and said, "I'm teaching the kid how to play dirty."

Joseph led the party up a path toward the dining room and introduced his folks to Dick Kenzie. "He's in charge of me," said Joseph.

"He's some swell-looking guy," said Joseph's mother. "I could use him myself. Do you like Joseph?"

"Yes," said the strapping Dick Kenzie.

"They've got some staff here," she said.

"I'll bet you could use him, too, you Irish bitch," she said to her friend, the woman doubling over with soundless laughter. "If I took my eyes off you, you'd have him behind a tree in two seconds."

"Well, your mother's here," she said to Joseph, kissing his ear. "Already she's got the place in stitches." She looked around at the path and the trees. "He runs quite a place here. You know what you'd have to pay for air like this at a resort? I'd hate to be the one to tell you."

"It's the same air you've got across the lake," said Joseph.

"You're starting in," said the mother.

At the dining room, Joseph showed his father the campers' tables he was to wait on, then pointed to the guest table area.

"So what do you do?" asked his father. "You take the food from the kitchen and bring it out to the campers, is that right?"

"That's right," said Joseph.

"What I'm getting at is you're a waiter, is that right?"

"Yes."

"That's what I wanted to get straightened out."

Joseph let his folks watch while he took care of his camper tables. They stood in the archway of the dining room, and at the end of the meal the young golfing pro walked over to them and said, "We're finally getting some service around here, thanks to your son."

Joseph, his T shirt drenched, bowed his head in spite of himself. "You're not very well liked wherever you go, are you?" said his mother. "People who deal with my son really lose money on the deal." She paused and when Joseph acknowledged her wink, said, "That's what I mean."

When the campers were gone, Joseph began to set up two

guest tables, one for Salamandro's brother and the hygiene inspector, the other for his folks.

"I want to get something straight," his father said. "How
come you're fooling around with these tables now? You just
finished with the kids. Aren't you through? Don't you go down
for a swim or something?"

"No," said Joseph. "That's the thing. Now I wait on guest
tables. I was supposed to wait on only guest tables but they had
the thing all set, so I have to do the children first. I do both."

"I don't know," said the father. "I hope you know what
you're doing. It seems like a lot of work to me. I thought when
you were finished you'd go down for a swim."

"You're making him good and crazy," said the mother.

Before the meal, Hortz brought over his mother and a third
dad, Joseph introducing the trio to his folks.

"This is my new friend and his folks," said Joseph.

"Hiya, baby," said Joseph's mother, shaking Mrs. Hortz's
hand. Hortz's third dad was a great gum-chewing man whose
fingers sparkled with expensive rings.

"They do a lot for the kids in a place like this," he said.

"It's a blessing," said Joseph's mother.

"The only thing I can't figure out," said Joseph's father, "is
that he's just finished waiting on two big tables and now he's
going to wait on some more. I can't understand these kids, you
know what I mean."

"You've just gotta give them elbowroom," said the gum-
chewer, "give them enough rope and hope they don't hang themselves."

After the Hortzes had left, Joseph's mother said, "That's your
friend?"

"And his folks," said Joseph.

"She's some little beauty, and I like her husband. He's quite
a father. I really like the two of them. A lovely couple. Parents.
Is that what they call themselves? I like her. I haven't seen her

kind knocking around the city, have I? A mother is what she is. From way back. And you know who else I like?"

"Who's that?" asked Joseph.

"Him. The father. I like his rings. He isn't one of the boys, is he? He hasn't been around much. I'd like to have a quarter for every guy he's had thrown into lime pits."

"You know that from just looking at him?"

"Your mother can't size up people? She really needs a lot of time with someone. Oh yeah, they're some two little beauties. Parents. And you know what they're interested in most of all, her with the slacks and him with the rings? Child welfare."

She slapped her Irish friend on the shoulder. "Bitch. You could be right in there with them in two seconds, couldn't you? I'll bet you'd love it. I'll bet you could use the big guy and he wouldn't love those legs of yours either, would he?"

When Joseph had his tables all set up, Joseph's mother peered over at the sister and her boyfriend who were standing aside, looking out of a window. "I don't like what happens to her in those shorts," she said to her husband. "Will you attend to it?"

"Why don't you take care of it yourself?" he said.

"You're starting in with me."

The father walked over to Joseph's sister. "Stick yourself in," he said. She clucked her tongue, wriggling back into the shorts.

Seated now, Joseph's father asked the boyfriend, "Are you going to wear that overcoat at the table?"

"Leave him alone," said Joseph's mother. "He's a little chilly. That's what my daughter wanted, that's what she's getting."

"Maybe I'm wrong but I never heard of wearing an overcoat at a table."

Joseph served the first course, cream of corn soup. "Is that tray heavy when you lift it up?" his father asked him.

"Not too bad," said Joseph.

"Because if it's heavy, be careful with it."

"Well, what am I supposed to do with it?"

59

"Now look, don't be a wise guy. You lift a heavy tray and you can strain yourself."

Joseph's mother took one spoonful of the soup. "Well, I've got news for you," she said. "Tomorrow morning I'm packing my grips and I'm moving right in here with you. I found a home. Is that a soup the son of a bitch serves! He doesn't know what he's doing with this camp, does he? My son wants to give him a few lessons."

She pounded the Irish friend's back. "She's eating. She doesn't know from nothing. Give her good food and a little boyfriend, young ones preferably, and she's off to the races. This is some Irish bitch I picked for myself, some little beauty."

"Will you stop it," said the Irish friend, who then exploded into the soup in silent convulsions. She had had some complicated, uneven things done to her teeth that made them glitter each time she flung her mouth wide.

When Doc Salamandro, passing from table to table, approached, Joseph's mother said, "I have to take my hat off to you, Doc. You serve a gorgeous table. How's my young prince doing?"

Salamandro put his hand on Joseph's shoulder. "He gives me a little, I give him a little, but we get along."

When the director moved to the next table, Joseph's mother said, "You're not very well liked around here, are you? In another week I'll hear that he's coming home with the whole camp." Then she looked over at Salamandro. "That's some man you're serving under. I'd like to know one-tenth of what's going on in that head of his. Mmmmph, the food he serves, and he doesn't have much charm either when he visits these tables. He doesn't know what he's doing."

"You think he's great?" asked Joseph.

"And you don't, is that it? Well, I've got a little message for you. He's there and you've got to get there."

"I've got to get where he is?"

"We should all be in his shoes. We should all have his head."

When Joseph brought the main course, his mother said, "Anything I don't finish is going right into this purse and I'm having myself a little picnic across the lake tomorrow."

She looked over at the boyfriend. "He's eaten meals like this before, hasn't he? In that neighborhood he comes from. That's all they gave him were meals like these. Where did you have to go to find him? With his overcoat on a day like this."

"Will you stop it, Mother," said Joseph's sister.

"I'm not butting in. You wanted him, you're getting him. Have you heard a word from me?"

After Joseph had served the dessert, his father asked him, "How do you feel when you're all finished here, all knocked out?"

"A little," said Joseph.

"I'll bet he does. This is hard work. I'll bet the kid feels plenty tired when he's all finished. I know that feeling."

After the meal, Joseph's sister got up, pulling at the shorts which had plunged into her backside.

"Will you please attend to that," Joseph's mother said to his father.

"Is that the kind of job you give me? What am I supposed to do?"

"You've always got an answer. Is that the way you want your daughter to carry on in front of him? The neighborhood he came from. Where she went to find him."

"All right," said the father. "It's over already."

Joseph told his parents to wait at the waterfront while he cleaned the tables. The boyfriend remained behind, saying, "Go out for a pass and I'll be a guy blocking you."

"I've got to clean up," said Joseph. But he ran through the dining room aisle anyway, looking up as though watching for a football. The overcoated boyfriend chased Joseph and suddenly grabbed at his crotch, bringing the boy to the floor. "Did you see how *I* went for the luggage when the referee wasn't looking? That's the secret. You look one way and with your hand get yourself a fistful. Nobody will catch nothing on you."

Later, at the waterfront, the camp girls put on a swimming exhibition. Joseph's mother, standing beside him, said, "I want to have some fun. Let me see if I can pick out your taste."

The French girl walked by, taking peevish little steps in the style of a female impersonator. She looked as though she had been bawled out by a château governess for acting restless during a petticoat fitting.

"Your mother doesn't know her son's taste, does she?" said Joseph's mother. "It took her a long time to figure out what you picked. Mmmmph, that's some little backside she's got there. And she doesn't know what she's doing with it, either, does she? It took me a long time to spot her. You're just like your mother. She always liked a pretty body, too."

The craner stood on her toes and waved, her legs pale and chilled in a tapestried Viennese-style swimsuit.

"I haven't picked out anyone," said Joseph.

Mrs. Hortz came over. "Hello, people. What did you think of my Louis? He plays the lute, you know, beautifully, and he sings ballads to me in my ear."

"That's all right with me," said Joseph's mother.

"You'd never know it to look at him, he's such a big man, but he plays so beautifully. He serenades me and I want to die."

"That's a musical instrument," said Joseph's father. "Is that it?"

"Yes," said Mrs. Hortz.

"I thought so." He nodded. "I just wanted to clear it up in my mind."

When Mrs. Hortz had joined her husband, Joseph's mother said, "That's just what I mean. He's a lute player, and he romances her; that's the new name they have for it. That's the first thing I said to myself when I saw him with his stomach and rings. There goes a lute player. And she sits back and allows herself to be romanced, her with the eye makeup and those little slacks of hers. I don't know. They've got all kinds of names for things these days. But it's all right with me. I'm visiting a camp."

"Bitch," she said, slapping her Irish friend's thigh. "Bitch that never says a word but that's good as gold.

"Is that a person?" she said to Joseph, holding her friend's chin. "Is that an angel? Is that as good as currency? Your mother doesn't have much luck with her friends, does she?"

"What am I supposed to answer to that kind of question?" said Joseph.

That night, at the social hall, Joseph's sister snatched him aside, holding his arm wedged in her cleavage. He stiffened, not sure whether he was supposed to enjoy it.

"I haven't had a chance to get my gorgeous brother aside," she said. "How do you like it up here?"

"I don't like it very much but I don't seem to be able to tell it to anybody. I'm waiting on thousands of tables a day and I wind up minus a hundred bucks or so."

"You're such a gorgeous thing," she said, clamping his arm even deeper. "What do you think of my new boyfriend?"

"He's all right. What ever happened to the engineer?"

"The engineer? Is that who you liked? He was all right."

"I liked him," said Joseph.

The boyfriend was at the corner of the dance floor, in his overcoat, doing intricate steps with an imaginary partner.

"Oh well, they're just waiting for him, with those little dippies," said Joseph's mother. "I'd like to know the neighborhood in which he picked up those prizewinning steps. It was in some wealthy section of Westchester, I think." She smiled back at the Hortzes and said, "That's the mother and father interested in their child's welfare."

63

When the music was turned up, she bit her lip and tapped her foot. "That beat, you should only know what it does to me. Tomorrow morning I'm packing a valise and moving right in here. . . . Momma," she said, flinging her head and stamping her feet. "I'll put an end to my life from that rhythm." The Irish friend tapped her feet, too, Joseph's mother pointing to her, saying, "A horse, a regular horse. She doesn't know which end is up, but she's got music and she's dancing. Nothing's going to stop her, I don't care if you put on the World's Fair here. A regular elephant. . . . You get this every night," she said to Joseph. "You've got a setup like this and I have to get telephone calls."

"It isn't that great," said Joseph.

The French girl came in then, her blouse damp, her upper lip beaded. Joseph wondered if he ought to ask her to dance and perhaps fake her into thinking it was the first night all over again. Without thinking more about it, he strode to her side.

"I wonder if you'd care to waltz through around during the music."

"You're not articulating properly," she said, "and I'm occupied."

He went back to his mother who said, "What's the matter, darling? Have you got your hands full?"

"I just wanted to find out something," he said.

"She's some little bitch," said the mother. "I spotted her behind the second I came in."

The Viennese fabric man entered then, pushing the craner on ahead, puppety, delighted, as though some new institutional section head had promised her a monkey show for the weekend. After which she and her entire craning group would get to go down to the lake and dip their toes in the water, all closely supervised, of course. In her fresh, clean, sailor-boy hat, she might have belonged to a ventriloquist breaking in a nautical act; he had been warned to get his dummy out of evening dress or be replaced by tango dancers. Her Viennese dad wore a tiny tweed suit and two-toned shoes. Bowing, he said, "I wonder if I might introduce myself. My Droshkula and your son have been getting along so nicely."

"Well, *this* is what I've been waiting for," said Joseph's mother. "Now you finally brought someone over. You're finally talking your mother's language. Oh, I *like* him. You know what I like most of all? His little suit. Yes, his little suit on those hips of his."

She spoke as though he was still across the room and could not hear any of her comments. Now she extended her hand and said, "I'm very pleased to meet you. And that's your Droshkula? Is that what you call her? She's very pretty." Lowering her voice, she said, "I know the whole setup already."

The Viennese man patted Joseph's shoulder. "She's terribly charming, your mother, a full-spirited woman."

Aside, to her Irish friend, Joseph's mother said, "There's one thing you've got to look at if it's your last act on earth. You've got to look at his shoes. The shoes, the little suit and those hips of his. And a daughter named Droshkula thrown in. That's the name he had to select for her or he would have passed out. Did you ever in your life! And that's my son's taste.

"Bitch," she said aloud, pinching her friend's cheek and collapsing in laughter. "I needed you along to see this." She pounded her again. "We have some laughs together."

The Viennese man bowed, then extended his hand to Joseph's mother in courtly fashion. "I wonder if you would honor me with this dance."

"Oh well, this is too much," said Joseph's mother. "I'd love to." To her friend she said, "I should have known. I should have known the second I spotted those shoes. That's the type that dances. The kind with shoes and little suits. He hears the music and you can't pry him off the dance floor. Oh, well, this is too much. I didn't expect this at all. I came to visit a camp and I've got a regular orgy."

The Viennese man whirled Joseph's mother around the floor; when they paused momentarily beside the Irish friend, the mother said, "I don't want to say anything, but I'm quietly being made love to. Those are the kind. With the shoes and the little suits. He comes up to my shoulder, but meanwhile he can teach Ronald Colman passion. In two seconds he'll have my brassiere off."

"Mother," said Joseph.

"All right, I made a remark. My mistake. He can't stand to hear his mother express herself."

"Nawwrrr," said the puppety girl, craning suddenly toward the ceiling.

"Who did that come from?" asked Joseph's mother, stopping now.

"The night air," said the Viennese man, throwing a shawl around his daughter's shoulders. "My little Droshkula."

"It's all right with me," said Joseph's mother. "I didn't hear a thing. As far as I'm concerned, it was part of the music."

They danced some more, the mother touching her head as though to check for fever. "Oh, I can't stand it. This is really too much. Steppies he's making with me. Intricate ones. The way he feels, Gene Kelly can take a back seat. Don't look now, but your mother's part of a new dance team."

The record ended, she came over to Joseph, her arm around the Viennese man. "Well, I want to tell you something," she said. "He's a swell guy. He can take a little kidding and he's a hell of a lot of fun. I haven't laughed like that in years."

"Your mother has a fullness of personality."

"Sure, that's what he noticed, a fullness. That's what they're calling it. In two seconds he'd have me stripped to the ankles. I'd trust him. About as far as you could throw the Washington

66

Monument. I like the way he looks you over, with his little suit. In one second you don't have a stitch on."

"Mom really understands people," the boyfriend said to Joseph.

"Oh, I'm Mom now. You've moved right into the family. That's okay. Just once, though, I'd like to know which area of Sutton Place you started out from with those overcoats."

The Viennese man asked the Irish friend to dance. "I knew it," said the mother. "She's moving right in. The horse. She could use him, too. But he's a swell guy. Don't sell him short. He probably knows how to spend a buck, too, but I didn't have much time to find that out. Look at her. A monument. She can't budge that behind of hers, but she's gliding . . ."

Joseph's sister took the craner aside to talk to her.

"Well, I want to tell you something," his mother said to him. "You won't find regular guys like that. And I've got news for you. He's loaded. Those are the kind. With the skinny suits. He's got his hands full with that daughter of his, but you're crazy. If I was you I'd move right in. You want that little bitch with the behind, you're just letting yourself in for a lot of aggravation. After the physical attraction, what do you think will be left? I'm not saying another word. So she's not that pretty, what do you care? You'll see how little that means. You get a little of that refugee cash in your system and you've got all your life to worry about prettiness. I'd like to know what he's got socked away in securities alone that the government doesn't know about. You're out of your mind if you don't move right in. How I wish I had someone to tell me these things when I was young. I wanted prettiness, too, so look where it got me. I think you're crazy."

"Then it's all settled," said Joseph. "Is that it?"

"I'm not saying another word. All I know is that if I were you I wouldn't make fun of that girl. She makes a little sound, don't listen. Turn on the radio. She's got some swell guy for a father. Think of that."

The Viennese father and his daughter accompanied Joseph's family to the boat dock. "We're right across the water, you know," Joseph's father said to him. "We get in this boat and on the other side is where our house is."

"I know that," said Joseph.

"And look, I want to tell you something before I forget. Look into that business about the tables. You shouldn't be working that hard. You're a young fellow. You've got all your life to work. Sometimes you're very lax about things."

"Listen to your father's brilliance," said Joseph's mother. "He really got far with it."

His sister wedged his arm between her breasts. "I didn't have a chance to talk to my gorgeous brother." She stepped into the boat. "Cover yourself," said the mother.

"Will you stop it," the sister replied, yanking down her shorts. Joseph felt a little sorry for her for her having all those globe-like appendages to keep sticking into her clothes. He worried about her having one sheared off, by a truck or a speeding train.

On the dock Joseph was flanked by the Viennese couple as he said goodby to his mother.

He tried to get her alone, but they stayed glued to his sides. Finally he whispered, "Look, it isn't that great here. I'm not that nuts about this girl and I don't really see what's so great about her father.

"Look," he said, "I'd like to come along. Couldn't I just get in the boat and leave my clothes? It's really lousy here." He thought suddenly of an old brocaded Oriental shawl with long gold tassels that lay atop an organ in the living room of his mother's apartment. He wanted to say more to his mother now, but it was as though the shawl had been dropped over his head and he was being carried down some steps, screaming through the brocade.

"I didn't hear a word you came out with," said the mother. "All I know is what I saw with my eyes. A healthy son, a bunch of swell guys, music, food I never heard of in my wildest dreams for a camp.

"My son is out of his mind," she said, breaking clear and sailing off into the moonlight.

The next morning, Joseph got a letter from Columbia University saying that although he was a well-qualified candidate, his application was being turned down. The thousands of newly returned World War II veterans seeking admission had made the competition for places especially fierce. Their applications, of course, had to be given priority.

"It is to be hoped," said the letter, "that this situation will ease so that future high school applicants will have an easier time of it than this year's unfortunates."

"Well, there goes the last one," he said aloud, snapping the fingers of one hand and then putting the letter down on the grass. He slipped it beneath his heel as though he had been handed an election brochure for some minor political candidate and did not want to be seen throwing it away. Then he picked it up again, saying "Oh Christ" and shaking his head, feeling he had to make an obvious demonstration of disappointment for an invisible crowd that expected such things. He went back into the cabin and lay down on the bed, trying to work up a few tears, helping them along by letting his shoulders tremble, in the style of actresses called upon to convey sorrow with their backs to the camera. Outside the cabin, he put his hands in his pockets and kicked some stones, wondering why he could react to tragedy only with movie routines. Now he was the high school hero caught stealing exam answers on the eve of the big game, waiting outside the principal's office to see whether he would be allowed to compete against State.

"You got troubles, kid?" asked Dick Kenzie, showing up suddenly.

"I had this last college foul up on me," said Joseph. "Now there are none left to go to. I just have to go home and sit around while everyone else is in college."

"You'll be all right," said Kenzie. "You're a helluva kid. Sometimes in life it's as though there's a whole street full of balloons. Everyone's catching them except you. I know that as a writer who hasn't grabbed one yet.

"You'll get your balloon," he said, rushing off.

"That's swell," said Joseph. "Only I'm not getting anything."

Ruffio accompanied him to the dining room. "We're cleaning up this season. We'll probably go over the $1,100 mark. Why'd you decide to come up here as a camp waiter? Sometimes we wonder how you *feel*, working your butt off and knowing you're winding up minus $110 after a whole season. The reason we let you have the one shitty table is that the inspector's only worth about three bucks. We had him last year and were glad to get rid of him. Salamandro's brother will give you a fiver for the whole season. All you'll get is what you make from your own folks. That's the thing we talk about. How you really *feel*."

"Something happened to me this morning and I'm telling you right now that I don't know what I'm going to do. All I

know is that I got this letter and I could really hurt someone."
He hit Ruffio in the stomach and was surprised to find his fist
going in so deep. Once, in a garden, he had come upon a
strange yellow cucumber that turned out to be hollow, filled
only with some white vegetable fluid. Now his fist went on and
on, finally bumping into something very much like the old
cucumber, making a soft popping sound. Ruffio shriveled into
the dirt and Joseph said, "I didn't want you down there," trying
to pull him to his feet. "I'm not getting up," said the boy, and
Joseph said, "Please get up." Ruffio got to one knee finally and
said, "Oooooch, I'm telling everyone about this." Trying to un-
punch him, Joseph rubbed the boy's stomach a little, said,
"Don't tell," and ran up the stairs to the dining room. At
the entrance he started to cry, amazed and grateful for the way
the tears appeared, a hot wash of them running up through
him in a completely non-movie way.

Waffles were the main breakfast course, Joseph making many
trips back and forth to the kitchen to get seconds for his tables.
He had once been taken care of by a Negro woman whose lovers all had animal names such as "Toad" or "Camel" and were
always walking out on her. He remembered standing on a toilet
seat to be dressed one day, the woman starting to cry, her tears
so profuse that some of them got into his underwear. She said
"Ole Bear" had left her, but what struck Joseph was that she
had had to go right on dressing him; there had been no arrangement for her to call a halt to her life and go off a while
to a special crying room. He remembered her weeping in bursts
that day as she worked, peeling potatoes, carpet-sweeping; chasing the milkman down the hall, she had gone into a bumpy,
heavyset cry. Now, as he waited for new platters to be made up,
it was maddening to Joseph that he had to keep tearing back
and forth with the waffles, that all crying had to be done on the
run, while serving up fresh batches. He told the grizzled, canny-

looking old Lemmie, "I don't want to be going back and forth with these. I got some lousy news this morning."

"I know'd there was something come up this morning," said the dish-scraping ex-seaman, peering at Joseph through a twisted eye. "You know how?"

"I know, I know," said Joseph. "By the expression around my ears or my mouth. None of that's going to help me now."

Back in the dining room, the golf pro said, "Thanks to your getting us all the food we want, we've really been able to stuff ourselves to the gills." He got his table of campers to give Joseph a cheer. "I don't want one," he said, but then he lowered his head, in the midst of his sorrow, proud to be helping send the young links star off on a series of successful big-money fall tournaments.

Serving the second breakfast to his guest table, Joseph saw Ruffio limp into the kitchen; he was thrilled, since the boy's appearance meant there had probably been no smashed internal cucumber. In a flash of daring he asked the hygiene inspector if he had any connections with colleges. "I've just gotten a turndown from my last one and don't have one to go to."

"We don't get into that area," said the inspector.

"I just thought that with the hygienic background you might do a little something with them."

Through the rest of the day, he could not seem to get a consistent pattern of depressed behavior going; he did some anguished filmdom dirt kicks but threaded them between a quite spontaneous burst of Negro Camel and Toad tears. He had no control, really, of his actions; it was as though he had stepped out of his body to race along beside it, observing himself with fascination, wondering what in the world he was going to come up with next. Once, Joseph's father had set a trap for a mouse which failed to kill the creature but stunned it instead, turning it dazed and spastic. Joseph remembered watching the mouse

73

stagger about groggily, putting on sudden bursts of speed, then lapsing into drunken wobbles. He reminded himself of the old kitchen mouse now, rudderless at one moment, lashing out with fury the next.

At midday he heaved himself upon his bed and caught his forearm on a mattress spring, raising a tiny hot nodule below the crease of his elbow; he took it to the European camp doctor who cringed backward, saying, "Where? Where? I don't see anything."

"It's there all right, if you look," said Joseph.

"I don't have anything here. I can't work. I am not equipped. Go away. I don't see anything. In Leipzig at least you had equipment, you could see good, there were others. There was a warmth . . ."

"Will you please do something?" said Joseph. "I got a terrible letter from a college this morning and everything's happening to me."

"All right, I give him a little schkveeze," said the doctor. He pressed the nodule between two fingers, applying gradual pressure. "There, I schkveeze him out good. You had a little something there, he's all gone now. All better?"

"It's still hot," said Joseph. "I don't think you got it."

"I didn't see anything," said the doctor, falling back in terror, opening and closing medicine bottles. "I schkveezed him out. Please, please, here's cotton, here's Band-Aids, don't make trouble."

When Joseph had served the first of his two dinners, the counselor with the pair of thin little sons said to him, "Look, kid, I see you've been acting a little funny. We've all got something. Here comes a confession. You saw me with those rolls the other day. Well, I'm not feeding them to the birds. I'm slipping them to my kids. You know why I do it? Look, during the winter my

74

wife works nights in a law office and sometimes I just have to get out and fox around a little. Once, in the lobby of one of your famed midtown hotels, I was out with a nurse and right under my coat, opposite the center hall elevator, I let her monkey me with her hand, people coming and going in front of us, some of them men of renown, pulling in thirty thou a year. So you see, I've got to do a little something for my kids. Otherwise, how could I look them in their faces?"

"How does that square with the fix I'm in? I haven't got a college in the world to go to and September's almost here."

"What's the matter?" said the old counselor. "You a smart little bastard? I just told you something." And Joseph suddenly feared he would be put at the old counselor's table as a third thin little son, served last and having to wait for stealthy midnight rolls to quiet his hunger.

At the social hall that night, the craner's Viennese dad said, "Your mother has a great femininity, you know. A rare charm. I am looking forward to continuing our relationship in the city."

"I'm not sure there'll be any city get-togethers," Joseph told him. "Not with the kind of college troubles I've got."

Outside, on the bridle path, the craner asked him if he would like a chocolate, then began to eat one herself, saying, "How do I love my chocolate fingers, let me count the ways." She chewed beautifully, licking her fingers with an elegance that confused Joseph.

"Sometimes I think you don't give a damn for me," she said, pronouncing "damn" in the manner of an English country marm, making it quite the loveliest word he had ever heard and multiplying his confusion. He decided finally she had picked it up watching old British films, a privilege granted between wallet-making and therapeutic baths to those nonviolents who were coming along in their treatment ("Movie night for nonvios").

"I don't know what you've got," she said, continuing the British inflection. "You're not a terribly deft lover and I've seen smoother-looking men. You do a sexy dance and of course your touch is good, the tactile wonders of your pinkies. I've decided I shall sleep with you if you like. All I demand is that you yield your soul."

"I can't talk about anything right now," he said. "I got a letter this morning that floored me. I'm without a college. That British accent might be getting to me a little, but I might as well tell you I haven't really loved any of these nights that much. And I've got something bothering me I want to take care of inside, if you don't mind."

"But I should like to share your problems," she said, her head puppety, smiling, as though someone were pulling at her mouth strings. "To sit at your feet spaniel-style while you read me lovely things you've composed. I believe I shall call you Alberto henceforth, a name that better suits you. Should we marry, I shall love you tenderly, although later there might be extracurricular activities."

"It's not going to get that far," said Joseph, turning to leave; but then he ran back to flash his hands beneath her clothes one final time, getting her to do a few silent, puppety things to him while her lips bubbled and she craned her head at the moon. Like a frenzied, thieflike squirrel, he stuffed his cheeks with winter sex treats and went through three warning plumbing buzzers before he held off. As he left, he wondered whether she would join in a compact to appear to him at all lonely stages of his life, in roadside hotel rooms while he was making trips for canneries, letting him make inspections of her body before he dismissed her until his next crisis. He thought of her responding to a small pocket-size buzzer he would always carry with him, hooked up to a receiver strapped to her wrist.

In the social hall, he walked past the tiny-footed Viennese dad, feeling oddly free of him, and stepped between the French girl and her poetic professional waiter. "I started out with you," he said, taking her wrist, "and we're teaming up again. Come outside, I've got something to show you."

"What?" she asked, with imported film coquettishness, and he said, "Never mind," tugging at her arm.

"No," she said, "I'm going steady and you're with the babies."

"Well, then, I'm telling you this," said Joseph. "Your complexion's lousy, you have no tits, and I don't like the smell of your stink either."

The waiter stepped forward and raised her other bracelet-enclosed wrist. "I bought her a lot of these."

"Never mind about that," said Joseph, letting her go. "All right, I'm dialing you after camp."

Dick Kenzie took Joseph around the waist. "Take it easy, kid. Let's go back and slam out some mood pieces. That's what I do when I'm roped off. There's a peace settles over you when you're banging away, creating witty-type characters; you'd be surprised. Get a little sophisticated repartee going and the tension drops right out of you. And then you never know when you're going to hit the slicks."

"I couldn't concentrate on that," said Joseph. He ran outside, this time getting up a fine cry in the night air, one that equaled all the short, uneven daytime ones. He had the feeling that if he were suddenly paraded before assembled bodies of Columbia deans, the cry still going full steam, he would be able to make an eloquent plea for admission, getting them to slip him into the school in place of some Anzio veteran, an engineering hopeful with no real potential for scholastic greatness. It seemed hopeless to think about college at this late date. He saw himself letting a year go by, then reapplying only to find himself regarded as a suspicious leftover fellow, his application tossed onto a pile labeled "repeaters," not to be read until all the fresh new ones had been gone through. Year after year would slip away, until finally, at thirty-seven, he would enter night school along with a squad of newly naturalized Czechs, sponsored by labor unions and needing a great many remedial reading sessions. With no plan in mind, he went straight to the professional waiters' cabin; yet once inside, he seemed to be carrying out stage 11C of an elaborate scheme concocted by men with pointers around a Danish conference table. Kneeling beside one of the trunks, he took out nineteen one-dollar bills, squeezing them a little, and then going round to other pieces of luggage, removing various sums from each one of them. The buckled boy turned out to have rich, fragrant clothing and Joseph stopped a while to rub his face in one of the luxurious sweaters, actually sticking his tongue in to taste its wealth. When he had accumulated roughly one hundred and ten dollars, he got to his feet and leaped a little with excitement. Ruffio, fully clothed, stepped out of a shower stall and said, "I've been back here. It paid off. I was there through the whole thing."

"So what?" said Joseph. "I'm not caught. I was just standing here and there's no rule against that. I was fooling around with one of the sweaters."

"Oh no, you weren't. You took dollars from each one of us, plenty of them, and they're in your hand. I guessed what would be inside your head, only making forty while we were going over a thousand. That's why I came down here. You couldn't stand it. I knew the kind of way your thoughts would work. I'm coming out now, only don't hit me in the stomach."

"Don't tell anyone, all right?" said Joseph.

"Uh-uh, not on your life. I got you with the money in your hands after taking it out of our wallets. You'd better stay right there. I'm coming back with a whole bunch of people and then we're going to take you up to Salamandro for severe punishment."

He made some hand gestures at Joseph as though they would chain him to the cabin. "Look, I'm crying," said Joseph. "Will you please not go up there and tell everybody?"

"Nossir," said Ruffio. "I'm on my way. They're all up at the social hall and I'm going to round them up and bring them down in a large group. Be right back."

"I don't have to stay here," said Joseph as Ruffio left. And then he hollered, *"I said I'm crying!"*

He put the money back in each of the trunks and then took it all out again, not really sure of what you were allowed to do under the circumstances. It irritated him that he was staying right where Ruffio had put him; in a show of independence, he stuck his arm out of the door. He wondered if it would be a good idea to hide out in some tall grass for the evening, then spend the rest of his youth on the countryside, living in a series of Vermont sheds. He would travel only at night, flying from village to village until the thing blew over. He wondered whether he could stay alive that way; it all depended on getting his mother to send him boxes of canned goods timed to catch up with him at various New England hamlets.

Ruffio came back with Kenzie and most of the camper and professional waiters. "I'm right here," said Joseph, ushering them into the cabin as though it had been his own idea to have them over. He saw Hortz and found himself going into the boy's apprehended thief routine, shaking his fingers gospel-style, saying, "But, but, but, I, I, I."

"Veddy, veddy sneaky," Hortz whispered.

"Kid, why'd you have to pull this?" said Kenzie. "You could've asked me for dough. This is the one thing we never went for out in the Pacific. We'd let a man get away with holy hell, but not swiping. We'd take that man out to the latrine and let him have it about the head."

"I just did it for a second," said Joseph.

Kenzie took his arm. "We won't work you over, but I've got to take you up to see Doc."

"I'm not sure I have to go," said Joseph.

Outside, the light was stained and glum as though the camp were a vast bus station urinal illuminated by a single men's-room bulb, swinging overhead by a cord. Joseph walked between Kenzie and Ruffio, the trio at the head of a swarm of petite manufacturers. "This kind of stuff is a pain in the ass, isn't it?" he said in an intimate, chuckling tone, Capone kidding along his guards on the way to Federal Prison. They were a pair of hired hands, just doing their jobs, as disgusted with the whole thing as he was.

Salamandro seemed almost pleased at the news. He had come out of a shower in a bathrobe and sat down, crossing his great bearlike legs, toweling his hair dry. Kenzie described the thievery, Joseph listening with a small blushing smile as though it were a description of a triumph; he had been the only one in school to get all the words right in a spelling test. In the stained and urinary light, Salamandro's crossed and bearlike legs seemed beefily seductive; Joseph found himself looking inside them, checking for nudity, hoping there was no way for anyone ever to know his thoughts. He prayed that years later he might not admit in a drunken slip that he had found a camp director's legs sexy.

"He sneaked, eh?" said Salamandro, toweling away, pleased, expansive. "Sure, I remember the way they came to my office. From three rooms in Bensonhurst. You should have heard them. Terms they had. Conditions. What does the father do? He cuts couches or some goddamned thing. I said what the hell, I'll give the kid a break. I'll show you boys a lesson though. You let turds in, you get turds on your hand."

On his feet, Salamandro slapped Joseph's face once, medium-hard, saying, "You sneaked, eh? In a camp. I'll give you sneaking." Once, Joseph's friendly neighborhod cop had stopped a carful of Negroes, yanking a two-foot-long knife from the driver's vest, then pulling him out of the car to slap and brandish the side of the blade against the Negro's face. He might have been sharpening it on a leather barber strap. Now Salamandro's slap seemed more of a Negro-brandishing than a real blow. Joseph turned to Dick Kenzie, much angrier at him for some reason. "And you're letting him do that. Violence. You're just standing there, a combat guy."

Kenzie looked as though he might consider taking on Salamandro, but the idea was only a flashing one that died suddenly in the corner of his eye. "He's been a good kid," said Kenzie.

"All right, then," said Joseph to Kenzie. "Your stuff stinks. I pretended I didn't know anything about writing, but actually I won an essay contest on 'Hemingway's Lost Generation.' Your stuff is lousy and there isn't even a sign that it's ever going to be any good. It's heavy-assed like you."

"It's over," said Salamandro, bored suddenly, businesslike, ending a dull interview. "Get your father on the phone and tell him I want him over here."

"You shouldn't make fun of the number of someone's rooms," said Joseph.

Taking the phone from Salamandro, he called his mother across the lake. "Hello, Ma, I'm calling you. Columbia turned me down today, you know, the last college I had. I was all upset and took some money. They caught me and I have to call Dad so I called you up."

"You took money with what I put into you? With the patience that was poured into you?"

"I didn't really take it. It's hard to explain. I felt awful having no college at all. Anyway, Salamandro, you know, the brilliant one, smacked me and said Dad has to come over."

"He what you? I don't believe I heard what you just said with my ears. Say that again. I've got to hear that if it's the last thing I do. Somebody smacked you?" When Joseph defied her, she had a way of putting her knuckles in her mouth, shooting her eyes wide, then biting down on the fist as though it were an apple; Joseph saw her doing it now through the phone.

"A light one," said Joseph. "It was just the idea. Look, I can't talk all day. Are you coming over?"

81

"I'll be right over, darling. Just you keep calm."

The group waited now in silence. Embarrassed by the tension, Joseph said, "What kind of season's this been for you?" To his amazement, Salamandro said, "So-so. Better than some, worse than others."

After half an hour Joseph's mother arrived, her mouth minty and fresh, his sister's boyfriend at her side. Joseph wondered what he wore under the overcoat, then remembered he had once caught a glimpse of dirty track shorts. Joseph's mother bent to kiss him, smiling at Kenzie. "You'll excuse me, but I have to kiss my son. He hates this, but how often do I see him these days?" He feared that Salamandro would lash out and wrestle his mother to the ground before anyone could step in, getting her in a hairy-legged scissors grip.

She took a seat opposite Salamandro and pulled out a cigarette, the director offering her a light. "You want to give me a light? All right, I'll take one. We'll start that way." She leaned back then and spoke quietly, pleasantly, as though to a would-be suicide. "All right, you wanted to be a gentleman, I let you show off. Why not? I've got time. I'm calm. I'm composed. You wanted to see someone, I came right over. No fuss, no excitement. I didn't raise my voice. As far as you were concerned I wasn't inconvenienced. You didn't hear a word. You called and I came. I was a lady. Twenty seconds and I was out of the house. No makeup. No girdle. Just the way you see me. I'm calm. I haven't raised my voice. I haven't said a word. You wanted to get busy with your match, I let you. Everybody here's my witness. All right, now, you talk. The stage is yours. I have a lot of time. I'm composed. So help me God if I'll interrupt. Talk. What's on your mind, baby?"

Salamandro began to speak, coherently at first, but then his voice took leave of him, broke into a faded crackle like sandwiches being wrapped behind a far-off door. "We're here on the subject of your son. He started off nice, but then he sneaked from the other boys. You brought him to me. I took him in. I was all signed up, but I made room. He sneaked."

Joseph's mother shot her eyes wide, apple-bit her fist and screamed, "Are you through? Did I hear you?" Then, as though he had jumped up on a suicide ledge, she addressed him calmly again. "I sat here. I was a lady. I was composed. Did you hear a peep out of me? Boys, are you my witness? All right now. You're the camp director, with delicious food, with uniforms, with acres, with fancy this, fancy that—right? You called and I was over in twenty seconds. You didn't hear a word out of my mouth about makeup, about girdles, about putting a drop of lipstick on my mouth. You were the camp director and you wanted to see me. That's all I had to hear and over I came. I listened to you talk. I was calm. I let you rave. Now I want to see something. It's my turn, right?"

Salamandro began again—"He sneaked"—but all he got were wrapping sounds. He opened desk drawers as though searching for another voice. "I like things told to my face," he wrapped, a fragment from another argument, held long ago. Joseph's mother shook her head in patient disbelief, the shakes in perfect dance-floor rhythm. She seemed then to be talking to a face on the cabin floor. "The son of a bitch isn't letting me get a word in. Nobody'd ever believe this." Then she turned to Salamandro and said calmly, "Are you finally finished? Because if you are, there's a little something I want to see. I don't ask for much. I live in three rooms in Bensonhurst. Everybody knows where to find me. I don't hide from anyone. I mind my own business. Once in a while I have a few laughs in my own way, but I don't own camps. All right? In the summer I take a little place and if I get some sun on my face, I'm happy. Granted? Here's what I want to see. I've been around. I've seen a lot of things. I've

83

seen Jolson at the Winter Garden. I saw Fanny Brice the night she broke in at the Belasco. I've seen a few things in my time, right? My daughter's crazy friend with the overcoat is a witness. Everybody else is suffocating, and he's a little chilly, but he'll tell you I've been around a little bit. So you know what I want to see now? I don't want to see much. I want to see you hit that child of mine again. No. I take it back. I didn't say a word. I should have my tongue torn out. That isn't what I want to see at all. I don't want to see you slap him again. As God's my judge, that isn't what I want to see. I want to see you go near him. I want to see you take a step in his direction. *That's* what I want to see. I'm calm. I'm rested. There isn't a steadier hand in the room and that's with all this smoking I do. I'm civilized. I'm a lady. Now hit the child. This is going to be good. Step up from the chair and walk toward him. Put a hand on him. You're a camp director, you've got acres, hit the child. *That's* what I came across the lake for in a rowboat."

"Show her the money he sneaked," said Salamandro, waving from his chair.

"That's what I mean," said Joseph's mother, rising now, kissing Joseph. The room began to stir. "That's the hitting I wanted to see. That's the show I broke my neck to get over here and view. I wanted to get a look at his face again and I wanted to see him come near you again. That's what I would've given my right arm to see.

"All right now," she said, standing over Salamandro, "shall I tell you something with your face and your bathrobe and your camp? The boy is leaving with me tonight. That much I've decided. I don't want him in here any more." She apple-bit her fist. "God forbid if I hear one word about money. God forbid if I really start in with you with what you gave me and getting me over here. Not only that, but I want every cent back for those uniforms you stuck him with, and if I hear one word out of your mouth you'll be sorry you ever started in with me."

Salamandro's brother came into the room and gave the director some papers which he began to sign.

"And there's another little beauty," said Joseph's mother. "I like the two of them, their faces. Just let that check not be in the mail tomorrow and I'll give you both papers you'll wish you'd never heard of before.

"Come, sweetheart," she said, leading Joseph back to his cabin where he got together his clothing.

Hortz went along with them. "Your mother's a wild gambler in the night," said the boy, pronouncing the word "gahmbler," Joseph aware the boy had broken in a strange new routine.

"That's the kind of comedy you like?" said Joseph's mother. "But he's a sweet kid. Look how he's stuck by you. Those are the kind of rare people you meet. His mother's been around a little, but she's regular and look at the fine boy she turned out. So it just shows you. Of course, she'd like to get a little close to your mother so she could have a new little friend in the city. I don't know what's on that little beauty's mind much, do I? Still, look at the son she comes up with. You can never predict these things. He could be a nice friend for you."

When Joseph was packed, he decided to take his mother and the boyfriend around to the kitchen to wish the dish-scraping Lemmie goodby. They found him snatching starched long underwear down from a moonlit clothesline. "When I was in the Merchants," he said, "a fellow once died in my arms. He opened up his eyes like he'd seen an explosion and then I knew he was off. After that a lot of the boys asked if they could die in my arms. They'd call for Lemmie if they felt it coming on."

"And that's your taste," said the mother. "It's all right with me. I'm glad I paid to send you to camp."

Joseph shook the old seaman's shined and heavy hand. "If he was your friend, you'd say he was brilliant," he told her on the way back to the dock.

"You're just like your mother," she said. "You like an underdog. You'll sooner stick with him than you will somebody who can do you some good. Well, that's why we are where we are today. In three rooms."

At the boat dock now, Joseph's mother entered the dinghy, her face suddenly reddening. "I'd like to see him touch you. I want the son of a bitch's finger on you. That's what I want."

"We're out of there," said Joseph. "There isn't any need to get excited any more."

"Your mother really handled him, didn't she, kid?" the boyfriend said some minutes later, steering the small boat across the lake.

"And wouldn't you really like to know how I handle people," she said. "Wouldn't you like to move right in on the family and find out. You could, we've always wanted a Rockefeller." She squinted at Joseph. "What kind of an arm is that?"

"What do you mean?" he said.

"I don't like the looks of it. Is that the souvenir you're bringing me from camp? Just what I ordered. A little trouble."

"It's nothing," said Joseph, rolling down his sleeve. "Besides, it's my arm. I'm the one who has it. It's my trouble."

They sloshed along in silence for a while, Joseph leaning over suddenly to kiss his mother's face. He put his head on her shoulder, taking a good smell of her sweater. It felt nice in there, but then he detected a mysterious cry starting up from the bottom of him. Before it got any further, he said, "What the hell am I going to do after that letter?"

"You're such a child," she answered. "Did your mother ever let you down?" She gave him an ear kiss that seemed overly wet and said, "Will you please learn to put your last buck down on this baby?"

book two

he next morning, in the house across the lake, Joseph's mother stood over him as he ate his breakfast, chewing along and saying, "Those are beautiful eggs I made for you. Now that your mother's got hold of you, you'll really see a difference. I'll have you back to your old self again. What else delicious can I get you?"

It felt nice being in his mother's kitchen in a bathrobe, but he turned glum suddenly, the eggs sticking in his throat.

"Oh, I don't know what's on your mind, do I?" she said. "I haven't been your mother for seventeen years for nothing."

"I can't help it," he said. "I keep seeing that Columbia letter."

"Well, you can stop seeing it," she said, "because there was no letter. There was no Columbia and there was no Mr. Mess across the lake with his heavy legs and his acres and you never saw anything. That's the way you should think. You've got three weeks of good times ahead of you the way only your mother can supply them, and if I hear the word 'college' out of your mouth I'll split your head open. At the end of the summer you'll see your mother will get you a college, I don't care if there's two minutes left."

"What type are you going to get me?" asked Joseph. "I'm a little curious since I'm going to have to go to it."

"*Now* you want an answer," said his mother. "This second, with the head that I woke up with that I don't know whether I'm coming or going."

His mother seemed to put colleges in the same category as sold-out musicals and jammed restaurants. Many times he remembered her taking him past lines of people to a theater box office, winking at the treasurer and saying, "I'd like my kid to see the show, sweetheart. Do you think you could find a little seat for him somewhere?" And Joseph, more often than not, would be paraded before outraged throngs to the one seat left in the theater. Once, a special kitchen-type chair had been set up for him in the aisle of a hit revue; he had watched the show tensely, expecting at any second to be tapped on the shoulder by higher authorities and told to take his chair out of the aisle. She did the same thing in packed restaurants; her mouth minty, a cloud of perfume flashing from her bosom, stopping only to hike her skirt and knot her stockings, she would pull Joseph through dense thickets of waiting people and say to the headwaiter, "I've got a hungry kid. Do you think you could do a little something, doll?" Magically, a table would appear and Joseph would eat an uncomfortable dinner, standees' eyes burning his back, wanting to turn and give them his food. Now he had a vision of her dragging him through lines of students to the bursar at nostalgic old Wesleyan or tradition-haunted V.M.I., asking him if he could "do a little something for the kid." And Joseph pictured himself in freshman classes, sitting in a special kitchen chair off to the side of professorial daises. With three weeks to go, however, it was too early for her to get rolling. Lines had not formed outside the theater; there was plenty of time for her to slip into her print dress, mint up her mouth, then stocking-knot and perfume-flash him past the bursar's office.

After breakfast Joseph's mother dressed and said, "All right, what do you want to do for your first good time? I'm yours for the day." She put good times on an official basis. When she took him to the movies, as a child, she would seat him and say, "This is some swell time you're going to have." "I know," Joseph would say. "Who knows how to treat a son?" she would ask, and he would say, "You do." He would then sit back and more or less enjoy the film, never really happy until he was home, listening to the radio, eating a pear, not having to have a good time any more.

"I don't feel like having any fun," he said to his mother now. The arm had nippled up pretty badly and he was wearing a long-sleeved T shirt to cover it. He had fooled around with the area a little and now he was sorry, certain he had allowed a colony of germs to troop in and get at it.

"I think you're crazy. You've got three weeks and you ought to really stuff yourself with good times. Can any of us predict what's going to happen then? Sometimes I think I don't know your head any more. All right, come with me and I'll show you your mother hasn't been napping."

They walked about a quarter of a mile until they got to the beach. A woman was sunning herself on a chair, reading a book. She had on thick troubled horn-rims and kept her eyes terribly close to the pages.

"That's the one," said Joseph's mother. "She looks crazy as a bedbug, but wait till you hear her head. And she's mad about your mother. Wait till you see the way I go over there and handle her. I'm the only one can get her to laugh."

"What's so important about her?" asked Joseph.

"Why don't you ask a few questions? You wanted colleges,

I'm getting you colleges. One of her husbands was high up on some board or something and she herself is on some kind of committees. She's had a mixed up life with divorces, but put your money on her brain. Wait till you see the books she reads. Your mother will find out the whole story before she's finished. Wait till you see how I have her eating out of my hand."

Joseph's mother approached the woman. "How are you, darling? You look gorgeous. If you parked yourself over here there must be a new fellow in the neighborhood."

The woman laughed shrilly, squinting through her horn-rims as though she had been asked to solve a difficult equation. The fact that she had been divorced all those times both frightened and intrigued Joseph; it seemed a very sexual condition to him. He imagined she even looked a little divorced. Her scattered hair had a worried quality to it; her breasts were wide and spread out as though exhausted by the strain of all these marital split-ups. Her legs were a little heavier than they should have been, but Joseph found them appealing; he was certain she knew how to do dark and divorced things with them. He wondered whether she did not smell a little pungently divorced, too.

"This is my son," said Joseph's mother. "He had a bad experience and I'm trying to fill him up with good times. Say hello to Mrs. Rhinelander, Joseph. You want to talk books, she'll give you books till they're coming out of your ears."

The woman shook hands with Joseph. "He's a sweet boy. Is he going to college?"

"He's having a little trouble. Tell Mrs. Rhinelander what it is, darling."

"I'm not in one yet," said Joseph.

"What a pity," said the woman. "Perhaps we can do something about it."

"You see," said Joseph's mother. "You see how it pays to get around and meet people. What did I tell you? And your mother hasn't always surrounded herself with nice ones either, has she?"

"Don't embarrass the boy," said the woman; Joseph's mother patted her head. "Read a little, darling. It's good for you. Read the pages, but keep one eye out for fellas." The woman poured out a shrill, neurotic laugh. "I'm the only one can get a laugh out of her," said Joseph's mother. "She's had some messed-up life, haven't you, darling?"

"I've had my difficulties," she said, Joseph wondering whether she would share some of her pained, sexual secrets with him if he got to know her.

"What good did that do?" asked Joseph, after they had left the woman and started off down the beach.

"Question me a little," said Joseph's mother. "That's what I need a little of. Doubt your mother."

Then she said, "Did you see me handle her? Smoothly. Like a baby. She thought she might be able to 'do a little something' for you. She should only know what's on your mother's mind. Before I'm finished with her she won't know what hit her. She thinks this is the last she's seen of your mother. Wait. She wants laughs, she's going to have to pay plenty for them."

"But what can she actually do?"

"Did you hear her brain? You heard what came out of her mouth and you're questioning your mother. Oh, this is rich. This is really good. This is one for the books."

They walked a little farther until they came to a grocery store. Joseph glared at two lifeguards he caught taking in his mother's heaving, full-flanked horsy stride.

"You're still worried about that," she said. "You'll still defend your mother."

"I don't see why they have to stare," he said.

"All right, come in here and there won't be any staring," she said, pulling him into the grocery store. "Your mother found a new little place and it's tailor-made for her. Lots of good little things. Only make sure you don't bring fifty dollars in here because it's the last you'll see of it."

She took a deep breath, holding her throat. "Ummmph, has he got stuff. Just for your mother with the way she's always shopped. The way she could always hold on to a dollar. They really saw me coming with this store. God forbid. I get in here and I go crazy."

She spoke that way about many stores, and Joseph did not see the appeal of this one. It was dark, pungent, crowded with hanging wursts and sausages that frightened him; he did not feel comfortable until he had spotted a rack of familiar name-brand vegetable cans.

A rough-skinned young girl in a tiny bathing suit waited for service. She looked as though she had been raised exclusively on wursts which had finally stormed forth to take control of her skin. He thought she would probably be good for some frantic pimpled sex under a boardwalk somewhere.

The grocer was an old man with fanatic eyes who looked as if he spent a lot of time marching in parades. He cut some cheese for the girl, all the while keeping one eye on Joseph's mother.

"Watch this. Is this a riot. This is your mother's new fella. In two seconds he'll cut his finger off. This is really cute. Ask him if he knows where he is now. Ask him if he knows he's in a store. He doesn't know there's a world. All he knows is that he's got your mother's chest. He could be in China right now, too."

Whe.ı the girl walked off with her package, the old fanatic took Joseph's mother around the waist.

"That's the kind I get," she said, running her fingers through his hair. "Lots of money but two years younger than God. Don't worry about him though. Ask him what he does back there in that little room of his. He doesn't count sausages, that's for sure. Young ones he likes. He likes them when they're big in front."

94

The old man took Joseph's arm in a pair of clear-eyed fanatical-old-man pincers. "Where do you think the trouble's going to start?" he asked.

"What do you mean?" asked Joseph.

"Down there," said the man, pointing to the floor. "The Mexes. Everyone's worrying about the Russians, but below us is where it's going to begin. Those are the guys we have to worry about. All because no one's keeping an eye on them." He tightened his pincers on Joseph's arm; the idea seemed to be that he would squeeze harder until you came round to his fanatical views. "They ain't sleeping down there," he said to Joseph.

"Listen to his thoughts," said Joseph's mother. "He'll get you crazy."

"You like fights?" said the old man. "I'll tell you something. You know why Schmeling took a dive in that second Louis bout? They didn't want to antagonize America. The night before the fight Schmeling knocked out Louis in a hotel room in the real fight. All you got to do is blow in a nigger's ears and he can't take it. Schmeling knew it."

"I don't buy that," said Joseph, yanking his arm out of the pincers; he felt like puncturing some of the store's wursts.

"Joseph," said his mother sternly. "You'll forgive my son. He's going through something crazy."

"That's the truth about a nigger's ears," said the old man.

"Like hell," said Joseph.

"I don't know where he developed that mouth," said Joseph's mother. "All right, I'd better order. I really needed a little friction."

Walking back to the house, Joseph's mother said, "All right, let's have it."

"There's nothing to have."

"You didn't see a Jew. Is that it? Is that what's bothering you? Well, your mother's really had to worry about that all her life, hasn't she? All her life she hasn't been respected wherever she went. Did you see how crazy that man is about your mother? Do you know what he would do for me? I could have walked out of there with the whole store. Ask him if he'd treat the Queen of England with any more worship."

"I didn't like the smell of the place," said Joseph. "I've been feeling that around here."

"You're such a child. You're such an infant. Who's looking at you? Do they know if you're a Hindu? You could be a Sioux Indian for all they care. Stop worrying about yourself for a change. The Jew thing should be my worst worry and I'd be riding on velvet."

When Joseph returned to the house, his mother's Irish friend was filling the refrigerator with fruit. Joseph's family rented the downstairs floor of the house from the woman, who lived above with her family. Seeing her now, Joseph felt a little trapped, very much aware he was not in his own home. The table did not belong to him; the chairs and the dishes were strange and unfriendly. What if they had a terrible fight with the Irish people? They would have to stay right where they were, using up the paid-for weeks. He knew he was not going to be able to take deep long breaths and be completely comfortable till he got back to his own apartment.

The Irish friend looked warm and breakfasty in her bathrobe. Joseph wondered what would happen if he suddenly swooped in through the opening and got at her legs for a few seconds. Would it all be glossed over with a few admonitions or would he actually be dragged into court to face charges? His mother put her arm around the woman's neck and said to Joseph, "You didn't know I had the bitch upstairs, did you? I'll kill it if they don't take it away from me. A few little pears she brought down in case I have to feed a sudden army. She's making sure that if the whole city of Chicago comes to the door her friend

Meg won't be caught short. Ask her if she's got a crust of bread, a crumb to feed her own morons upstairs."

She pinched the woman's cheek. "Sweetness. Is this good. I'll absolutely kill it in two seconds." Taking Joseph's hand, she dragged him to the linen closet. "You want to see sweetness. You want to see your mother's kind of friends. Look in there. A few covers she brought down in case someone should get pneumonia. In case there's a sudden snowstorm. Ask her if she has a rag to cover her morons, but she was worried your mother would get a little chill."

"You stop it, Meg," said the friend. "You're really making too big a fuss."

"If it says another word I'll choke it to death," said Joseph's mother, taking her around the neck again. "Is this an angel. Is this a goddess. Could you just faint. It made sure your mother had fruit in case she got hungry. Four in the morning the day I moved in here she was on her knees scrubbing your mother's floors so I shouldn't get a little depressed when I moved in. You want to know about your mother's friends. And guess what? It's really affected her face." She squeezed the woman's cheek. "Puss. Have you ever seen such a face? And dimples it had thrown in just in case it wasn't gorgeous enough. I'll die. Four in the morning it gets down on her knees to sterilize floors and you know what else is affected? Her body. Oh yeah. Here, I want you to see a pair of bitch legs." She flung wide the woman's bathrobe. "Did you ever. And I'd like you to see what she's got doing on top. Sixteen years old. Mine I could toss over my shoulders, but look what she's got standing out there. Look at a pair of legs on a woman. A behind." The friend had seemed cozily maternal in the robe, but beneath it her body was lewd and midnight-sleek. She wore no bra, her panties a fleck of redness which Joseph could not be sure were panties at all.

"Meg, darling," said the woman, closing her robe. "You're embarrassing the boy."

97

"You're getting the hell out of hand," said Joseph.

"What's the matter?" said the mother. "He saw a body? That really fazes me. That's one thing I never had to worry about with the way I brought up my children."

Shivering, she pinched the woman's behind. "Saint. Queen. Worry a little about me. And this has always been your mother's luck. Wherever she's gone there's always been one of these things around. The same sweetness. The same charm. Oh, I'll meet a little beauty like the mess with the heavy legs across the lake, but then I'll always get one of these around me to wash away the crap.

"And it doesn't know what I would do for it, either, does it?" said the mother, kissing the woman's cheek. "It doesn't know that it could have my blood if it asked."

"Your mother and I have always been good friends," said the Irish woman. Joseph was not sure of the protocol on handling them, but he prayed for another bathrobe separation.

The woman said she was preparing a barbecue that night for Joseph and his mother; when she went upstairs, Joseph's mother stood limply in the kitchen, her hand at her throat. "I can't breathe. When I see what that thing does for me I get absolutely weak. Do you know what it's meant for me to have her here? Only life itself. And you wonder why your mother never needed a Jew. A Jew would sterilize floors for your mother and a Jew would care whether the refrigerator was filled or not? Oh yes. Mr. Corngold who lives in 4L above us in the city would run down with blankets if he heard your mother give a little cough?"

"Aren't you paying for all this?" asked Joseph.

"And you know what? That's just the kind of remark I'd expect from you. You're going through quite a stage. When you grow up you'll see that you can really pay for what your mother's getting from these people. Guess what I'd have to leave at the end of the summer to pay for what I'm getting. Only my skin, that's all."

Joseph's mother had invited the college-connected divorcée to the barbecue; in the early evening he went to his mother's room and found both women with their skirts hiked up, comparing girdles. Joseph's mother wheeled about and said, "Look at the lines, the stitching. Well, make up your mind you'll never see such work as long as you live. A little fellow named Sol does it for me. He's as big as a second and you could trip over him in the street, but you should see a pair of hands. And he'd do anything in the world for this baby. You don't see work like this any more." Turning to Joseph, she said, "Mrs. Rhinelander spotted your mother's shape. She's the first one, isn't she, darling? Tell her about it, Joseph. How many people have fainted."

"She has the figure of a young girl," said the woman. "And she's got exquisite taste."

"Well, she really would know taste with her head in volumes for the last thirty years. When she gets to the city, your mother is going to take Mrs. Rhinelander around to see a few cute little tailors and corsetieres if she behaves herself. But for that she's going to have to pay plenty."

The woman laughed, lowering her skirt. "How does it feel to have such a young mother?"

Joseph felt he should say something intellectual and college-worthy. "Oh, I don't know, it's all relative." He hoped she would not ask him what he meant.

His mother pulled a tissue-covered negligée from a drawer and stuck it under Mrs. Rhinelander's arm. "Here, darling, you keep this. She wants to meet a few fellas. When I get finished with you, you'll meet so many you won't know what to do with them."

When the woman left, Joseph's mother said, "Those are the

99

kind. You should listen to the smartness that comes out of that head of hers and yet when it comes to clothes she doesn't know whether she's coming or going. Did you see the dress she was wearing? She could be a fast matron of ninety years old. I looked at her brassiere. It makes her look as though she's carrying a lovely bunch of flowers in there. But don't worry, she spotted your mother's shape. With all the books and the smartness she found time. Oh, I'll take her in hand all right, but she should only know what it's going to cost her."

"Did you ever find out what college she's connected with?" asked Joseph.

"Yes, I found out," said the mother, tucking shields into her armpits. "She's with the college that I'll tell you when I'm ready and not one second before. You're going through some period. You saw the way your mother just twisted her around, and you're worried. You're worried about your mother's sense of timing. About her way of handling people. You've got a lot to worry about."

The barbecue was held in the rathskeller; Joseph saw three golden children's heads bob up over the bar, each with wildly scattered smiles as though they had gotten their teeth by making empty-mouthed leaps for them, never bothering afterward to have them arranged in even rows. "The morons," said Joseph's mother, running toward the blond trio, grabbing the chins of two. "Hello, imbeciles. I don't think I ever heard you say a word. Ask them if they ever gave a cry in their lives. And if they did, who would come to listen to them. Just like the way you were brought up," she said to Joseph. "Just like the care that was poured into you."

Joseph's mother took a fistful of potato chips from the bar. "Taste these. The stuff she's laid out. Ummmph. And I have to think of a way to repay her, too."

"I don't get your meaning," said Joseph. "All she did was put out these potato chips." The camp nipple had spread out now and was definitely taking control of his arm.

"I can't handle your mouth," she said. "Not the mood you're in these days."

Chris, the Irishwoman's husband, a tall, round-shouldered man in a coat sweater, was cooking meat on a tiny open oven that barely had room for one steak. He said very little and was given credit for having a great deal of reserve. Joseph had met him once before and decided he really was not reserved so much as he had no ideas and nothing to say. He held down an important sales executive job, and Joseph imagined it was because they were all waiting to hear what he was going to come out with when he finally broke his silence. He could probably keep them guessing that way for about ten years, it seemed to Joseph. When his bluff was called, he would simply move on to a second company for another wordless decade.

"There's my doll," said Joseph's mother, running over to hug him. "Prince. He knows how I feel about him, too. His quietness. His reserve. Don't sell him short, though. I'd like to have a nickel for a few of those little ideas that are going on in his head. Some of those little deals that he puts over in that quiet way of his. His smoothness. His ways. Watch him handle the morons if you get a chance. One word from him and they're paralyzed with fear. Let him give them a little look and they'll have diarrhea for a week. Just like your father's control over you."

"You've got a wonderful mother here," said Chris, patting down the one steak. He said it as though he had put her through a series of rigorous tests before reaching his judgment. Joseph, who could not meet his warm, mensy fishing-trip eyes, said, "I know."

"Joseph," said his mother, beaming, her arm around the man's neck, presenting him as though he were a display at a regional sales conference.

101

"What?" asked Joseph.

"Your mother's choice of friends."

The divorced woman came in now, wearing a flowered print dress that billowed round her in great tentlike circles. "Isn't that pretty?" said Joseph's mother. "I'd like to know where she had to go to get that dress. What connections she needed. I'll bet anything it was Paris. That's all right. I'll dress her in the city, but she's going to have to pay heavy for it. Not in money. My way."

Joseph's mother always ran down other women's dresses and underwear; he had come to think of all female garments that weren't hers as ill-fitting, ridiculous and somehow a little shabby and unclean. He felt sorry for the divorcée in her terrible, poorly chosen clothing and was certain that if she had spent a little time on girdle and underwear protocol she would have been able to fend off several of her divorces.

When some Latin music started up, Joseph's mother took the divorcée's hand and began backing her way toward the sound as though she were inching up to a campfire. "Music," she said, tearing at her throat. "I'm lost. The piece de resistance. What it's done to me ever since I was this high. Could I ever stop these feet when I hear strains? They'd have to kill me first. And they don't know how to butter up your mother around here, do they? And she won't pay them back in spades when she gets back to the city?"

"Come," she said to the divorcée. "You want to see life, watch me. You never saw this in colleges." In the center of the rathskeller she began to dance alone, leaving the divorcée to stand and watch her. She did that often, guiding people out to the center of dance floors, then abandoning them so she could dance by herself. Much of her dancing consisted of standing in one place, eyes at the ceiling, arms at her side, tapping one foot and shaking her chest, as though her breasts were on a shelf, the idea being to shake them down and win a prize. Sometimes she would tap herself around in a tiny circle; always it was as though the music were coming from a shower spigot and she was letting it wash down all over her. It was a style of dancing that did not require spacious dance floors. She would sometimes go into it in elevators and on subway platforms, humming musical backgrounds.

The divorcée watched her now, forlorn and squinted in her teen-age tents of flowered chiffon, her lips soaked as though a sour liquid had been hurled in her face to commemorate one of her divorces, the way rice is thrown at newlyweds. Shaking her shelves, Joseph's mother told the divorcée, "You're living now, baby. Forget you ever saw a college. You've got Meg now. Get a little of her into your system. You want to see grace, a sense of rhythm? Those are things they could never take away from me. Watch. I'll show you sex." She bit her lips, tapped and shook some more, saying, "There's your sex. Someday I'll get out of this girdle and show you real choreography." In the middle of the song, the divorcée suddenly contributed a single, slow, twirling pirouette, her skirt flying above her waist, ending the movement by settling into a deep, heavy-legged Victorian curtsy. "That was cute," said Joseph's mother, not breaking the rhythm. "Where did you learn such a thing? You know who'd like that? Men. They really would."

The old wurst man appeared, wearing an apron, and took Joseph's arm as though continuing a conversation that had been going on for hours. "I'll tell you why you get so many colds," he said. "What do you do when you take a shower? You dry yourself, right? Well, you're drying up the pores. They like to be wet and loose like people. Next time you take a shower, you sit around wet for a while. Keep the pores soaked up. You'll see your cold go right out the window.

"Hey," he said, pointing to Joseph's mother on the dance

floor. "You see your mother? She's a sausage." He held the apron out in front of him daintily and began to imitate her dance. "A night at the burlycue with the boys."

The two beach lifeguards came in now. One had a short-snouted dog's face set on a fortresslike neck; he looked as though he ran into walls to keep himself toned up. Joseph's mother danced close and said, "I saw him, too, and I know just what you're thinking. He loves Jews. You have the same head as your mother. But you want to know something? Those are the kind that surprise you. Never go by a face. I'll show you that I'll have him eating out of my hand."

She asked the boy to dance and in a few minutes led him back to Joseph, saying, "Don't look now, but your mother's got a new boyfriend. A young one. How old are you, sweetheart? A fast nineteen. Ugly as sin, but he's cute as a button. Meet my son. He decided he didn't like your face, but I bet him I'd win you over."

"What kind of thing is that to say?" said Joseph. But he shook hands with the smiling, short-snouted boy and felt a little better about him.

The rathskeller began to crowd up; the second lifeguard was a powerful, cheery-looking blond boy with low-slung hips who gathered several drinks in one arm and began to weave slowly through the guests, in imitation of a halfback, one arm stuck out to stiff-arm the opposition. Someone named Rafferty appeared, angry, open-collared, reciting anecdotes about how he had told off various people during the week. He kept his face half an inch from listeners' mouths as he told his stories; Joseph heard him wind one up with the line "And so I said to him, 'Fwar-rrkk you,' and he didn't say a word back to me."

"Who invited that bargain?" Joseph's mother asked Chris at the tiny grill. "He's all right," said the tall Irishman. "He just gets a little hot under the collar."

His mother turned to Joseph now, as though a translation

were needed. "He's a swell guy. He gets a little steamed up, but two seconds later he's a sweetheart."

"I heard," said Joseph. "You didn't have to repeat it."

The tiny grill had finally produced two cooked steaks. Joseph's mother took off a piece for him, saying to Chris, "God's your judge, is there anyone under the sun you'd do this for?"

"Just you, Meg," said the host.

His mother turned to Joseph now and began to cry, her nose growing red and bulblike. "Sometimes it gets to me the way they treat me. They know it'll take me my whole life to pay it back."

"Mom, it really isn't that great a spread," said Joseph, putting his arm around her. The tiny grill had misted up the rathskeller; the man named Rafferty was beginning to worry Joseph. He was not sure whether it was all right for the man to be hollering out "Fwarrrkk" within hearing range of his mother, and he wondered whether he ought to spirit her out of there. He had the feeling his last chance to apply soothing, minor medications to his arm had slipped away; now that he had blown his chance, something major had taken over and was snapping along through it. He wondered whether the Irish friend had passed the word along that Joseph and his mother were the only Jews at the party and if they were to be unmasked at a special midnight ceremony.

When his mother returned to the dance floor, Joseph spoke to the divorcée. "How's the college season shaping up?" She said something vague about accreditation and he wondered why there did not seem to be any way to ask her point-blank whether she could get him into one. The words would not form in his mouth, just as he had not been able to rap out fresh applications to other colleges once the Columbia letter had come. As she turned slightly to watch the dance floor now, her nipple slipped out of her bodice for a second. She covered it casually, the way you might adjust an earmuff, but Joseph felt a wash of shame that all his hopes for college entrance should be tied to someone whose nipple could slide out so unexpectedly. What if she were pleading his case in some last-ditch effort before an assembly of deans and one emerged? Wouldn't it all be over? Or might it not work another way, her total lack of concern for personal tidiness being taken as a sign of academic integrity?

The music began once more, a group gathering around Joseph's mother to watch her dance. The man named Rafferty took his place in the circle, Joseph afraid he'd bombard her with fwarrrkks. "My son's passing out," said Joseph's mother, getting her shelves started. "Look at his color. Sometimes he wishes he had another kind of mother, a gray-haired sweet little old one, don't you darling?" The pimpled beach girl stood in the crowd, Joseph certain he smelled wursts. "Comin' through," said the cheery lifeguard, weaving through the crowd to Joseph's side. He was the kind of fresh-faced rascal who made people say, "He's a wise kid, but you've got to like him."

"That your mom?" he asked. "She's great, really stacked. I saw you two down at the beach today. My name's Vinnie. Hey, you know what you ought to take up? Free-style fighting. I been putting in a summer on it. A guy's teaching me. You use anything you can get your hands on. The first thing you do when you come into a place is look it over for things you can use on guys. Could be a lamp, a picture on the wall, your enemy's tie. You make it a habit. Right now, if we had a little something between us, I got ten ways to come at you. You want to hear the first one?"

"What?" asked Joseph.

"I'd have this right up in your face," he said, tapping the bottom of Joseph's steak plate. "Then I work you over to the bar and come in with that tray of glasses about your head. I thought of those the second I saw you. You fall into a pattern of thinking. Anytime I go into someplace, the first thing I do is figure out ways to come at guys." He saw the pimpled girl in the crowd and whispered confidentially to Joseph, "Hey, you know who she looks like? I saw her on the beach. Like one of those little Jersey City Jew broads. You ever seen any?"

"I've never run into them."

"Yes," he whispered. "We used to call them Jewies."

The three scatter-toothed blond children appeared suddenly, harpylike, dancing by with Joseph's secret. The grill smoke had beaded the windows. Joseph glanced at the divorcée and grew panicky; framed by steak mist, her face seemed ethereal and holy, as though all of her college years had been spent standing in campus chapels and her connections were only with small heavily Baptist colleges that would automatically be sealed off to Joseph. The dancing had stopped now, the hostess announcing a game involving the switching of clothes by some of the men and women at the party. "None of that," said Joseph, but his movements were groping and syruplike and he could not seem to get through the crowd to take his mother away. His arm was quite hot now and he heard another "fwarrrkk" from Rafferty. He imagined that the next game would be one in which he and his mother, as the party's only Jews, would have to stand in a corner and fight the whole gathering. He wondered whether the short-snouted boy who had been so nice would be neutral. One vision he tried to scoop out of his head was that of his mother poking out a harmless, thin-wristed jab, then stopping a roundhouse right and falling to reveal a pinwheeling cloudburst of complicated undergarments. Joseph's mother and the wurst man were the first couple to volunteer for the switching. They stepped behind the bar and the grocer soon emerged in his mother's skirt; she came out then wearing the wurst store apron over her blouse and girdle. The old man picked up his skirt, displaying thin, fanatical old legs. "You should know what I had with him behind the bar," said Joseph's mother as everyone laughed and applauded. "As far as he was concerned, the girdle was part of the deal, too." The cheery lifeguard had turned to watch the game, and Joseph, fascinated by his own behavior, brought his steak plate down on the boy's neck, saying, "I'm using it on you first, you bastard. I'm Jewish." The lifeguard held his neck, wiped off some steak juice and looked around, saying, "Just let me get my hands on something."

Joseph ran out on the dance floor to his mother. "I knew it," she said. "What happened? I could see it coming all along. I saw your mood. You had to get it out of your system. From the second you got here you were going to not like it. All right, hold that moron back there, someone," she said, motioning toward the lifeguard. The host and the short-snouted boy pinned his arms. "There's nothing to use in this goddamned room," he said, straining toward Joseph. When he had quieted down, Joseph's mother said to the host, "Chris, darling, what can I say? You have three sons. Someday you'll appreciate it. He's going through a stage. God alone knows what's on his mind."

"I understand, Meg," said the tall Irishman.

"I've got to take him back now. Promise me one thing," she said with a wink.

"You name it."

"That you'll stay as sweet as y'are."

Joseph followed his mother up the stairs to the main floor now. The apron left the backs of her legs exposed and he tried not to look up at her flapping girdle straps. "You had to spit it up, didn't you? It was like a stone. You had it in there from the second you got here and didn't see a Jew. So now you got it up. You feel cleansed. And what did you accomplish?"

"Maybe you'd like to go back there and find out what that son of a bitch said about us."

"That's the way you talk in front of a mother?" she said, wheeling suddenly. But then she walked on, entering the kitchen. "He said, he said, he said. Always what someone said.

My son's going to change the world. You saw the spread they put out for me tonight. The liquor. The taste of those steaks that you could faint. The charm. I get swellness like that and I'm supposed to worry because someone said a word? You know what I have to do for these people, those saints? Get down on my knees and thank my lucky stars."

"I still don't think they're that great," said Joseph. "Not if they have a guy like that lifeguard as their friend." He wondered if the divorcée had seen him hurl the steak plate. "Do you think Mrs. Rhinelander will hold this against me?"

"You let me worry about her," said his mother, getting him a pair of pajamas. "That's the last thing on my mind. Just you concentrate on being a little less crazy."

he next morning Joseph's arm was so full in his sleeve that he could not roll back the pajama material to get a look at it. He said "Uh-oh" aloud and that second remembered he had said the same thing, years back, upon hearing of his beloved uncle Samuel's death, the first person he had been close to who had ever passed away. "Is that all you can say?" his aunt Muriel had asked. "Is that the depth of your feeling for your uncle?" It was not that at all. He had loved his uncle Samuel and wished he could snatch him back from the dead. But he was bad at responding to tragedies, could summon no Churchillian eloquence when one came up.

When his mother entered the room, he said, "That arm I got at camp is all blown up."

"What, am I blind all of a sudden that you have to tell me?" she said. "I could see it from two blocks away. Well, you really fixed yourself up this time. That's some arm. And I needed it, too. I was feeling too good. I had a day of peace. This is what you're presenting me with, eh? With the way you've been acting, it's a lucky thing you don't have a swollen head.

"All right," she said, sitting on the bed, "let me have a look at it. I sent out a special order for it. I needed this." She bent over him and gently guided up the pajama material. He could see the roots of her hair and said, "Why don't you just let it grow back to the natural color?"

"Now you want to make cutesy with me," she said. "I've got time.

"I don't like the looks of this arm," she said, touching it lightly. "I could very easily do without it."

"That's surprising," said Joseph. "I thought you'd eat it up."

"You know what'll make it go down?" she said. "Your comedy." She touched his forehead and said, "How do you feel?"

"Pretty good," he said. He actually did not feel bad at all; the arm gave him no pain, although this in itself seemed an ominous development.

Biting her lip, she stood up and said, "Now look, I don't like the looks of that arm at all." It was as though she were debating a giant body of people who loved the looks of the arm. "I know what an arm can lead to."

"Is there anybody here saying they like the way it looks?" he said.

"And I'm getting Doc Hurwitz up here to take a look at it. If he complains about how far it is, I'll fire him out of my house. I knew him when he charged fifty cents a visit and he used to beg you to come. Let him say a word to me about distance when I need him now."

"Why don't you give him a chance?" asked Joseph. "He'll probably run right up here."

"He'd better if he knows what's good for him. I'll remind him about how his wife used to take in wash to keep them alive when he was finishing school. Those are the kind that don't remember. He's very fancy now with stocks. Let him open up his mouth to me."

When she left to make the call, Joseph heard his father drive up outside. "An hour and thirty-five minutes to the second," he heard him say. "Last time it was an hour and forty-two minutes."

Joseph dozed off momentarily and was awakened by his father's voice. "What are you doing there under the covers?"

"What do you mean, Dad?" asked Joseph.

"With your hands. You know."

"Nothing."

"You're sure you're not fooling around with yourself? All right, all right, I'll take your word for it. Listen, Mother told me about your arm. Let me have a look at it." Joseph held it aloft, some broken voltage running through it as though he had been plugged into a toaster.

"Well, that's not right, I'll tell you that to your face," said the father. "It's bigger than the other arm, there's no argument about that." The father shook his head worriedly. "Look, let me get straight on something. You were going to go to college, weren't you?"

"Yes I was, Dad."

"Well, let me ask you, how do you expect to go with an arm like that?"

"I don't know."

"They won't let you in. I'll tell you that right now. I mean I don't claim to know much about it, but I'll bet you dollars to doughnuts you don't get in."

"You're probably right," said Joseph. "I wasn't really in one anyway. Mother had some woman who was going to see about it, but it's up in the air."

"Well, I don't know about any woman, but no college will

let you in like that. Why should they? You think a big college has time to bother around in this day and age? They have their own headaches, believe me. They've got their hands full. You want them to stop and worry about you and you've got a surprise coming. You're just one person."

"Maybe it'll get better in time," said Joseph. The arm felt warm and cozy and Joseph guessed it was only when you raised it that you were toastered.

"I could give you an example," said Joseph's father, removing his shirt to shave. "You don't have to go any farther than my own business, although it's no college. Would we send out a couch if we didn't like the looks of it? How long do you think we'd be in business?"

He lathered up his face, shaking his finger at Joseph. "I'll bet you never gave it a second thought about college. You've always been lax about things. Wake up, I'm warning you, wake up."

He had great mats of hair on his back and chest and Joseph wondered if he himself was slated to have equal amounts; and if so, why had not significant growths yet gotten under way?

"I used to get about five shaves a blade," his father said, beginning to stroke off the lather. "Now that my beard is tougher, I only get two. The same thing will happen to you.

"Did you just laugh at me?" asked the father, wheeling around.

"No," said Joseph.

"Don't be no wise guy. You worry about that arm of yours." Then, as though to lighten the atmosphere, the father pointed out the window and said, "You know what's out there?"

"What's that?" asked Joseph.

"Your camp. That's where we rowed across to visit you. I'll bet you didn't know that."

"I had an idea," said Joseph.

"Well, that's where it is," he said. When he had finished shav-

113

ing, he wiped his face and dressed, pausing at Joseph's bed.
"You may have your hands full with that arm, you know. You're
taking it like it's a joke."

"No, I'm not," said Joseph. "I realize its seriousness."

The father dug down into his pocket and pulled out several
coins. "Here, you want some change?" he said.

"What for?" asked Joseph.

"To keep," he said. "Keep it in your bathrobe while you're in
here. You ought to carry a little money with you."

"Okay," said Joseph, taking it with his good hand.

Alone now, he studied his great arm with a certain concern,
but with the feeling, too, that if the going got rough, it would
have to shift for itself. There was something separate and
peninsula-like about the arm; once, his geography teacher had
drawn giant square maps of Asia on the blackboard, adding, almost as an afterthought, several appendages, the main one being Kamchatka in the northeast. He thought of his arm now as
that remote, snowy peninsula, sentimentally related to the main
body of him, but expendable in a real pinch. He could not imagine any of the arm's badness sweeping over and getting into
the rest of him. He was sure it would be headed off at the
shoulder checkpoint, forced to retreat. He remembered, too,
that if you had an infection, sooner or later a small army of
good corpuscles would rally together and beat back the trouble.
Looking at the arm now, he decided that his had not swung
into action quite yet, and wondered when they were going to
get rolling.

The Irish friend carried in some soup on a tray. At her side,
Joseph's mother said, "The bitch made some broth. She heard
your mother was in trouble. You know what kind they are? The
kind that wait for a formal invitation to give help when they
hear there's sickness.

114

"Taste this soup," she said, giving Joseph a spoonful. "You want to know love? You want to know decency?

"What did you put into this soup, puss?" she said, pinching the woman at her waist. "A pint of your blood? Don't look now, but a whole month's savings went into the concoction you're eating.

"Is it delicious?" she asked Joseph.

"I can't tell on just one spoonful," said Joseph.

"You'll forgive my son's comedy," his mother said to her bathrobed friend. "He's laying with an arm the size of a house and he's got time for jokes. Someday, when he grows up, he'll know friendship and decency."

Joseph ate the soup, stopping after each mouthful to see if he could feel any of it pouring across into his arm to do battle with the tide of fast-multiplying bad cells. The Irishwoman sat on his bed now, offering Joseph a clear view of a large, nervous section of her pants. He wondered whether he could trade the soup for a silent twelve-minute exploration of her body beneath the covers. There was no way to ask her this, of course; but what if he wrote her a brilliant letter, setting forth with exquisite logic all the reasons it was harmless and would mean so much more to him than bowls of chicken gumbo?

"I think if you slipped in next to him, and gave him your chest, he could forget all about the soup and the arm together," said his mother.

"You oughtn't talk that way in front of him, Meg," said the woman, covering her pants.

"Why, it hasn't been done?" said Joseph's mother. "And I don't see where he's staring? All right, not another word, that's the end of it."

Later, in the afternoon, Joseph's mother greeted Doc Hurwitz by saying it was a lucky thing he had gotten there when he did. "Because if you'd taken any longer I'd have split your head open.

"I don't have to take any crap from him," she said affectionately, smiling at Joseph, her arm around the doctor. "I know this guy from way back when. Do I know you when you and your wife had to eat dry cereal for dinner so you could finish school? I gave his wife stockings when she didn't have a pair to her name. He can't get fancy with me, can you, Doc?"

"Your mother's got my number, sonny," said the doctor.

For many years the family had been taken care of by the skilled Dr. Baum, Joseph's mother certain that when his abilities became known generally, a shrine would be built in his honor. "And your mother will be there with the first stone," she had said often. "If ever there was a king, he's your man." One day, quite suddenly, authorities had swooped down on the kindly medical man, seizing him on a tax-evasion charge and leaving Joseph's family without a physician. Hurwitz was a slightly built neat little man with a toothbrush mustache who lived in the neighborhood and had enjoyed some success in chasing off strokes whenever Joseph's spinster aunt Lorraine came down with them. When Baum had been packed off to jail to serve his sentence, Joseph's mother grudgingly turned to Hurwitz; she gave him some small credit for having a "good head," but held against him his way of always working his relatives in on cures. They were all in related professions, such as podiatry and vaccine manufacture. "God forbid if you don't fill your prescriptions at his brother-in-law's drugstore," Joseph's mother said. "I think he'd drop dead." She resented, too, the amount of his fee. Feeling he was entitled to more than $5, yet lacking the confidence to shoot for $8, he had settled on the odd figure of $6.50, giving patients change from a little purse he kept in his medical kit. "It's very becoming for a doctor to handle change," she said. "When I see that purse come out I could vomit."

Now, as Hurwitz approached Joseph, a figure slipped furtively into the kitchen. "Who was that?" asked Joseph's mother. "I caught him. And if it's who I think it is, I'm throwing the both of you out on your heads."

"He just came up for the ride," said Hurwitz.

"I knew it," said Joseph's mother. "You have to watch him like a hawk. I knew he'd try to slip his brother in on me. Well, I'm telling you right now that if he comes within ten feet of my kid's bed, you'll both be sorry you ever met me."

"I don't see what you've got against my brother," said Hurwitz. "I don't say I'm calling him in here, but he's a very good man."

The brother was hiding behind a stove; through the door, Joseph could make out his khaki army jacket. He was a surgeon who had just been discharged from the armed forces; Joseph heard that he had performed thousands of operations under battlefield conditions, doing daring and complicated incisions you would never get to handle in ordinary practice.

"If he's a good man, you can have him," said Joseph's mother. "He's not going near my son. I got a look at what was doing under his fingernails in the city and that was it then and there. God forbid if he approaches this bed."

"He's not, he's not," said Hurwitz. "That isn't the point. But you really ought to give him a chance. He saw things in Germany another doctor wouldn't see in a lifetime. Do you know what that's worth?"

"Well, you can have him. On toast. I saw his fingernails. That was enough for me."

Hurwitz sighed and tapped on Joseph's arm. He said he needed wet cloths, and Joseph's mother, as she left the room, said, "Did I tell you or didn't I? He's got a good head but he'll always work some goddamned brother in on you. Let him try it on me and he'll never try it again."

When she was upstairs, Hurwitz's brother, in combat boots, flashed in through the door to take a quick look at the arm.

"She told you not to," said Joseph, who never felt completely confident in standing up to doctors.

"He just wants a little look," said Hurwitz. "You want your arm to get better, don't you? How are you getting along at college?" he asked with a mirthless smile, while his brother studied the arm.

"I'm not in one," said Joseph.

"Thaaaat's good," said Hurwitz, buying time.

Joseph's mother came back with the cloths, passing through the kitchen, where Hurwitz's brother was cooking a potful of surgical instruments.

She walked into the bedroom to find Hurwitz on his feet. "Did that hulk in the kitchen see the arm?" she asked Joseph.

"Just for a second," he said, not knowing whether to cover up for the medical team or tip off their game.

"The son of a bitch," she said, unbelievingly. "I turned my back for a second. I knew it. I knew it the second I saw him with his dirty jacket. I ought to have my head examined."

"Meg," said Hurwitz, "it needs twenty-seven little drainage cuts up and down the arm. He can do it in half an hour and it'll be all done."

"He did look at the arm," she said. "And now he wants to make little cuts. He didn't get enough in four years in the army and now he wants to practice on my son. From that little kitchen pot that God knows what was in it. How about if I made a few little cuts on his head? Because if I get my hands on him he won't know what hit him."

"I don't think I want to have those cuts," said Joseph.

"Do we roll?" asked Hurwitz's brother, marching to the door.

Joseph's mother closed her eyes and with her back to the brother whispered, "I'll give you two seconds to get him out of here with his jacket and his fingernails and take the pot with him, because if I turn around I'm not going to be responsible for my next move."

"All right, all right," said Hurwitz, "but I think you're a foolish woman. In half an hour he'd be on his way to recovery."

The brother retreated into the kitchen, and Joseph's mother said, "He'll defend his moron brother, too, right to the end. And this is called medicine with what I had for twenty years with a saint who this one couldn't shine his shoes. Everything today is called a doctor. Didn't I know it? Didn't I see it coming? I knew he was going to drag that beauty along with him. Wait, any second now he'll pull out his purse, which is very becoming for a doctor."

"I'll give him a shot and you can try soaks around the clock," said Hurwitz. "I still think you should have let my brother have a chance." He gave Joseph the injection and then, cleaning his hands, said, "I'm still $6.50."

"I know what you're still," said Joseph's mother, giving him six dollars and fumbling for some change.

"Look, owe me the half," said Hurwitz. "I'm not going to quibble."

"And you know what?" said Joseph's mother. "This is a delightful conversation to have with a doctor. Very confidence-inspiring."

"I'm glad there weren't any cuts," said Joseph, when the Hurwitz team had driven off. "I've never had any before and I'd rather not start in with them."

"There aren't going to be any anythings," said Joseph's mother, stuffing up his pillow. "So don't you worry. You know why?"

"Why?" asked Joseph.

"Because your mother's starting in on you. I think it's about time."

Rolling up her sleeves, she slapped and sloshed her wet cloths against his arm for hours, at first with vigor, saying, "Now you're getting your mother. I should have handled you from the beginning, but first I had to deal with dirt. I had to learn my lesson. Now I'm grown up." Then her eyes glazed, the sloshes became slow and trancelike, and her own arms, which had seemed powerfully ruddy, began to soften. She told him of her dead father's wisdom, translating a few of his pronouncements from Yiddish to English. They were succinct and should have been little nuggets, but each one missed Solomonlike heights by a fraction and lacked practical application. They were on the order of "With a fool what can you do" and "To deal with a stubborn man is like rushing down a hot soup."

"If that man were alive," his mother said, "all you'd need is one word from him and you wouldn't have to go to any college." She said that because of the toughness of the neighborhood, her two brothers had to walk at the old man's side to keep his beard from getting pulled. Joseph thought of his two thin and tiny uncles, unable to imagine them of any use against a team of determined beard-pullers. She switched then to the length of her blond hair as a girl and to her beauty, how one rich merchant had come before her father and laid three hosiery stores on the line, hers if she consented to be his bride. "But I made fun of him because of his cockeyed eyes. I should have grabbed him, but what do you know when you're that age." She said she had seen Joseph's father playing a vibraharp one night and fallen for his hands and his charm, having no idea he was a fainter. "How many times I had to pick his head off a sidewalk somewhere and pull his nose to keep him alive. Those are the things you can't know about a person." Joseph could hardly feel the sloshes now on his arm; it occurred to him that it might take six years of round-the-clock cloth applications to equal a single Hurwitz drainage cut in effectiveness. They had a nice sound to them, however, and provided a fine background for the stories. She remembered an old boyfriend who used to throw newly arrived Poles into cellars; her mother standing beside a pushcart with cold feet; and clothing she used to wear as a young girl that was much more expensive than anything she had in her wardrobe now. The thought of those expensive long-gone dresses got to her and she began a muffled heavy-nosed cry right into Joseph's arm basin. "I can't help it," she said. "Your mother's a real person and she's got feelings. I look at what I've got now sometimes and I get sick."

"Is there anything we can do for you, Meg?" asked the Irish-woman, standing in the door.

"That's what I mean," said Joseph's mother, drying her eyes. "That's what I have to live for. If it wasn't for a thing like that—What is she after all? She came out of God knows what kind of a home—I think I'd give it all up. But when a thing like that, a nothing that probably didn't go past the second grade, can step out of her way . . . then there must be a God in heaven."

It seemed to become dark in an instant as though a new stage setting had been wheeled in on runners. The woman's husband stood at her side now, looking up at the ceiling, Joseph getting the idea the man thought he was making too big a fuss over his arm; in a similar situation, any one of his own sons would have laughed it all off and gone to play volleyball.

"Stand there, angels," Joseph's mother said, starting up the hot soaks again. "Stand there and give me strength. And I'll try to think of a way to repay you. Maybe in a million years I'll come up with an idea."

Almost in the time it took to go from one slosh to another, Joseph felt a branch of voltage snap through him and settle in his cheeks. He felt that the worst had happened, invaders from his arm somehow getting through checkpoints and pouring down through his body. He thought he might be going into his first faint and this frightened him, although he had been fascinated by tales of his father's fainting exploits and had always wanted to see what one was like. Not wanting the Irish people to see him now, he whispered to his mother, "Can you ask them to leave?"

"You're completely out of your mind," she said, but then she felt his head and said to the couple, "You don't mind, do you, sweethearts? He isn't feeling well."

"Maybe if we went home I could get better," said Joseph when they had gone.

"I know, darling," she said, kissing his cheeks over and over. "When you're this way you want your own bed. I'm the same way. And you don't want anybody around. Don't I know. You try and you try—what else can you do? But much as you love them, when you're sick, you don't want to look at shiksa faces."

The sun was out full the next morning. Joseph's mother had first bundled up his arm and then thrown an overcoat around his shoulders. "Aren't I going to be too hot in the sun?" he asked.

"I'm just about to take chances," she said. "This is the kind of a day when you could faint, the cold is so treacherous. But people see the sun and they think they can go naked. Thank your lucky stars you have warmth to put over you."

Joseph had always admired slings; whenever he saw someone rigged up in one, he wanted to slip his own arm right in beside theirs. His mother had arranged a black woolen one for him, and now, outside the cottage, his legs feathery, his coat arranged in capelike fashion, he felt terribly romantic, seeing himself as the rich woman's son who was always being whipped on and off international airliners to see specialists in Lausanne. He would be spotted often in cafés, alongside his wealthy mother, aging uncle and the longtime family friend and admirer of his mother named Ian. All terribly wealthy, grave, wondering whether the new clinic in Berne would be able to deal with his strange malady. He would force himself to be gay, and to get off a great many head-tossing laughs, knowing this would double their sorrow. When his ailing lungs permitted, he would slump over a piano, coil his neck in a muffler and compose sonatas. Sometimes they would start him in a fashionable Eastern college, but his chest would always grow spindly and he would have to be whisked off in mid-semester to recuperate on ocean liners, romantic dormitory legends sprouting up after his departure.

When his father turned over the motor of the car, Joseph, his head light, floated across the lawn and into the back seat.

"Do you want me to carry you?" his father asked.

"I'm in here already, Dad," said Joseph.

"Don't be no wise guy," his father said. "You don't know what you've got. Sometimes a little thing like that can surprise you and turn into something big. You feel a little better and right away you want to take on the world. I admire a spunky kid, but I don't like to see one step out of line either."

"Say goodby to the saints," said Joseph's mother when the Irish couple came out to the car. "Jesus Christ himself wouldn't have poured more care and more sweetness into you." Certain the silent Irishman felt he was faking, Joseph said, "I hope they can fix up this arm when I get back to the city." The man smiled and shook hands with Joseph's father behind the wheel. "Say, you have a car, too, don't you?" the father asked. He had bought his first car late in life and still could not believe he actually owned one; he tried to work the subject of cars into conversations whenever he could.

"Yes, I have one," said the Irishman.

"I figured you probably did, but I'd never really seen you in it so I thought I'd ask. Almost everybody you run into these days has one. I drive this little job here. As far as I'm concerned, cars are just transportation.

"Look," he said, fearing he had been a little too obvious. "You might not have had one, right? There are still some people who don't."

"I agree," said the Irishman.

"Give the gorgeous thing a final love," Joseph's mother said, and Joseph hugged the Irishwoman through the window, burrowing into her chest and wondering what she would do if he licked her nipple once. Perhaps then his father would do something miraculous and wonderful, speeding off instead of punching him, leaving her with no course but to make a token phone call when they arrived in the city.

On the road, Joseph's mother said, "Maybe you'd like to spread out on the floor back there. You'll be out of the drafts."

"I think I'd get nauseous down there," said Joseph.

"You know when *I* get nauseous," she said. "When you fight me."

"If he has to vomit, that's not so terrible either," said Joseph's father. "It's no shame. Plenty of famous people vomit. You bet your life they do and you don't hear about it. What do you want them to do, make an announcement in the *New York Times*?"

Joseph tried the floor and his mother asked, "How is it down there?"

"The bump in the middle makes it bad."

"But you're out of the wind. I knew he'd love it down there, but he'll always fight me."

He peered out of the window when he sensed they were passing the beach, wondering if he ought to ask his father to stop so he could fight the lifeguard who had said "Jewie" one last time. Maybe he could swirl him up in his romantic cape and flail at him with his good arm. He thought he had better get in any fighting right now, feeling that if his arm ever got better it would be only through the sheerest luck. Joseph thought this was true of all illnesses and was amazed when even colds got better. It surprised him that they didn't simply go rampaging onward to end as death rattles. He really did not believe there was any such thing as a germ too small to be seen by the eye and that clear-colored medicines would be able to fight them down. One day, he felt, it would be announced that the whole germ theory of disease was a hoax, that there was no such thing as a germ (unless you could actually see it, like a cockroach), that all medicines were silly, doctors could learn all they needed to know in two weeks of school and that when people got better it was by wild coincidence.

He got back down on the floor, and in maneuvering his arm, realized that it was not really a romantic arm at all and that even if he were miraculously summoned to a college at the very last second, there would be no way for him to get it thinned down for the trip. He hated the arm then, wondering if he could just snap it off at the shoulder and toss it out the window so that at least the rest of him would be all fresh and new, enabling him to start all over again, pared down but healthy.

"I could have been the best driver in the world if I'd been able to master the wheel," said Joseph's mother. "The instructor said I had the best foot action he'd ever seen and that I could be a crack. I have to tell you about my rhythm, my sense of timing? Have you watched this baby dance? But that wheel always scares me."

"If he has to vomit I don't see why he has to do it in a new car," said Joseph's father. "He should tell me so I can pull over to the side of the road. Otherwise he deserves a smack."

book three

In the early evening they pulled up before Joseph's apartment building, his father saying he would go and park the car while they went upstairs. "Remember when we didn't have a car and used to have to come home from the country in a bus? Well, we have one now. Remember how I always said we'd get one?" Joseph was glad to see the apartment building and still could not believe he lived in it. Ten years before, in his one great business triumph, Joseph's father had done some surreptitious free-lance couch work for a moneyed Swiss who was new in the country. He had been paid with a stack of bills which he carried in his pocket, whipping it out every once in a while and saying to Joseph, "Look what I got." One night they had gone to look at an apartment in a new building and Joseph could remember dancing through it, smelling the rooms and closets, saying, "Look how new it is." His favorite part of the building was the hall incinerator; after they moved out of their dumbwaitered apartment, he remembered taking dozens of trips a day out to see it, emptying foods out of new cartons so he could have fresh garbage to toss into its mouth. When he poured things into the incinerator, he would dart back, afraid he might be swept in with the refuse; once, when he was slipping in a small batch, a cloud of coffee grounds dropped from the floor above, smacking the back of his wrist. He loved to be asked where he lived so he could answer, "The new house up on the hill," and he kept saying this years after he moved in, when the white brick had become smudged and neglected and after a colony of cleaner and taller buildings had sprouted up around it.

Standing in the street now, his arm napkined to his neck like a sick baby, he could see the window of the apartment's only bedroom and remembered his father's two years on a board; minutes after they had moved into the apartment, his father had come up with a mysterious back ailment and had to lie on a plank in the dark for two years, bathrobed and unshaven, saying, "It hurts, it hurts" whenever Joseph came by to check his condition. Joseph played beneath his father's window with a strong-willed fatherless older girl, she taking the part of an international smuggling queen, Joseph doing a lackey who was to carry out her bidding. She would break off the playing after a while and begin to hiss, "Your father's sick, your father's *sick*," Joseph answering, "Just a little bit." One day Joseph fought a laundryworker's son on the sidewalk and found himself being scooped off the ground by the tattooed laundryworking arms of the boy's father. "Let's go up and see your dad," the man said, holding Joseph in a bleached and angry vise. A crowd gathered, taking Joseph's side, saying, "Go ahead. We'll go with you," but Joseph, not wanting his father to have to come off the board, had said, "Not tonight." After two years, Joseph's mother went into the bedroom one morning and said, "You're getting up today."

"No, I'm not!" he cried. "How can I?"

"You're getting the hell up," she had said. Joseph wanted to punch her; but his father rolled off the board onto the floor, hunched through the apartment and the next day returned to the couch factory.

He went upstairs in the elevator now, his father pointing out that he should press only the button of the floor he wanted. "You press more than one button this thing'll break and we'll never get upstairs." His aging aunt Faith, a tall purpling woman, waited mysteriously in the shadow of Joseph's apartment door. Forty years a wardrobe mistress, she lived several miles away now in spinsterly retirement, her small flat crammed with gowns that had been worn in Belasco productions. On his way home from school, Joseph used to stop off at her place for bread-and-butter sandwiches and to read movie magazines, wading through tons of them in the vain hope that just once he would turn a page and see Ann Rutherford or Marsha Hunt naked. Since her retirement, she spent her time seeing to it that Joseph's father (her younger brother) got enough to eat and was warm. Grateful stage stars had rewarded her with trunkloads of jeweled pins, and sometimes it seemed to Joseph she went around wearing all forty years' worth at once. Now, tinkling and beaming in the shadows, she said to Joseph's mother, "How is he?"

"How is he?" she said. "How do I know? He's got an arm and we'll hope for the best."

"Has he eaten yet?" asked the aunt. "If anything happened to that baby brother of mine I don't know what I'd do."

"I knew it," said Joseph's mother. "For a second I couldn't believe my ears, but she's starting in already. Is this one for the books! First the Jew thing, then the arm and now this. Can a human being stand any more?"

"Dad's all right, Aunt Faith," said Joseph. "I've had a little trouble with my arm and that's why we came home."

"I heard there was something," she said. "But first I want to see if your father's all right.

"Let me go back to my place and bring you some bread and butter," she said, touching her brother's cheek.

"And that's about what she'll bring, too," said Joseph's mother. "That's what the great love amounts to. Ask her if she ever shelled out anything when for two years he was laying on a board and we couldn't buy toilet paper. You should only know what she retired with that we could all live on the Italian Riviera if she was the kind that parted with a nickel. And I have to stand here with a son who's got an arm like a house and listen to her dole out bread and butter."

The aunt took out a five-dollar bill, stuffing it into Joseph's pants pocket. "I don't have any use for money any more," she said. "What does it mean to me? All I want is for my brother to live and be well."

"Fives she'll give," said Joseph's mother. "Don't worry about that. And she'll get a reputation for being generous. I'm waiting for her to pull some real money out of those purses. I'll have to croak first."

Something about finally being in the apartment loosened up Joseph's legs and he collapsed on the floor, face first, unable to twist his neck and get the carpeting lint out of his nose. "He can't stay there," said Joseph's father, tugging him through the kitchen into the tricky combination dinette-bedroom, the aunt hollering, "He'll strain himself!"

"And I've got you for a background chorus, too," said Joseph's mother. "I always have, all my life. Get the hell out of my house while I have a nerve left in my skin."

"At least let me bring some bread and butter," said the aunt, tinkling out the door. "That's all I've ever asked."

Joseph's father turned the dinette lounging chair into a bed, saying, "I can't stand sleeping on an unneat bed." He made his voice high and piping, then said, "So who's asking you to? It's your son's bed." It was a variation of his only joke, the basic one being "How can you eat that ice cream when I'm full?"

Joseph grabbed at furniture legs, supporting himself in that manner until he got to the bathroom; sometimes, with lightning speed, he wrote dirty stories in there, read them over in an instant and then hurled them into the toilet, flushing them swiftly out of sight, always a little afraid the paper would not pass through and come bobbing into view, soaked but still readable, to greet the next bathroom occupant. After a minute, he heard his father begin walking up and back outside the door, saying, "What does he do in there all that time? Does he have to stay in there that long?"

"And I'm the one you picked to ask," said Joseph's mother. "Why don't you break down the door and find out? Ask him for an itemized list when he gets out and then you'll know."

On an impulse, Joseph inhaled the flannel of a pair of his sister's pajamas, then slipped into them, his eye on the doorknob, wondering if he would be allowed to continue living in the apartment should his father plunge through the door and catch him. He stood on the sink for an instant, and looked at himself in the mirror, editing out his head and arranging his legs so that he might have been a girl. Then he tore off the outfit, caught his breath to look calm and snapped open the door.

"What were you doing in there?" asked his father.

"I was just in there, Dad," said Joseph.

"For two hours?"

Joseph dove into his dinette bed as though it were a pool; the sheets were cold and delicious, making him feel he might be able to siphon off a little health from them. But the kitchen light was in his eyes and it occurred to him that no matter how his mother insisted he had his own room, he was still a fellow who slept in part of a kitchen. Joseph's mother appeared near the refrigerator with her arm around a Negro woman. "Look who I brought here for you to do a little cleaning. Winnie. She took care of you when you were a pup. Who else in the world would give her work in her condition but your mother? Well, maybe someday it'll be all totaled up and they'll see that I'm not the bad one around here."

Winnie was the Negro woman who had been in charge of Joseph for years, taking him to see movies each Saturday, on Christmas Day paying the admission with her own money. He remembered being tense on those days, knowing he had been paid for with pathetic, poverty-stricken colored dimes. She had been a good cleaning lady until the day she began mysteriously to tumble down flights of stairs in subways and private buildings. Time and again Joseph's mother had to go to Harlem to retrieve her from alcoves. "At night, too, with cute little colored drivers that I never knew from one minute to the next if I'd be hit on the head. Still, that's your mother. She gave me devotion when I needed it." After the falls, her cleaning had become lopsided and bleary-eyed; once, brought back from a hallway with her head in gauze, she had come into the apartment and fallen against the sink; Joseph, pretending he was playing healthy childhood fantasy games, rolled over on the floor and peeked beneath her dress, getting a slice of pink behind. She nabbed him, saying, "And when I is busted up, too."

Her eyes blurred now, listing slightly, she knelt to kiss him; he was never sure of the protocol of kissing beloved Negroes and solved the problem this time by giving her a light, fast one on the cheek and a deep, sincere shoulder squeeze. She went off then to do some dim, absent-minded cleaning, Joseph's mother saying, "Look, even if she only gives a wipe here and a polish there, I still need somebody like blood itself. I can't take care of a whole house." People began to stream in through the doors now, the first a vegetable market deliveryman who spoke no

English and who had been in "the camps." His face was hollowed and torn, yet he had great mountains of vigorous concert-pianist hair, as though the horrors of Auschwitz had perversely thrown his pompadour into flower, each new Nazi degradation aerating and strengthening his follicles. Liberated, but stripped now of all family and possessions, he delivered phone orders for the vegetable store. "And believe me, he's tickled to death to be doing it, too," said Joseph's mother. "Say hello to Schreiber."

"Hi," said Joseph. She poured him a drink and tipped him a quarter. "What did you do that for?" asked Joseph. "He didn't deliver anything."

"You're telling me how to operate?" she said. "I should stiff that man with what he's been through, with what his eyes have seen that we should never know from it? You want me to com-mit the greatest crime of the century? You'll take everything away from your mother, but you'll never touch her religion." And in a softer tone she said, "They look for that, sweetheart. I've got to have the respect of my tradespeople. What is it, a quarter here, a dollar there . . . but when I walk outside I know I'm a lady. And if I should sneeze, he'd be up here in two seconds."

"Who would you lay down your life for, Schreiber?" she asked, sticking her hand into his hair. The Hitler refugee blushed. "And he doesn't understand any English either, does he?" said Joseph's mother. "Only when he wants to. I'll tell you something else. With all his camps and his aggravation I still wouldn't be caught alone with him in the back of a store."

A small, dapper neighbor named Fedders rang the doorbell, came in and got a drink, too. He was eighty-five, his main virtue being that he had aged beautifully. "Did you ever see such a gorgeous thing in all your life?" she said, putting her hand on his head and presenting him to Joseph. "That goes to business and that still takes a drink and if it sees a pretty leg, that reacts, too. Turn around there and show my son how beautiful you look." The dapper old man pivoted slowly and Joseph's mother said, "Could you just die from how beautifully this thing has gone through the years?" She wheeled suddenly to shove the Negro cleaning woman. "Other women would tolerate your kind of cleaning, too, wouldn't they? For about forty seconds. Someday there'll be a shrine with your madame's name on it." The doorbell rang. "They'll come from far and wide," Joseph's mother said. "They heard your mother's home and they'll look for her." She led in an ex-fight manager from the neighborhood who had suffered a stroke and now talked in words that no one had ever heard such as "kaw" and "ziffer." "Could it break your heart?" she said, bringing him into the dinette. "He swears he'll only take a second of your time." The old man laid down his cane on the floor with a clearly visible black thread attached to it that no one was supposed to see. Then he pulled on the thread and made the cane stand up as if by magic. "Do you know what you would have done to that man if you hadn't let him perform?"

"What?" asked Joseph.

"Killed him."

Joseph was beginning to feel all bunched into a corner and imagined himself hanging outside the window, clinging to the bricks until everyone left. He could not tell whether his fever had risen or he was reacting to the joint body heat of the fast-gathering kitchen throng. He caught himself pedaling his feet beneath the blankets as though trying to cycle out of the house. A giant square-bodied lady neighbor ducked in through the door now and crouched into the kitchen; Joseph remembered her face always being angered as though she were receiving continual telegrammed reminders that petiteness was forever beyond her grasp. "Hello, angel sweetness," said Joseph's mother, pouring her a drink. "Look," she said to Joseph, "you think it's

136

a picnic she's got on her hands? Your mother's the only one who won't discuss tallness and who'll treat her like a human being.

"Isn't that right, doll?" she said to the woman. "And once in a while we'll go downtown and find her a cute little guy who likes big ones. Your mother doesn't know how to soothe people, does she, Joseph?"

When the Negro cleaning woman had finished washing the hall woodwork she staggered through the kitchen and said, "Here y'are, honey," pouring the pail of cleaning water over Joseph's feet. It did not feel too bad through the blankets and for a second Joseph thought it might have been part of a new treatment he had not been told about. "What, she did a little something again?" said Joseph's mother, turning about. "Son of a bitch. All right, I had enough of your cleaning," she said, ushering the woman to the door. "Put on your hat and coat and I'll see you tomorrow." She turned to the gathering and said, "What am I going to do, put her in a colored institution that it would break her heart and she'd last maybe two days if she's lucky?"

"Could you change this blanket?" Joseph asked.

"I'll be with you in two seconds," she said. "I'll give you so much care you won't know whether you're coming or going."

"What's going on here?" said the landlady, wheeling in through the door, a slow-moving tanklike woman who wore flowing ankle-length dresses, giving the impression that entire personal fortunes were strapped to her legs.

"And your mother will melt this cold-hearted bitch, too," said Joseph's mother. "Try and get a paint job out of her. Ask her for some extra heat someday and you'll hear what she says. The tightest bitch that God ever created, yet who's your friend, Dichter?"

"You are," said the landlady, capitulating immediately and

137

hugging Joseph's mother. "Your mother's a peppy woman," said the landlady, "and I never could resist peppiness."

Then, as though she were captioning a picture for a newsmagazine, Joseph's mother extended her arms in the kitchen and said, "Your mother's friends. They heard she was in trouble and they came. Do you wonder why I could bust sometimes? Why I go on? Anytime you ever want to know who the bad one is, just remember this picture. Remember that you saw love."

Joseph's purpling old aunt flashed in the door then, carrying a plate covered with wax paper. "I'm getting this bread and butter in here," she hollered, "and I don't care what you say. You give it to that brother of mine."

Joseph's mother bowed her head patiently. "Tell me if she's still standing there because if I open my eyes and I see her that'll be the end of her and that'll be the end of the whole house, too. I'm standing here with solid gold, with friends that if I coughed they would come all the way from Puerto Rico somewhere, and that filth comes into my house that's scrubbed from top to bottom . . . I can't talk. Is she still there? Because if she is *I'll fire her out of my house.*"

The scream went right inside Joseph's arm; from that second all noise seemed to register inside it somewhere, as though it had turned into a meter. When the aunt had disappeared, Joseph said, "I really mean it, Mom. I've got to get a dry blanket. I may be at my all-time worst now."

"All right, sweethearts," said Joseph's mother, herding her friends toward the door. "My son can't stand duress. He never could and I've always had to shield him." When the assemblage had gone, she said to Joseph, "What's the matter, darling? I know. You want the benefit of your home, don't you?"

"Yes, Mom," he said.

"Sure," she said. "But those are your mother's friends, and I had to show you realness. That's who she turns to when your father's on a board and you have an arm. God knows, ever since you were a pup I've tried to present you with a set of rules. So that when I'm not here any more, at least you'll be able to recognize genuineness and you'll know how to spot dirt, too."

Joseph's mother ushered in the evening with a stepped-up schedule of arm soaks, sitting beside him in the dinette-bedroom and saying, "I'll give you care, darling, don't you worry. But I can tell you now that after I had your sister I could have done without a son. I went at midnight to get you pumped out of my stomach." She said that later, when she had been forced to nurse him, he sucked once and blood flowed from her nipples.

Joseph remembered an earlier time when his mother had done a great deal of voluptuous midday lying around in the living room, asking him to get her things. He brought a friend up to the apartment one day, a short needy one whose family Joseph's mother had mocked for eating low-priced gas-producing vegetables. Massive-breasted in a white brassière, she had lounged over on her back and asked Joseph to hurry and get her a drink of soda.

"Is that your mother?" the vegetable eater asked.

"Yes," said Joseph.

"She doesn't act like a mother."

Joseph could not be sure how long that voluptuous lying-around period had lasted, and now he asked, "Why did you have to tell me this new stuff right now for?"

"Because I'm not suppressing it any more," she said. "You've been shielded all your life and it's about time you knew a few things."

Hurwitz appeared later, saying, "Now let's see, what'll I give you, green pills or purple ones? What's your favorite?"

"That's supposed to be charm," said Joseph's mother, "to go with his new office and his new prices. And you're supposed to forget that his wife used to run eighteen blocks to a colored neighborhood to save three cents on vegetables that it turns my stomach when I think of it. And how do you like how I've stuck with him, too, and I'm letting him examine my son? I should have my head examined. What did you find?"

"We don't know much about these things," said Hurwitz.

"I'd give a nickel to know what you *do* know about with your new appeal that I could do without."

Hurwitz walked a few steps into the kitchen. "Can we talk here?" he asked Joseph's mother.

"Who're you worried about, my son? He might as well be in the next country."

"I'm afraid we're going to have to take it."

"Repeat what you just said. I knew that's what you were working up to. And it's supposed to come as a big surprise to me who you'd like to do the taking, too, eh?"

"You can have him, you can have someone else, whatever pleases you. He's very good."

"And he isn't right outside the door by any chance, is he?"

"Outside, inside, what's the difference? I can have him here in twenty seconds and you'll be pleased with his work."

"How would you like to pack that little wholesale beauty of a bag of yours and get the hell out of my home, Hurwitz? Because if you stay here two more minutes you'll be minus a head. And I'm not paying you for this kind of a visit either, how do you like that?"

Hurwitz ran off giggling. Hands on her hips, Joseph's mother said, "I love it when he turns on the charm."

"I heard the whole thing," said Joseph. "Is it coming off?"

"You don't have to worry, darling. As long as I'm your mother, there won't be any coming off. Don't I know what's on his mind? His brother was away in the war, so he's drumming up a little business for him. If it was up to the two of them with that great brotherly love, there wouldn't be an arm left in the country."

"Now go to sleep, darling," she said to him later, "and when you wake up you'll see that you'll forget you ever had an arm. Your father has an announcement he'd like to make to you."

Joseph's father carried in three shirts and said, "I was about to throw these away, but then I thought you could get a few wears out of them. You can be as hard on them as you like. Kick the hell out of them if you want to and I won't say anything. After all, I was going to throw them away, wasn't I?"

"He'd give you the world," said Joseph's mother, "but his trouble is he never knew how to express himself."

The father kissed Joseph on the forehead. "You don't have to worry," he said. "Fellas kiss their dads." Once, laid off by his couch factory, he had torn through the apartment to awaken Joseph, then a fevered reader of big-little books, and to whisper, "I can never give you dimes for big-little books again." Now, each time he bent down to deliver kisses, Joseph expected to hear him announce he was revoking some long-treasured activity. His father turned out the light, and as he left the room, his shoulders looked lonely in their undershirt; Joseph felt like asking him to come back and tell him some stories about Harry Kastner, a boyhood friend who had died five years previously. It bothered Joseph that his father had no friends now and he liked to look at photo album pictures of his father and Kastner, both soft-armed and hairy, standing on a beach in 'twenties tank suits, arms thrown over each other's shoulders in comradely fashion. They had both been factory payroll guards one summer, escorting bundles of money in an elevator, with guns at the ready. Aside from the payroll yarn, Joseph's father had actually told him no detailed stories about the friendship; but the idea of his

141

father having a pal was warming to Joseph, who would ask over and over, "What did you two guys do together?"

"Oh, you know," his father had said. "We were just a couple of friends, I guess you'd say," and Joseph would grab the album and love the pictures some more.

Now Joseph snuggled beneath the covers to wait perhaps as long as eight hours for his sister to return from her date and possibly undress in the foyer. He had been doing this for years now, sometimes staying awake until it seemed his eyes had turned to ashes. Most often she would say goodby in the doorway and head straight for the bathroom, but on occasion she would reward his vigil by flinging off her clothes in the foyer where he could see her. His best haul was an early morning in which she decided to examine her breasts by lamplight, serving up first one and then the other, studying them quizzically as though they were twin world atlases. Another time she stood nude for a minute and worked on a behind pimple; he was not sure whether he liked that session or not, although, if pressed, he guessed he would have to admit he was glad it had come off. He remembered her, too, sitting in a chair at dawn to make a hushed and nude telephone call; he had just barely stayed awake for that one, fighting his way though veils of tiredness; it seemed to him that when it came her time to listen, she had put the receiver against her nipple. He was not at all sure it had happened, yet he kept the sequence in whenever he thought about it. Most things between them, it occurred to him now in bed, were patched and dim, vague, full of maybes, half recalled. He remembered becoming stronger than her one day, wrestling her for a grapefruit, holding it in one hand and letting her claw and struggle for it futilely, her chest thumping against his nose, her skirt washing his lips. "Now, let me have it," she had said, after fifteen minutes of this.

"Why didn't you ask?" he had said, flipping it to her.

142

She saved greeting cards, thousands of them, wrapped in neat stacks, kept in a drawer under lock and key. As she added new ones to the collection, she threw some of the old stacks away, Joseph asking if he could keep some. "What for?" she would say. "You don't need them." Once he pulled a stack of them from the garbage, scraped honeydew melon seeds from the top ones and kept them in his own locked drawer. She had many girl friends, and for a time, when they appeared at the front door, he would run at them with his head lowered and butt them below their waists.

As they grew older together, they seemed to circle one another in a great dampness. One night, alone together in the apartment, she sat in an armchair, coiled and moist in her slip, while he walked in and out of the room, trying to catch his breath. "Look," he said finally. She polished her toenails and told him the only dirty joke she had ever recited, never taking her eyes from her nails. It all hung on a confusion between mules and asses. When she was finished, he said, "Jesus," and apologized for not having any to tell her back. He had a recurring dream in which she settled comfortably in his bed and allowed him to explore her body, her face sweet, patient, neutral. He loved the dream, wishing he could arrange to have it run on schedule. Sometimes, late at night, in lieu of an undressing, she would come and stand alongside his bed, eating some cookies, stooping to touch his hair. He had a hanging, half-awake shred of a memory involving cold, wet, milky, low and lassoing half-mad kisses in the darkness.

He thought now of all the hours he had invested in waiting for the undressings, and it occurred to him that had he spent them poring over books, he might be the world's expert on Neanderthal man or the pancreas. He did not mind being awake now, but he thought it was a shame there was no way for him to ship his arm off to sleep independently, so as not to deprive it of any health benefits. Looking at the hall, he wondered for the first time whether it was possible for his sister to peer into the dinette darkness and see the open slit of his eyes as she was getting out of her things. He walked out to the hall, then looked back at his empty bed, unable to make up his mind whether you could see a fellow's half-opened eyes on the pillow back there. He had been suspicious one night when his sister and a thin girl friend had undressed and taken turns posing in front of the lamp, one getting next to it while the other jumped into the clothing closet, then changing places as though they were relay runners passing a baton. Beside the lamp now, he felt a loosening in his lap and lowered his pajamas for an instant to give a quick treat to some imaginary fellow back there in the bed.

Later he heard the front door open and dragged himself out of a chained sleep to see his sister and her overcoated boyfriend enter, along with a second couple, someone named Pic and the pimpled, wurst-loving girl he had first seen at the country grocery store. The boy called Pic was a pal of the boyfriend, and Joseph, one night, had seen them have a fight after which they ended up howling at each other beneath a lamppost, peeing on each others legs in the deserted city street. The friend was tall, had black hair that was always soaked, and Joseph thought he would make a better boyfriend for his sister than the shorter, overcoated scatback. Pic and the wurst lover disappeared now, in the direction of what Joseph thought was the bathroom; for the next fifteen minutes he heard a great deal of scuffling and periodic toilet flushings. He could not see his sister and her unshaven boyfriend, who seemed to be in the living room. After a few minutes he heard her repeat, "You promised. Good God, you promised," a whimper then getting into her voice. He slipped out of bed, remembering his arm for the first time, and found himself mysteriously blowing on the bandages. Standing in the dinette now, he wondered whether he could get out the window to creep suction-footed along the bricks to his parents' bedroom, rousing them in secret and then creeping back along the bricks so that no one would know who had sounded the alarm. He inched along in the kitchen, panic-stricken, reaching a point where he could see his sister and the boyfriend on the living room rug. She wore cotton anklets of a sort she had always put on for basketball games; her legs were wishboned, the cotton panties that circled one of her knees of a whiteness it seemed to Joseph you could not produce in apartment building washing machines. He made himself visible then, waited a second or two until he got up a few tears, then strode forth and said, "Didn't you know about my arm?"

"The kid," said the boyfriend, throwing up his hands in mock defensive posture. Joseph ran in to pound him on the neck, the boyfriend saying in a falsetto voice, "Don't, don't, he's killing me," then running with exaggeratedly high steps into the dinette. Joseph felt pretty good for a second, having a championship quarterback in retreat, and came after him, cornering the grid star against the dinette radiator. When they were alone, the boyfriend sullenly bared his teeth and said, "All right, quit or I'll cut 'em right off for you."

Joseph backed out to where his sister was collecting herself. "Didn't you know I was sick in there?" he said. "What were you doing?"

The boyfriend came in and told Joseph's sister, "The kid was murdering me in the other room."

The other couple emerged from the bathroom, the girl saying, "Oh, I know your brother from the lake." Pic sent forth a series of howling institutional lamppost bleats, pouring them into one cupped hand. As awful as they were, Joseph knew that as soon as he was alone, he would be trying several himself.

"Everybody go home now," said Joseph's sister. On his way

out, the boyfriend poked Joseph and said, "Hey, no more murdering me, okay, kid?" When they were gone, Joseph said to his sister, "You won't tell Mother about any of this, will you?" She kissed his nose, then raced crying into her tricky combination bookshelf-bed, yanking the covers over her head.

ach time Joseph got to his feet and walked a few steps the next day, he would sail headfirst to the floor as though tough judo instructors were stationed at three-foot intervals along the carpeting, getting him by the pajama tops and demonstrating armpit tosses. Now that he had reached the judo stage, it occurred to him that he would probably die and that it was not such a bad idea since it would save him the embarrassment of going around without a college. If only there were a way of getting a guarantee that it did not hurt too badly and that perhaps life was not completely over when you died, that there were a few bonuses at the other end, such as getting to return periodically and take looks from a high, shelflike place at how things were coming along. Or if you were a fellow who found death really unbearable, that you got a chance to change your mind and come back with only a small penalty, say, such as having to be a Negro. It was the word "death," actually, that frightened him more than anything. He thought the whole idea might not be too bad if there were another term for it, such as "whiffle."

Joseph's mother sent for his Aunt Hester, a small, bowlegged woman in the wholesale test-tube business whose opinion on medical matters was respected and who knew when it was time to bring big men in on cases. She lived twenty miles away yet feared all vehicles and walked to Joseph's house when summoned, curling up little papers along the way and dropping them into her purse for use on arrival as ear stickers. "Her poor feet," Joseph's mother said after Aunt Hester had called to say she was getting under way. "Why doesn't she take a cab?" Joseph asked. "I wish I knew," she answered. "She always walks."

Arriving that afternoon, Aunt Hester said, "Where is he?" and was led to Joseph's bed. "How long do you know me, darling?" she asked.

"A long time," said Joseph.

"Would your Aunt Hester harm a hair on your head?"

"No."

"Then let me see the arm." She stared at it for a while, working up a batch of new stickers from an old *New Yorker* cover, and then said, "Shall I tell you something, darling? You know your Aunt Hester wishes you no harm and would do anything in the world not to hurt you."

"What's that?" asked Joseph.

"You're a sick boy."

"I know, Aunt Hester."

"And shall I tell you something else, though God knows I don't want to alarm you."

"What?"

"It's making your mother a nervous woman."

She stood in the dinette with Joseph's mother and said, "Are you my younger sister?"

"Yes," said Joseph's mother.

"Then can I talk frankly to you?"

"Please, I have no time for philosophy. All right, yes."

"He needs a big man."

"You really think so?"

"Yes, I saw his arm."

"Who should we get?"

"Peretz," said Aunt Hester.

"Is he big enough?"

"The biggest."

"You know I *have* a big man," said Joseph's mother. "Hurwitz. He's about two inches tall. He's so big that if I see him I'll take off his head from what he did to my son's arm that I now have to hear the child needs a big man."

"I'll call Peretz," said Aunt Hester, using her first sticker. "A man like that doesn't come to houses. Too big."

Joseph heard the next morning that his mother had ordered an ambulance. "I didn't know I was that sick a guy," he said. "I don't think I'm going to like it in one of those."

"Do you think you'll even know where you are?" she said. "You'll think you're in Dad's car. If I had to worry about ambulances with what I've been through, it would have all been over a long time ago."

He could not warm up to the idea at all and was worried about the ambulance smell. There would be dials and metered hoses in there that really made you sick once they were fastened onto you. He pictured putting one foot inside the door, losing control of himself and then really needing an ambulance. His father came to the door and said, "Do you think I ought to stay home from work today? I'd do it, but what would be the point? It stands to reason they have a driver for these ambulances and it would be a waste. You mean to tell me they don't have facilities for handling someone when they come to pick him up? Of course they do."

"Go to work, sweetheart," said Joseph's mother. When he had left, she added, "Like you could always face an emergency."

A little later the two attendants came in carrying a stretcher, and Joseph got onto it, making a special grim ambulance-style face.

The fact-gathering Himber's blond mom was in the elevator. "I didn't know your son was sick," she said.

"Didn't you get our announcement?" asked Joseph's mother. "I thought we sent them out to everybody."

"I didn't hear," said Mrs. Himber.

In the downstairs lobby, as Joseph was being carted along, his mother said, "I'm surprised she didn't start in about her moron son."

"At least he's in a college," said Joseph.

"If you wanted to have a face like that you could be in thirty colleges."

In the street Modell, the stooped, unshaven grocer's son, looked up from his milk crates to see Joseph being whisked along toward the ambulance. The subject of many jokes because of his sexual retardation, Modell had vacationed in West Virginia and found a small insectlike girl whom he had taken back East to become his bride. The wedding date was elastic, and Modell kept her chained to the grocery counter, forking out cream cheese while he tore through piles of marriage manuals in the back, looking for surefire methods of laying siege to her sexual fortress. Joseph had the feeling that Modell was tossing him a loose, salivated laugh, the first he had ever thrown at anyone, and as he sailed by he said, "I'm not that sick, you bastard."

Inside the ambulance Joseph steeled himself, ready to have tubular coils fastened onto his pressure points, but was merely deposited on a neat bed, the sheets almost suffocating in their cleanliness. One attendant sat beside Joseph while the other drove. After several minutes Joseph's mother said, "Are they two swell boys. Did you ever see such clean-cut types in your life?" She leaned over and whispered, "Listen, what do you think I ought to give them?"

"How should I know?"

"Does five and three sound all right?" she asked. "Five for the driver and three for the other kid."

"Will you leave me alone," said Joseph. "I'm supposed to be sick. You're the mother."

"That's the difference between us," she said. "I worry about those things."

Joseph began to enjoy the idea of being in an ambulance and yet not actually as a fellow whose life was slipping away. After a while he looked out of the window.

"You see how you were worried," his mother said. "What was it? A joke. You're having the time of your life."

Later the attendants deposited Joseph in Peretz's outer office. It was in what seemed to be an ordinary building; Joseph felt it was a tribute to Peretz's bigness that he could just be a regular apartment fellow and yet get ambulances to sweep up to his door. Joseph's mother pinched the cheeks of the two attendants, tipped them and said, "You were two sweet things. Consider that just a down payment. If either of you two boys ever want something, some underwear for a girl, a couple of fight tickets, I want you to promise me you'll call me right up. I don't forget so easily."

Joseph's Aunt Hester was waiting in the anteroom and sat beside him. "Are you worried, darling?" she said.

"A little."

"Well, shall I tell you something? Don't be. You know why?"

"Why?"

"Because a man like this doesn't have time to hurt a boy."

It bothered Joseph that there were no other patients in the room; even after pocketing Joseph's fifty for the visit, he could not see how Peretz with empty anterooms could be hauling in an income massive enough to go with his bigness. Perhaps when he had gone to fifty he had priced himself out of the business and he was too embarrassed to go back to twenty-two. Joseph wondered whether there was a way for his sick-armed patients to get word to him, perhaps by anonymous note, that his office would once again be flooded if he dropped back to the lower figure and that there would be no shame in it.

Peretz came in, small and dapper, wearing civilian clothes. Hooking his arm, Joseph's Aunt Hester said, "Doctor, darling, how long have I known you?"

"A good many years."

"And do I come around every afternoon and pester you?"

"Of course not, dear. What can I do for you?"

"Will you take a look at a very sick boy?"

Peretz said he would, but when he moved she held his arm and said, "And can I tell you something else about him?"

"What?"

"He's a sweet boy. You know what I mean. A good boy."

Joseph realized then that there had been no appointment and that his getting to see Peretz had all hinged on his aunt's reception room plea. If Peretz had decided he did not want to see a sick boy's arm that day, the whole ambulance ride would have gone for naught. But that must be how big men operate.

Once he was inside Peretz's office, Joseph's respect for his bigness multiplied. It seemed to be just an ordinary living room, Joseph unable to see one sign of a medical instrument anywhere. He decided finally that Peretz kept them all crammed in the corner closet; if backed against a wall, a patient suddenly erupting with new symptoms on his carpeting, he would fling open the door and start hauling out scalpels. But what if there were only overcoats in there and he was big enough not to have a single bandage in the whole place?

"It doesn't look like a doctor's office," Joseph whispered to his mother as Peretz pulled aside the drapes.

"You should worry about that. Someday when you get a little time, see what's doing inside his brain. Then you'll stop worrying."

For a second, as his mother unpeeled his arm wrappings, he felt ashamed there wasn't something more exotic under there. What if Peretz took a look at it and became offended at their bringing a routine arm before him, one that any number of small men could have handled?

"All right, where's a good place?" said Peretz. "Over here near the window where there's light. Hold 'er up while I get the blinds."

Joseph presented his arm, and Peretz stared at it, holding it close to his face like an ear of corn, running his finger along it while Joseph's mother said, "Ummph, his way, his style." He dropped the arm, sat down on the sofa and tapped his nails on an end table, then got up and walked along the bookcase, running a pencil along the bindings of a row of best sellers. "Shhhh," said Joseph's Aunt Hester, putting a finger to her lips. Then Peretz said, "I'd leave 'er alone."

"Thank God," said Joseph's mother. Joseph's Aunt Hester ran up and kissed the back of his hand. Joseph was excited and thought about someday himself becoming an arm man, getting a fine apartment and having people bring their arms to him, saying "Leave this one alone" to certain of them, "Tamper with this one" to others, then raking in the fifties. Most likely, you would even be allowed to be wrong on a few since the chances were there were no averages kept on arm decisions. It occurred to Joseph for an instant that maybe his Aunt Hester was confused, that she had gone to the wrong office and that the real Peretz was one flight down, his office full of patients, his shelves bulging with medical equipment. That this fellow was really in investment banking, but, posing as Peretz, was able to siphon off the one out of forty people who left the elevator on the wrong floor.

"Doc," said Joseph's Aunt Hester, modestly peering up at him. "Shall I tell you something?"

"What?"

"I don't think you minded helping that boy. Not a man like you."

"My sister's told you something," said Joseph's mother. "Now sit back and relax and *I'll* tell you something. My son, the one with the arm, he came in here—now I can say it—and he was worried because he didn't see equipment. He looked around—he's a young boy—and he didn't see an X-ray, he didn't see a drop of medicine.

"Now do you want to know what the something is?" she said, spinning the bandages back on Joseph's arm and then getting up to pinch the famed specialist's jowl.

"Okay," said Peretz.

"His mother wasn't worried."

Several days later a small riverlike tingle began to curl through the bandages; Joseph knew his arm, as though satisfied with a set of fresh proposals, had decided to end its strike and do business with the mainland. This depressed him because soon he would have to stand in the sun and explain to people why he wasn't being shipped off to college despite a neighborhood reputation for smartness. To celebrate his arm's return to health, he was shifted into the apartment's only bedroom, his parents', to get a few days of stretching out in a real bed. This was upsetting, since it reminded him anew of the apartment's tininess. Tucked away in the dinette, he could imagine it was palatial in size, that his father's clothing closet opened onto vast paneled playrooms. But once inside the bedroom, he knew perfectly well the closet shielded only herringbone overcoats.

The number of rooms a fellow had was always a key factor in Joseph's being able to make new acquaintances. If the new man was a two- or three-roomer, Joseph warmed to him readily, whereas he put immediate limitations on friendships with those who lived in four and up. Once he met a new boy who needed two shaves a day and sold insurance policies at fifteen. The fellow said he lived in eight, but there was something about his manner that failed to threaten Joseph. He told his mother, "I've got a new friend. He has eight rooms." Joseph brought the boy home, and afterward his mother said, "I saw your friend with the eight rooms. He really looked rich with that overcoat and those socks he was wearing." It took Joseph a long time to wangle an invitation to the boy's apartment, but finally he succeeded; it was behind a theater; inside, the boy's father sat shoeless and gray-ankled in a chair. The stove was in the same room, right alongside the dad, and a newly menstruating sister ran through the apartment, holding her fist between her knees. The entire apartment was more or less a long hall, smelling of coal. But Joseph counted the rooms and there *were* eight, if you included a rear section that was divided in two by a board. Later that night his mother said, "I heard you visited your rich friend." Beginning to cry, Joseph said, "Yes, and he did have eight rooms." At that, he would have preferred a gray-ankled, menstrual eight to his own neat three.

On the day of the shift, Joseph's mother got him comfortable in her bed, then went to a bureau and began taking out perfume bottles. "You want to see what I have?" she said, lining them up for him. "Your mother's got plenty socked away. In case there's trouble, your father, God forbid, lays down on a board again, this time I'll fool everybody. I'm ready. You want to see some more? I'll show you underwear, too; you never saw the likes of such stuff."

"I don't want to see any," said Joseph. "That's no treat for me."

156

"Just in case you were worried about your mother. Don't ever worry about this baby. Not any more. Not since she smartened up."

She leaned out the window then, folding her arms at her waist, and carried on long conversations with women below, flagging them down as they walked along the street. "Hey, Rifkind," she said to one. "Well, I finally calmed him down. I've got him in here with me. There's no arm any more. He's resting peaceful as a doll. I had some time with him. Ask me if you want to know about sons."

When she had been talking to the woman for half an hour, Joseph told her behind, "Why don't you invite her up?" His mother leaned back and said, "Because this is how I love it," then hollered down to Rifkind, "The son of a bitch will try to change his mother's habits. He's got some case."

Some friends came to the window to inquire about Joseph's health: the handsome, black-haired Schnayerson who had seemed a doctor all his life, reserved and humorless as though pondering tricky surgical incisions at the age of six, off to Louisville for premed; the charming Negbar twins who had toured Europe with their widowed marmalade-importing dad and then begun to entertain needy Bensonhurst girls at home in dressing gowns and ascots, both Michigan Staters for liberal arts; Stretch Hirsch, the block's first declared masturbator, who had come to his window one night and shouted down an unashamed report on how great it was, political science at Western Reserve; the vast-hipped and sorrowful Goldbeck, a two-roomer who at eight had seen his father, the appetizing store king, slump over a carp counter with a fatal coronary, business law at Manhattan College; sticky-fingered McKeown, the block's only Catholic, who had never missed a fly ball and attended all Bar Mitzvahs, there to be patted on the head by grandmothers and told, "Isn't it wonderful, this day and age, that he can be here with a face like that," Duquesne on an athletic scholarship; the gibberish-

157

speaking "Immigrant" Kitay, who good-naturedly let his strange Latvian-type mumbles be ridiculed, then stepped forth at seventeen to announce he had been deaf since birth and had never heard human speech—off to a special Midwestern school for gifted deaf guys.

Joseph came over to the window and elbowed in alongside his mother in time to see his Ivy League-bound friend Rodell, richest boy on the block, approach the building. His father, Guy Rodell, the elegant, homburg-wearing haberdashery tycoon, believed in an "earthy high school education" before you got to "your Brown or your Harvard." He had sent the boy to the public school, where he sat opposite Joseph during lunch hours and wolfed down fat little filet mignons and thick ketchuped-up chicken sandwiches to Joseph's light and frothy lettuce-and-tomato-salad numbers. "Why don't you like meat sandwiches?" he would ask Joseph, who would say, "Because I don't like to get all heavy." Rodell lived in eight carpeted honeys across the park; his father, who talked to Joseph as though he were an old, rich guy ("Get your capital the hell out of electronics"), had the first television set in Bensonhurst. All of Rodell's games were electrically operated, and he had a way of teasing Joseph with his richness at least once a night. "My father has a thousand-dollar bill for every fake dollar on the board," he said to Joseph, who had just beaten him in Monopoly. "My father has one for some of them," Joseph replied, but the remark cut into him for weeks. Rodell's only weak spot was that his father got divorceᵤ a lot, the youngster inheriting a series of moms, whom he refused to call "Mother," referring to them as "Jane" and "Toots." At that, Joseph wasn't sure he would not have traded off his own mom for electrified games, fat little filets and entree to your Brown or your Harvard.

A year previously, Joseph had borrowed Rodell's expensive Big League catcher's shin guards and face mask, then left them on the subway. He was too sick to tell Rodell, afraid to tell his parents, and so he had said nothing to anyone, unable to sleep comfortably for months. Rodell tormented Joseph by never asking for the equipment; instead, every now and then he let a distant shin-guard expression come over his face. "See how you're loved," Joseph's mother said now, as Rodell stopped beneath the window. When she went inside to the kitchen, Rodell said to Joseph, "I'm going up to Cambridge next Saturday. I just wanted to tell you that you can keep the goddamned shit."

"Which shit?" asked Joseph, but Rodell had wheeled around and was walking paunchily up the street. Joseph wanted to run after him and tackle him hard at the waist, to shake the richness out of his stomach. Standing near the window had made him dizzy, and for a moment he thought he was going to do one of his carpeting dives. He made it to his mother's bed, smelling some of her leftover perfume in the pillow, and wondered how rigid South Iowa Deaf was on its requirements, whether they ever absorbed an occasional fellow with keen hearing who just happened to want to go there. He got a slight flex in his healing arm, cried a little, and then his mother came in and said, "I just talked to the divorced bitch with the cockeyed eyes, and she's got you into a college. Just in case you were worried your mother was sleeping."

"Oh Mom," he said, and when she came to him, he spread a latticework of tears across her chest.

What's it called?" asked Joseph later when he had stopped tingling. "What kind of place is it?" He got out of bed and walked around, kicking the walls with excitement, not caring whether he was risking another arm revolt.

"You're starting in again," she said. "Two minutes ago you would have given up your whole head to get into a college and now you want sworn testimony that you're going to love it. It's in the Midwest someplace. You'll find out later when you get there. Meanwhile, you're not even in it unless you have an address out there. She gave me the name of someone I have to get to. Commander Vanderhuysen."

"What do you mean, 'get to'?" asked Joseph.

"What are you trying to do now?" she said. "You want to see

how far you can push me? You're worried about your mother's manipulations? I have to see him so he can get you a hotel room. Every room is taken and if you don't have one they don't let you register. You might as well not even start out. Meanwhile you don't even have a decent suit if I want to present you to someone."

"What about my sports jacket?"

"That's just the thing to walk in there with. He sees that and you can forget about the college. Vanderhuysen. That's a lovely name. I can just about imagine what his face is like with a name like that. He must smile a lot, about once a year on Thanksgiving. That's all right. This baby's handled tougher nuts than him in our time."

The swift Bensonhurst wind seemed to hook him below the ribs, and Joseph, on his way to Flavens & Gordon for a suit, wondered whether it was possible for wind to actually take control of a thin, recuperating fellow and fling him beneath a bus. He imagined himself in such a situation, being blown along like a candy wrapper, trying futilely to grab telephone poles and fire hydrants.

Gordon, a nephew, after being taken off the streets by Flavens and nursed along in the business, had suddenly pulled out to set up a shop across the street, selling exactly the same suits, "only with a more of an Ivy League cut to them." Younger and more charming than Flavens, Gordon had pictures of himself in the new store's window, tape-measuring celebrities such as George Burns. Unashamedly, he went right after the old Flavens & Gordon customers, calling up Joseph's father and saying, "Just do me a favor and come down here. I guarantee you I'll fit you up with something you never had on your back before." He then told him he had Jimmy Dorsey in the store right that second. But Joseph's family sided with the older Flavens, agreeing that they had never heard of anything so ungrateful in their whole lives. The sign atop the old store had a black panel across half of it, now reading "Flavens &." From the moment his nephew deserted him, Flavens had been clutched by gall bladder difficulties; now, as Joseph and his mother entered, he acted as though he had been talking about his nephew continually, around the clock, with time out only for bladder twinges. "What was he?" said Flavens, a small man with great exhausted shoulders. "A young fresh kid who didn't know how to button his fly. He couldn't tell a herringbone from a baked herring. I taught that boy so much that if I'd had fourteen sons I couldn't have done more for all of them combined. I had him up to a hundred and a quarter in a month and he'd never seen more than forty in his life. He wanted to promote a little salesgirl in the supply room, I closed my eyes, I didn't see anything. So look at him over there now. My new neighbor. He's standing in the window laughing at me and I'm lucky I have a chair left in the store I can call my own."

"He got some tough kicking around," Joseph's mother said, gesturing toward the betrayed Flavens. "I don't know how he stands it. I never liked the way the kid gave me the personality and smileys when I used to come in here. Didn't I see this whole thing coming? I could've told him if he'd asked me."

When Joseph stood before the mirror, Flavens adjusted and smoothed down his sports jacket, saying, "How does she fit across the shoulders? We got beautiful stuff here."

"I wore this one in here," said Joseph. Flavens let his arms go slack and said, "See what he did to me." He shook his fist at the store across the street. "You dirty whippersnapper. You lousy charm boy."

Each time his mother bought a suit for him, Joseph would shrivel up with guilt as though she had to pay for it with an internal organ. He would protest, saying, "I really don't need it," and she would say, "And I know what he's worried about, too. You're crazy. What is it to me? A snap." And then, plucking crushed dollars from a pushcart-peddler-style purse, she would add with a grimace, "You know your mother's very rich." After he had settled reluctantly now on a gray pinstripe, his mother got a very small-voiced, glazed, whipped expression on her face. "Now would you let your mother buy you an overcoat," she whispered, as though begging to face a firing squad in his stead. "No," said Joseph, hearing his voice come forth as a wail. "For Christ's sake, no."

"All right," she said. "I can't deal with a crazy head."

"How much is the suit and I'll get out of here," she said to Flavens.

"Eighty dollars."

"He's being cute with me," said Joseph's mother. "And I really have time for that."

Flavens put his arm around her shoulders and said, "I'm crazy about your mother. She's from the old school and they don't make them like that any more. All right, Meg, give me $70 and I'll forget about making a profit on this one."

"I'll give you $60 and I could still support a family of five for a month on what you're making on the one suit."

"I'm mad about your mother," said Flavens, wrapping it up.

"And look," she said to him, as she and Joseph were at the door. "Forget about him across the street. You'll see that he'll break his neck. All that charm wears off and then he'll still have to know clothing."

"He'll come crawling back here," said Flavens, "and I wouldn't give him a job as a stockboy."

Joseph's mother took his hand as they wheeled out into the night wind, walking toward the subway. "Do you love your new suit?" she asked.

"Yes, but I didn't really need it," he said.

"I wouldn't be a bit surprised if he clipped me on the price," she said. She stopped then, tapped her foot on the sidewalk, then whisked him across the street and back down the block.

"Let's just go in and see what the kid's got. You need another suit and I'm dying of curiosity."

The name of the school was Kansas Land Grant Agricultural. It sounded just outrageous enough to make it seem a deliberate choice. You could not possibly be going to such a school without a reason for selecting it above all others, and it was this tack that Joseph used when presenting it to his neighborhood friends. "Oh yes," he would say, "I'd had my eye on it for a long time. Terrific liberal arts, and the farming thing is something you don't have to bother with." He said it was either Kansas or Nebraska Land Grant in the Midwest, and the others out that way such as Oklahoma Dairy and Missouri Shepherd were just jokes by comparison. Oddly enough, he found he did not have to defend it much; its name had a fresh robust uniqueness to it somehow and even such prestige-conscious fellows as the heavy-pompadoured Brown-bound Hilly Cantrowitz good-naturedly hollered "Hey, Kansas" to him across the avenue. Loving it, he blushed and said, "Cut it out." One morning Minter, the bow-legged, slightly Mongoloid City College-slated athletics expert, attacked Joseph's college along sportsmanship lines. He remembered every score since ball games began and said a Kansas Land squad had once been booked into Madison Square Garden where they did a lot of shoving and spitting on the court. "They're not all like that out there," said Joseph, his temper aroused. It felt fine having a college to go to; now, when stopped during strolls at his dad's side and asked about his plans, Joseph would say, "I'm going out to Kansas Land Grant," to which more than one questioner would respond, "Oh, I know that school. It's got a good reputation. It's in the Midwest." Only with Vonzel, king of the sewers and Joseph's closest friend (if a softball were lost, he would climb down into any sewer to retrieve it), did Joseph give voice to any of his doubts. Whenever Joseph and Vonzel were together they would begin to rain amiable blows on one another's bodies; one night, pounding away at each other on Vonzel's fire escape, Joseph said, "I don't want to wind up a farmer or anything. I hope I don't have to take a whole bunch of courses in dairy fat," to which Vonzel, a Brooklyn Polytech-er for ad layout and design, said, "If we play you in football we'll beat your ass."

The divorcée assured Joseph by phone that he was not to worry about the agricultural side of things. Kansas Land was a fine, solid school, the various courses only slightly tinged with a farming overlay, this to placate several wealthy wheat planters who through the years had been tendering it grants. She herself, as a matter of fact, had spent her freshman year at the nearby Windsor College for Women. Joseph thanked her and sent her a box of dress hankies with a note that read: "Thank you for getting me into K.L.G.A." As an afterthought, he added: "I'll try to do you right proud out there, ma'am," putting "Heh, heh" in parentheses to point up the satire on folksiness. Joseph's mother, who had gotten a little prouder of him now that he was a college fellow, read the note and said, "She'll faint when she reads my son's wit, his humor."

One morning, a week before registration, Joseph's mother shook him out of a sleep and told him to get dressed; she had an appointment with Commander Vanderhuysen. "I had some party," she said. "Fourteen operators I had to go through. Your mother's courage. Someday you'll see it written on a monument. And you should hear his voice. You could go quietly into labor while you're waiting to get a word out of him. But those are the kind. Win them over and you don't have to worry any more, you're riding on velvet. Get into your suit. He sees the way it fits and he won't give you a room, he'll give you a whole college."

■ ■

Commander Vanderhuysen was a tall, unsmiling turkeylike man who Joseph felt would have looked right at home in Founding Father-style wigs. He had been one of the Navy's great fighting skippers and there were pictures of him about his office walls shaking his fist defiantly at Axis captains who had blown ships out from beneath his legs. Retired now, he headed up a nationwide network of lowly ex-seamen, spiriting them into trivial jobs across the country and calling them regularly to remind them who had put them in their menial slots.

"May I call you Commander?" asked Joseph's mother as they entered his office. "I'm Meg and this is my son. He dressed up all morning, I want you to know, to look pretty for you."

"Where does he get his clothes?" asked the Commander.

"Oh, a place we've been dealing with for years," said Joseph's mother. "Flavens and Gordon. I know the boys since they were pups. They've got gorgeous stuff."

"You think they've got room for someone in their stockroom?"

"I don't know," she said. "You could ask Gus Flavens. He's a little aggravated, but I'm sure he'd tell you."

The Navy Commander sprang to his feet, made a call and said, "Hello, Leach. You got a pencil? Get over to an outfit called Flavens and Gordon. They may have something for you. A few very good friends of mine are tied in with them. And you keep yourself in line or I'll get you out of there as fast as I'm getting you in." He spelled out the name of Joseph's mother, who whispered, "This is a new one. I thought I knew maneuvering. Wait till Gus Flavens hears what I'm doing to him, he'll faint. I only hope he has something. This is some cutie I started with. Well, look where he's gotten."

"Where's that?" asked Joseph.

"Where you should only be someday," she said.

"Commander, darling," she said when he had slammed down the phone, "I'm going to make a remark to you and unless I miss my shot I think I can. My son will bear me out that I know people. Now, if I'm not mistaken we've both been around a little, is that right?"

Joseph did not mind the Commander while he was talking; but silent, his face became colonial as though he were about to levy harsh penalties for acts of sedition. When he nodded that he had been around, Joseph's mother said, "I thought I knew my customer. Now tell me, have you looked into that little matter in the Midwest my son is passing out about?" He picked up the phone, dialed long distance and soon said, "Commander here. Any word on my single at the Goatback for September 15? Look, I want to hear from you on that promptly, Krusy, or I'll lay it into you. I had seven men wanted that job, hear?"

"His use of power," whispered Joseph's mother. "The way he gets his message across. Quietly. All I can say is I'm glad I'm on his side. Well, that's what you get when you're playing in the Big Leagues."

"Would it embarrass you if I said you were a doll?" Joseph's mother said to the Commander. Joseph wanted to say it would embarrass *him*, but was afraid the Navy man would see him as a sarcastic New York type and decide he was not Kansas Land after all. "I'm getting him $300 a month," said Vanderhuysen, his lips bitter. "Only this Christmas I sent him four strips of heavy-grade plywood to patch up the west wall of his office. He'd better shape up, all right." It seemed to Joseph that the Commander's affairs were trivial; he felt a little sorry for him.

"I know what you mean," said Joseph's mother. "I've always been the same way. But you find out as you go along that very few people are real. We all grow up eventually, but for some of us it takes a long time.

"Now look," she said, getting to her feet. "I don't know what your schedule is, but we've got the whole day ahead of us. It would be my greatest pleasure to do a little something for you. Would you let my son and I show you New York?"

"Maybe the Commander's *from* New York," said Joseph, wondering if it was Kansas Land to question your mom. "I don't care if he's the mayor," said his mother. "He's never seen your mother's New York."

The Commander said he thought he might be able to get away from his desk; then he disappeared into a small adjoining room.

Joseph had the feeling he could be away from his desk for four years without a single affair of consequence being affected. His mother made a fast call to Joseph's Aunt Faith, the ex-wardrobe mistress who despite her elevated age still wielded ticket-getting power in the Broadway theater. "This is Meg," said Joseph's mother, "and I want three for this afternoon's matinee at the Lyceum if you know what's good for you. I'm not seeing the show if that's what you're worried about. It's for your brother so his son can get into college."

"She'll get them if she has to croak," she said, laying down the receiver. "Wait till he hears where he's going. Those are the kind that see a lot of hit musicals. You can tell from his face. Wait, your mother's just starting to work on him."

"Do you think the hotel room will come through?" asked Joseph.

"He'll get you more than that," said Joseph's mother. "I saw where his eyes were for the last twenty minutes."

The Commander was first to get out of the cab alongside Lindy's, the famed Broadway restaurant; Joseph's mother paid the fare, saying, "He must take a lot of cabs, too. I'd like to know the last time he took a dime out of his pocket. Just like your mother always worried about the almighty dollar."

The outside windows of Lindy's were lined with volumes written by show biz celebrities; the Commander slipped a book out of an envelope, showing it to Joseph and his mother. It was called *Naval Ceremonies for One and All* and signed with his name. "Something I wrote," he said. Over her shoulder, Joseph's mother said, "Who the hell can keep up with him." She took the book from the Commander, and when he had gone to check his coat, she said to Joseph, "I'd like to know the name of a trick he hasn't thought of yet. And that's with his little navy uniform and with his not ever saying anything. You really have to worry about that beauty." She went over to one of the headwaiters; the restaurant was not terribly crowded, yet he was making elaborate hand signals to other distant headwaiters, as though a new anti-slothfulness edict had gone into effect and he was fearful of losing his job. "Jimmy darling, I have a favor to ask," she said. "My son's friend wrote a book. God only knows what it's about. Could you maybe sneak it into a window for me like a doll?"

"What's he, a comedian?"

"He's some comedian. I'd like to learn some of his material. Meantime, will you do that for me, angel, and I'll give you something nice."

The Commander ordered baked herring for an appetizer. "He's living," Joseph's mother muttered. She told the waiter, "Look, sweetheart, tell them to make it nice. We have a very important person here. If he likes it, he'll bring in the whole Navy." Then she said, "Tell the truth, Commander, did you ever eat baked herring in your life?" The Commander let fly a gray, toothless, historical laugh; Joseph's mother pinched his sleeve and said to Joseph, "I can kid around with him." When he had ordered corn fritters for a main course, she said, "Corn fritters you want. That's all right with me. They'll love that in the kitchen. I think it'll be the first time since the restaurant opened." When the Commander began to talk to the waiter, Joseph's mother said, "Leave him alone, he's eating a little baked herring and corned fritters. That's the combination he insists on. You don't give him that and he won't be happy. They were just waiting for him in Lindy's." She rocked back and forth with laughter, slapping Joseph's arm and saying, "Leave him alone, he's eating in a restaurant."

When his fritters arrived, Vanderhuysen asked the waiter, "Have you people ever thought of bottling these?"

"I'd like to bottle them, all right," said the waiter. Joseph's mother, turning serious, explained to the Commander that they did not get much call for fritters at Lindy's. "Someone from out of town comes in," she said, "they'll make them up as a courtesy, but usually they don't bother around with them."

"But Commander Vanderhuysen's from New York," said Joseph.

"My son's very technical," she said. "You'll have to excuse him."

A man in a loud sports jacket approached their table now, Joseph's mother averting her head and saying, "Watch the son of a bitch come right over here. This is just what I need." Joseph recognized him as a famed Broadway comedian.

"Hiya, Meg," said the entertainer. "Hearty indigestion to you all."

"Hello, sonny," said Joseph's mother. "Watch your filthy mouth because we're here with an important out-of-town person, something you don't know anything about."

"I've noticed the Commander," said the comedian, bringing his cuff down to the Navy man's mouth as though it were a microphone. "Would you like to tell the folks out there in the water a few nice words about drowning? I'll bet you're having gobs of fun here, sir, am I right? Oceans of it."

Joseph's mother seemed to be trying not to laugh, but her body began to shake in spite of herself. "He's funny as hell," she said, "but I can do without him now." She said to the Commander, "I'll bet you'll never forget this day as long as you live." The comedian said, "Watch this," and took a piece of ice from Joseph's water glass. Concealing it in his palm, he walked over to a pair of young girls who were dining alone, made a mock sneeze into his hand and then shook the ice drops into the girls' faces. "Disgusting," they said in unison, cringing backward, but Joseph had the feeling they secretly admired his kind of earthy fun; he pictured the comedian in bed with the two of them later on, his white-on-white shirt hanging on the doorknob. "He's some screwy bastard," his mother mumbled, Joseph wondering how his chances were for Kansas Land at the moment. The comedian hopped back to the table on one leg, saying to Joseph's mother, "It's been wonderful seeing you, Mrs. Coolidge." Then, through her dress, he shook the tip of her breast as though it were a hand, and said, "And you, too, sir."

"Get out of here, you crummy bastard," said Joseph's mother. "Can't you see, I'm here with my kid and his friend." Joseph reached across the table and grabbed the comedian's tie, pulling hard, yanking him down into some split pea soup; his mother eased him away, saying, "All right, all right, he'll always defend his mother. Get out of here with your lousy comedy."

The comedian dried his tie, said, "They don't like my asparagus, I'll sell it somewhere else," and hopped over to the cashier's desk. Joseph wondered how the Commander would feel if he were to pursue the comedian, leap on his back and drive him through the cigar counter. He wondered if a gentle nipple shake actually hurt a woman; when he saw the comedian hop out of the revolving door, he found himself oddly at ease. Restaurants were one of his favorite places; sitting in them alongside his mother, who knew how to get around headwaiters, he felt luxurious and sure of himself. There was no way for anyone to tell he was a three-roomer, no bedroom door to guard so that people would not peek inside and see his apartment was diminutive. The waiter came over and said, "The food was our good news, now here's the bad news," putting the check before the naval officer. He began to probe for his wallet and Joseph's mother took the check, saying, "Now look, this is our treat." "Heh, heh, heh," said the Commander, laughing at an untold joke as though he was going to be generous and fail to pay this one check after having picked up forty thousand in a row. And he was only doing it because he had been touched by a special remark Joseph's mother had made. When he went to get his coat, she said, "I like the color his face turned when they put the check next to him. We're with a big spender."

Outside, they checked the restaurant window again. The Commander's book had been wedged between a best-selling Joe Penner memoir and a Sonja Henie autobiography on the joys of the skating game.

During the war Joseph's father had taken his air-raid-warden duties seriously; Joseph often made blackout rounds with him, standing by as his dad hollered in to lax apartments, "Hey, you'd better put those lights out. What if a bomb really did fall?" Joseph loved to try on his father's gas mask, even long after the war, wondering if it still had protective powers and how long he could hold out with it in a city of lethal fumes. His father was very patriotic and whenever newspapers ran a picture of some silver-haired American general, he would take it over to Joseph and say, "Look at that man. Is that a guy?"

In the theater lobby now, Joseph's father introduced himself to the Commander, tapped the Navy man's chest decorations and said, "You must have seen plenty of action, I'll bet. That war was really something, wasn't it? And that Hitler. Hmmmph. Every time you think about what he did it seems unbelievable. He must have been crazy, don't you think? That's my theory. Otherwise, why should he have done all those things? A sane man doesn't act that way, nosirree."

The Commander seemed to have a different personality for all-male groupings. He leaned over to Joseph's father in a confidential style, poked his ribs and said, "Hey, the little ladies of San Juan." He formed his hands into open globes, winked and began to twist them in the air, simulating the massage of large

172

breasts. "Back Bay, Boston," he then announced, continuing the twists but making the hand-globes tiny.

"We have a comedian with us," said Joseph's father, putting his arm around the Commander's shoulders. "Do you know what he was just putting across?" he asked Joseph.

"I'm not sure."

"He's still a kid," Joseph's father told the Commander. "Listen, when you think back, we didn't know about those things in the old days, either. Am I lying? If we knew about such things, we'd get our heads rapped."

An usher announced five minutes to curtain time and Joseph's father said to the Commander, "You didn't see any shows like this during the war, did you? Of course not. That would be some deal to take a show like this on a boat. People, sets, you'd have quite a problem on your hands." He seemed to be imagining himself in charge of the engineering job and said, "Hmmph."

Walking down the aisle, the Commander pointed back toward the Negro attendant who had taken their tickets. "Dis am de voice from de motor pool, boss," he said. "De two half-ton trucks are ready, sir, black ones, of coase."

"He's quite a boy," said Joseph's father. "We don't even need a show."

The Commander sat between Joseph and his father, settling into his seat and then tapping the armrests. "Say, I'll bet you folks never even thought of using these." He seemed to think Joseph and his father were involved somehow in the theater's ownership. "What if you were to work a tie-in with your restaurant? Each one of these armrests has a little glassed-in plate says 'Lindy's for fritters, after the show.'" He made a two-fingered slash in the air to show how it would look.

"You think that's a bad idea," said Joseph's father. "I wouldn't laugh at that. People have made money on even crazier schemes."

There were many young chorus girls in the show; as was his

173

habit, Joseph selected a favorite, one he would concentrate on through the production numbers; during dance twirlings, he would fasten his eyes on her pants alone, and only when his favorite's skirt had settled would he scan about and try to pick up bonuses from other late skirt-droppers. He wondered whether glimpses of pants were intentional in musicals and were assigned by producers, say seven to a scene—and if so, how producers went about telling the girls they were required. On occasion it occurred to him that they were all accidental, an honest by-product of vigorous dancing, and you were supposed to lower your eyes when they turned up. Sometimes he felt like writing shamed letters to the girls confessing that while they were dancing their hearts out, putting into play hard-to-accumulate skills, all he had done was sit back and wait for panty flashes.

Now, seated beside the Commander, Joseph wondered whether his father had favorites, too; he speculated on how it would affect his chances for a Kansas Land Grant hotel reservation if the Commander knew what was his real interest in intricately worked-out dance routines. He gripped the armrests tightly, laughed deeply at the jokes and applauded the melodies with vigor as though the catchy dialogue and tuneful strains were the real lure for him in musical comedy. Several times he craned his neck around impatiently during the choreographed numbers, wasting twirls to throw the Commander off. Before the first-act curtain, the Commander nudged Joseph's father, said, "Third one on the left," and did some globular twists below the seats. "Hey, that's not supposed to be what you're watching," said Joseph's father with a laugh. During the intermission Joseph's father suggested orange drinks and the Commander said, "Okay, but only on a no-host basis." Joseph's father said nonsense and bought the drinks, the Commander saying, "Heh, heh, heh," as though the idea of letting people pay for him had a certain novelty, and he was going to make a full evening of it —just to see what would happen.

Joseph enjoyed standing in the lobby with his father and the heavily decorated Navy Commander. He rocked back and forth on his heels, chuckling warmly, feeling people in the lobby would see him as part of a rich and influential family, the Commander his uncle and mentor who was squiring him along through a series of impeccably chosen prep schools, shaping his career for naval greatness. He was just in from Andover for a crowded weekend of theater, cotillion dances and private, leisurely, expensively tailored lunches at the club.

After the show Joseph's mother plowed her way through the audience to their seats, dragging along one of the usherettes. "I'll bet you had a gorgeous time," she said to the Commander. "Leave it to Meg to show you the real New York." She introduced the usherette, a homely woman with pained, collapsing feet, saying, "Jeanette works here and was dying to meet three handsome fellows. We've been connected with the theater for years, Commander." The usherette seemed at a loss as to what her role was and then said, "Would you like some extra Playbills for the show? I can spare about a dozen if you like." The Commander smiled and said he could certainly use them for his outer office.

"And he'll treasure them, too, the dope," said Joseph's mother, cupping her mouth as though delivering an aside to some audience. "They're worth a fast two cents a thousand. Well, he really knows his way around the legitimate stage."

"I'm not finished with you yet," she said to the Commander. "I'll bet you'd give your right arm to go backstage." The Navy man said he had met Frances Langford during the war. "Oh, that's nice," said Joseph's mother. "Everyone's heard of her. All you have to do is to meet Frances Langford and you don't have to say hello to anyone else. You've met the entertainment world." She took his hand and led him through the curtain, Joseph and his father following. "Would you folks do one of your shows on naval stores?" the Commander asked. He seemed to have the idea that Joseph's family was responsible for the production, too. "I can get one to you on that if you think it'll go."

"Oh, now you're writing a musical, too. Well, why not?" she said. "Everyone else is in the theater, why not you?" She steered the Commander over to the leading man. "I've got a gentleman here from out of town who thought you were wonderful and would like to say hello to you." The male star seemed to get the idea he was being interviewed by *Stars and Stripes*. He sat down in his robe, threw his legs up on a chair and said, "I won't do small clubs because I can hear my medium nasals hitting the walls and bouncing right back at me."

"Is this a riot," said Joseph's mother. "The two of them, him with his naval stores that the theater is just waiting for and this one who's talking to Brooks Atkinson. Your mother's combinations.

"Well, Commander," she said, "you wanted to see the real Broadway, the theater that the average out-of-towner never gets to see, you're getting it right between the eyes."

"Look," said Joseph's father. "Maybe the Commander doesn't like it back here. It's possible. Maybe he likes to watch the show and when it's over he likes to go somewhere else."

"And you know who would have the answer to that question," said Joseph's mother. "You. You'd know what another human being likes and doesn't like. I ought to let you show him New York and he'd really see a lot. He wouldn't see his own behind."

They took the Commander back to the apartment for dinner; on the way, Joseph's father talked to him about his business, using the word "goods" often, explaining how you could ship many more couches if only you could get enough of them. The word began to sound funny to Joseph and he wondered about its origin, why it had not turned up as "greats" or "honeys."

Joseph's grandmother was waiting in the apartment with a

college sweater she had just finished knitting. She was a slip of a woman with lovely hair and distended stomach, and her sole activities were knitting and slumping over into dozes. All her sweaters were in the outdated slipover family, and their vast areas of Central European ribbing embarrassed Joseph. He had a drawerful of them which he wore under great tension, ready at all times to beat up fellows who insulted their antique styling. His mother grabbed the freshly knitted slipover and showed it to the Commander. "Look at the workmanship on this, the warmth that went into it. God bless her, you'll never see such fingers again.

"The Commander would give his right arm to have a sweater like this, so shut up before you make a remark," she said to Joseph.

After the Commander had removed his coat in preparation for dinner, Joseph's mother said, "You know what? I think the Commander could use this family a little bit. Its intimacy. And he's the first one, isn't he?" When dessert had been served, Joseph's father sat at the organ while the family took turns singing. His sister came home early and sang a medley in a Dinah Shore style, Joseph pitching in by crooning "All the Things You Are." His father played only in one key, making it impossible for Joseph to hit several of the high notes. He wondered how he would sound if he ever got to sing in his real key. When Joseph sang the lyric "Some day my happy arms will hold you," his father stopped playing and said, "That really gets me. Happy arms. How can arms be happy?", then continued, chuckling to himself. The Commander looked on with Declaration of Independence solemnity, but Joseph was not worried about him. He was sure the naval officer was being charmed out of his skin. Joseph felt fine at these songfests; he forgot about being a three-roomer and was sure that if he had had chancellors of leading colleges in to look at them, to see the kind of warm and rich homelife he had, he would have been flooded with college acceptance letters. When he did the reprise of "All the Things," Joseph's mother said, "That kid's voice could always tear my guts out." "That's enough," he said to her, but he did another refrain, pouring even more tenderness into it. His father followed with a sweet, old-fashioned tenor solo that made Joseph's eyes water; he felt like recording it so he could have it forever, playing it often after his father was dead. The party all gathered round the grandmother then to hear her hum "They Say," and tap her bunioned feet to the melody. "She really does do it," Joseph said to the Commander, kneeling at his grandmother's feet. Whenever she hummed the melody, the family would howl with glee, but now, as he watched her fall over into a sudden doze, it seemed to Joseph that they were exploiting her to amuse a stranger. "Hey, let's quit," he said. "She's tired."

"Pull on her ear if you want to get her up," said the Commander, and Joseph told him he did not think it would be a good idea.

"Tell the truth, Commander," said Joseph's mother. "When was the last time you were among such warmth in your life? This is your real New York. Will you treasure this day as long as you live?"

"Fine," said the Commander. Joseph took out the neatly kept family photo album and spread it on the Commander's lap. It was another thing he wished he could do for chancellors instead of making out applications. He flipped the pages, saying, "Here's my mother in a flapper outfit" and "That's Dad with an outboard motor he once won," but he sensed the Commander was not responding and shifted the album onto his own lap, pretending he had brought it out for his own entertainment. After a while the Commander made ready to leave; at the door, Joseph's mother grabbed his elbow. "Nobody has to say anything. He had some treat, didn't you?"

"He's been in other homes," said Joseph's father. "What are

you making such a fuss about? I don't mean during the war when he was at sea, but when he got back he got plenty of invitations, I'll bet."

"Oh yeah," said Joseph's mother, looking into the naval officer's eyes, "and they were just like this one. He had the same good time. Meanwhile, don't look now, but the poor guy is so grateful that if you asked him he'd give you the whole Navy."

The next morning Joseph seemed to run flailing out of his sleep rather than to awaken; his mother called on the telephone and told him to meet her at the Commander's office in the early afternoon. For a second he thought his arm might be up again; rather than look at it, he reached tentatively for it with his other arm, grateful to find it slender and ribbonlike. The Negro cleaning woman had his breakfast ready; her eggs, once considered the best in the world by Joseph, were loose and uncertain these days and he wondered if this had any connection with the pails of old cleaning water she absent-mindedly left about the apartment. She told him that she would be fine if it were not for her son who worked in a nightclub and made lots of money but periodically got himself "all jiggered up." Joseph wanted to feel sorry for her but could not for the life of him see what was so tragic about her circumstances.

He went downtown in the subway, moving to the front car and pretending he was the conductor. He scanned the corridor up ahead, wondering whether a man standing along the sides would be crushed or might slither by. Later he sat in the Commander's anteroom, leafing through magazines, waiting for his mother the same way he had waited so many hundreds of times —at corsetieres, hosiery stores, in millinery shops and beauty parlors. After a while he heard a scattered grumbling of voices and went inside. He saw his mother leaving the Commander's inner office, buttoning her blouse over great sunburned breasts, tucking it into her skirt and snuffling as though she had just been given bad news. The Commander followed her, his jacket off, his freshly starched sleeves rolled up.

"What happened to her?" asked Joseph.

"I don't know, boy," said the Commander. "Don't ask me."

"Come," she said. "I'm glad you're down here."

"Are you hurt?" asked Joseph.

"No," she said. "But let's get out of here."

Joseph supported her out to the hall. Years back, she had gone without fuss one morning to have a fistlike growth taken from her by surgeons. It had turned out to have a long threadlike connection that ran along the side of her, making the operation a long and major one. "I never told anyone," she said afterward. "That's not your mother's way." Now, leaving the Navy man's office, he felt he was helping her after the complicated fist removal. Downstairs he hailed a cab and said, "Look, did he do anything to you?"

"He didn't do anything," she said; in the cab she began to cry in great heaving fat-nosed whulps.

"Look, I'll go back there and get the son of a bitch if he did anything. I tried to get my grandmother to sing for the bastard. How do you think I feel about that now?"

"No," she said. "I know you would, but don't. He's a crumb, he's that kind of a man, he has a face like that, you can't change him. Nothing will. He'll be that way till the day he dies."

"But what the hell did he do, Mom?"

"Nothing," she said, whulping into his shirt. "In two seconds I'll forget all about it."

"I don't like the idea of someone getting away with something like he did," said Joseph, back at the apartment. "Wouldn't it be all right if Dad and I went down there to pay him a little visit?"

Backed up by his father's great couch-making forearms, Joseph was sure he would be able to handle the aging war hero. He thought that perhaps he would take the air-raid-warden gas mask along, too, and work it in somehow. He was certain they would come out all right, especially if they jumped the aging sea dog before he got to summon fresh young lacrosse-playing ensigns from the Naval Academy.

"That's all I need is for you to tell your father. He's just the one to handle a situation. Look, you might as well stop kidding yourself, there's nothing you can do in one of these. It's like beating your head against a stone wall. Forget it."

Joseph fully intended waiting several hours before asking the next question. He went ahead without waiting, though, feeling terrible about it, as though he had wolfed down a sardine sandwich seconds after the burial of a good friend. "Mom, I know something lousy just went on, but am I allowed to ask you just one quick thing? Did he get me the reservation out there for college?"

"You're such an infant," she said. "There never was a reservation. From the second he saw your mother there was only one thing on his mind. He saw your mother's form."

"I really would like to go down there," he said, "and just give him a short one in the neck."

"I know, darling," she said, "and I love you for it." She gave him one of the new kind of kisses she had introduced in the past few days. They were wide, and gurgling, and had some suck to them. As he received each one, he felt as though a large, freshly exposed, open-meloned internal organ had washed against his face. She pinched him often, too, saying, "Ooooooch, that child. I could die. My life."

"Come on, none of those," said Joseph, wiping the kissed area with his sleeve.

"A mother's kiss you're ashamed of," she said.

"I don't like wet ones," he said. "I guess all this means that I'm washed up out at Kansas Land."

"You know what I have to give you before another day passes

181

by?" she said. "A course in your mother. You're going out there tomorrow and you'll see whether you'll be in there or not."

Then, without warning, she went into a wide-nostriled, mascara-tinted series of whulps, drawing her lips back over teeth that had had much bridgework done on them and just barely got by. "I'm going to let a man like that, with what that person *did* to me, what he thought of, stop my child, my life and my blood, from going to a college. . . ?" Her cries brought into play all her worst features; they involved plenty of heartbreak for him, but down beneath all of that he wished she had a neater, more conservative way of doing them.

That night Joseph had the feeling that in small towns all over the Midwest, incoming freshman Kansas Landers were all congregating at fresh and scrubbed teen-age hangouts and having farewell parties, getting their final milk shakes from proprietors named "Doc" and "Skeets." Joseph decided he would pay a visit to the Koke Kanteen, a teen-age dancing hall which in theory was youthful and wholesome. Actually, it was a sinister place where at least once a night fellows in great navy-blue fitted overcoats went at each other with weaponry. On one occasion Joseph had seen a group of them all join hands in a circle as though for a session of dodgeball and kick at another overcoated fellow on the floor, all the while casting looks over their shoulders for the police. Joseph peeked into the circle and saw the fellow protecting his head, but was sure after a while the boy was dead. When the police came, it surprised Joseph to see him get to his feet and saunter toward the door, the only sign of his beating trails of blood which appeared at his cuffs and continued on down along his fingers. There was something frightening about the overcoats and the fact that a fellow could be all cut to pieces yet make a natty appearance afterward except for blood cuffs. Joseph was not a Kanteen regular, yet he had visited the hall several times, mostly because of its wholesome name and always in the hope that new policies would have gone into effect turning it into the kind of hangout he was sure you could find every ten feet in Abilene. For each of his visits he would grease up his hair, put a jacket on over a turtle-neck sweater and spend most of the evening on the side of the hall, making tough faces and trying to avoid all overcoated fellows.

On the night of his farewell, he stood momentarily at the Kanteen entrance and, to his surprise, found himself striding confidently up to a girl named Tricky and saying to her, "I'll take this dance if you don't mind." She was the finest dancer in all the Kanteen, a girl whose sweeps and bobbing dips were the talk of the floor and whose performance dominated most of the entrance area. She was a favorite of the overcoated crowd, Joseph remembering them having thrown protective cordons about her during knife battles. Each of her dances was with a different boy, and she seemed inexhaustible, able to follow the most elaborate of tosses, finishing each frenzied number with only a single chest-heave and the word "whee" before sailing into others. Joseph thought she was pretty and had always wanted to touch her behind to see if it was muscular and lindy-hop-hardened. He aspired to dance with her, too, but since he knew only three breaks he had always held off, figuring you needed at least thirty to get through a single fox-trot with her. He encircled her waist now and it seemed to Joseph he had used up his three almost as soon as the music began. He did the same three again, deliberately now, as if he had not been satisfied with his execution, and when she said, "All right now, let's really cut," he had no choice but to bring forth the trio a third time, saying "spat, spat," with each of them, making a new set of faces as though he could disguise them that way. "We did those," she said, and Joseph led her to the side in disgrace, saying, "They're all I had time to cook up." An overcoated fellow went in for him, and he headed for the door, but then decided he was in no frame of mind for striking out to new Midwestern colleges. He whirled about, snapping his fingers and squinting his eyes, as though suddenly overcome by the music; then he headed back into the Kanteen where he spotted a short fellow with bad posture named Brown he knew from high school. The boy had been a fair student who had suddenly retired from the academic race, preferring to hang back and remark on the brilliance of other fellows in the class. "That Gold has a math mind like a steel trap," he would say to Joseph. "And how about Seldamari on current events." At the time of his retirement, Joseph noticed Brown had begun slipping into great fitted overcoats, word getting about that he had gangland connections who were going to get him a break in crooning. He was making a phone call now, alongside a small cluster of overcoated fellows and one sullen, massive-breasted girl. Beckoning Joseph to come closer, he took his mouth away from the receiver and said, "We're placing a large order at the Chinese restaurant which we then won't pick up. Order something."

Ever since he had begun showing up in large coats, Joseph had been a little afraid of the thin-armed Brown. He cleared his throat and placed an order for eight portions of Chow Har Kew. Brown then introduced Joseph to his friends, Joseph telling them he was off to Kansas Land the next day and had wanted to get in a few final laughs before heading out that way. "Education is an important element," said Brown. He seemed to be the leader of the group and invited Joseph to go prowling with them after the Kanteen closed. At midnight they piled into a black sedan, taking Joseph to a darkened elementary school nearby.

They all vaulted the pronged fence outside, Joseph amazed at how nimble they were in their large, flowing overcoats. Inside the abandoned school the group worked its way through the rooms, kicking down the doors with their feet, keeping their hands in the coat pockets as they proceeded. Joseph did a few batterings himself but was terribly frightened since it was his first experience as a vandal; he was sure someone was going to leap out and catch him, forcing him to pay for seventeen expensive double-hung school doors. It would come to the same amount as two years' tuition at Kansas Land. "How come you guys are doing this?" Joseph asked Brown as they kicked through the boys' lavatory. "Because the school system's all fouled up in red tape," Brown explained, booting away with extra vigor. Not really sure he had been enlightened, Joseph said, "Well, I've got to get back and do some packing if I'm going to get off tomorrow." When they had all returned to the car, Brown said, "It continues over at my place." Joseph got in alongside the silent girl and was driven to Brown's apartment, where the group removed their overcoats for the first time. On the way there, the girl had asked Joseph if he respected her and told him she had four brothers who were soldiers. She had then taken his hand and made him swear he would not go above the knee if she dozed off on the way.

At the apartment Brown removed his shoes and distributed bars of halvah, then snapped his fingers and told the girl to take off her clothes. She got out of them, as though she always disrobed after halvah servings; three of the fellows put her in the bathtub, the entire group then standing around the tub and scrubbing her down with washcloths. She hunched over, folding her hands across her breasts and taking most of the scrubs on her back. Joseph stepped up to the tub, briskly did her shoulders and then told Brown, "All finished."

She stood up after a while and began to dry herself, Joseph looking at her and deciding she was much too good to be mistreated in tubs. The other boys filed out of the bathroom and Joseph had the crazy thought he would whisper an invitation into her ear, one for New Year's Eve which would represent his first Kansas Land mid-semester break. There would be no way for anyone to tell by looking at her that she had been gone at with cloths. He pictured himself falling in love with her and thought that would be some fix, marrying a girl and having to go around always knowing that she had once been gang-tubbed, when you were in movies and out with other couples.

In the next room, Brown and his group had begun a dart game. Still hanging behind, Joseph asked her what she was going to do with herself, whether she was going to college.

"Oh, I don't know," she said, toweling her hair. "As long as I don't have a farty little life."

"Why do you hang around these fellows?" he whispered.

"Brown," she said with a disgusted wave, stepping into a pair of gay little red panties. "Those guys. What do they know. They just cruise around." He was a little relieved to find her lethargic of speech, killing her off slightly as a romantic possibility. They went back to the living room together, Joseph a little guilty about their appearance as a team. He thanked Brown for a swell evening, saying he really had to get rolling now. To his relief, Brown excused him from the other scheduled activities and told the group that Joseph had the best head for grammar he had ever run into.

On his way home Joseph hunched through the streets, glad he had seen nudity, trying to memorize all the details, yet feeling this was hardly the fresh and clear-skinned send-off he had in mind. He stopped at a neighborhood soda fountain and packed in a hot fudge sundae, trying to line his insides with a little last-minute wholesomeness. It was run by a man who had admitted to being a little pink in the thirties. Joseph listened to some cigar-smoking old guys, the only other customers, go at each other's throats in a debate on Wendell Willkie.

book four

The following morning Joseph awakened to find his mother lining up perfume bottles in her valise.

"Why are you packing?" he asked. "You're not going anywhere."

"I knew you'd start," she said. "If you make a fuss I'll kill you. I'm just the one to let you go out there with an arm that we still don't know what's doing with it. That you should thank your lucky stars twenty times a day that it's still on. If I let you get on a plane with that arm, you know how far you'd get? They'd throw you right off. You certainly know your mother. You really have a portrait of her down pat."

"But I don't want to go out there with a mother," said Joseph. "I don't even know if you're allowed to have one out there."

"I'll be there all together two minutes," she said. "I just want to get you set. So that maybe I can have a few seconds of sleep for myself in the future with what this has cost me in peace of mind that I don't even want to go into now."

Joseph's send-off was a casual one. When he was packed, he opened the closet door to say goodby to his sister. She was sitting in there, with bathrobes and overcoats pulled down about her head, her only way of making private phone calls in the small apartment. She covered the mouthpiece, said "Goodby, gorgeous," and went on talking, her legs in a great yawn. "Did you see where he still looks?" said Joseph's father, carrying the valise.

"I don't have time to worry about every little thing," said Joseph's mother. "Thank God, I've got good kids and nothing ever happened."

Riding down in the elevator, Joseph's father said, "Now do you know where you're going?"

"To college," said Joseph. "Is that what you mean?"

"Now, I'm not fooling around," his father said. "I just want to make sure you've got your head screwed onto your shoulders. You know, sometimes you do some funny things. Like putting on your pants first, tightening them and then trying to jam your shirt in through the belt. You won't be able to do things like that out there. You'll get sent home and you'll be damned sorry, get what I mean? You can act any way you want, I won't be there, but you'll get into the soup if you act crazy."

In the lobby a stocky, flirtatious woman stopped them and said, "Oh, is that your new coat, Meg? I don't like the way he did it. Not at all."

"Watch how I handle the son of a bitch," Joseph's mother whispered. She opened the woman's fur wrap and said, "Look at you." Then, unbuttoning her own coat, she said, "And look at me. Now maybe you'll stop worrying about coats."

"Did I cut her to ribbons?" she said, when the woman had marched off. "Her shape, and she has the nerve to go around with a mouth like that." Joseph thought it over and decided his mother's wit had been far from rapierlike in handling the neighbor. It bothered him and he imagined her coming up against saber-tongued Kansas Land deans and being made to seem clumsy and illiterate. Her hennaed hair and mammoth breasts began to disturb him now, and he wondered if there was any way to tone her down, as though these features, too, would make her easier to hit with verbal blows. "You're looking at your mother's outfit," she said, catching his eyes on her in the street. "Well, all your life you've really had to worry about what kind of an appearance your mother would make, haven't you, angel? She's always let you down."

On the way to the car they ran into Mr. Latzen, Joseph's high school trigonometry teacher, who was better than any other instructor at keeping classes disciplined. With menacing glances and catlike darts over to suspected talkers, Latzen was able to maintain a tense, tomblike silence, though frankly inhibiting loose and freewheeling trig discussions in his classroom. Joseph's final grade in the course had been taut and restrained, but since Latzen lived in the neighborhood, Joseph's mother forgot and assumed her son had done brilliantly.

"Guess where your favorite student is going," she said to the trig man. "To college. You were one of the first to spot him and we owe you a lot."

"Good luck," said the heavy-browed Latzen. "Which one are you off to?"

"Try to get two words out of my son and it's like opening a clam," said Joseph's mother. "Those are the kind, the brilliant ones, who'll be quiet while the morons holler. To Kansas Land, a very good school in the Midwest."

"Well, you're a nice fellow," said the teacher, walking off. Joseph wondered whether Latzen expected him to maintain high discipline at all times or whether you were allowed to cut up a little when you were graduated and ran into him on streets.

At the airport Joseph's father asked him if he had ever been on a plane. "Well, that's something to think about," he said. "How do you know you're going to like it?"

"I don't, Dad," said Joseph.

"Well, there you are, you've saved this for the last second. A lot of people get up there and they find they don't care for flying. They get nauseous. What are you going to do then? Look, I can't run your life. If that happens, tell your mother, and the people on the plane will get you something. They must have something for people in that condition. What the hell, the airlines are big business today. You act as though you're the first person ever flew a plane."

They stood in the waiting room, watching the plane take on fuel. "Jesus," said Joseph's father, "that's some strong plane. I'll bet you that's one of the strongest they got. I remember back when they didn't have 'em at all. No fooling. I'll bet you thought they always had 'em."

Joseph kissed his father's cheek and said goodby, enjoying the toughness of his beard and wondering, if you really came down hard against it, whether you could actually slash open your face.

On the ramp Joseph's mother pinched his shoulder and said, "Ooooch, look what you're going to get out there—girls. Lots of pretty ones. I'll bet you didn't know they were going to be in store for you." The pinch hurt Joseph; he remembered a time when she had pinched him very hard on the rear end, getting him to say, "I'm leaving home." The angrier he got, the more she laughed and the harder she made the pinches until his eyes had filmed over and he cracked his nose against a butter dish.

"Hey, watch those," said Joseph. The girls were very pretty and were waiting for the last second to get on the plane. Joseph wished he was very far along in friendships with all of them so that he could just go over and hold their behinds without causing a break in their discussion. "Are you going to have bitches out there," his mother said. "And they'll be able to use you, don't worry. I'd like to know what those mothers spent on their little skirts and dresses. Those are the kind that are going to be very interested in courses and have no time for men. Oh yeah. Don't look now but they'll all have lovely stomachs out to here in three months."

Joseph and his mother took their seats, and when the girls entered the plane, she said, "Do you want me to get you started? Why not. There could be rich ones in there. Then you can stop worrying about solving fractions." She called the girls over and said, "May I ask you a question, dears? Are you going out to Kansas Land? That's where my son is going. He's sorry I started in with you."

The girls said they were headed for an all-girls school several miles from Joseph's university. One of them looked like Ann Rutherford and kept digging her hands into the pockets of her jumper as though searching for some small lost seashells. Joseph wished he knew her well enough to get right into her pockets with her. He wished, too, there were a way to put across how great he was, to give her a little pellet containing all his wit and good qualities which she could swallow like gum and know upon digestion that he was special, not just a fellow with a mother. The girl asked if Joseph and his mother were a show biz team going out to do an act in Kansas. "Ooh, a mouth on it," said Joseph's mother. "I'll kill myself. It must be these," she said, sticking a brown scarf Joseph had given her for Christmas into the cleavage of her low-cut dress. "We're not entertainers," said Joseph. "Just a mother and her son." When the girls had walked off, Joseph's mother said "There goes a little cutie. She's going to have a lot of trouble attracting fellas. Oh yeah. When she's not studying higher geometry. Meanwhile, I think she could have forgotten the whole college and used my son and gone back to become a lovely mother."

"She couldn't have used me," said Joseph, wondering if the girl looked upon traveling performers as glamorous or merely silly.

"No, huh?" said Joseph's mother. "Someday you'll look in a mirror and see your face."

When the plane was aloft, she took a deep breath and said, "Don't look now, but your mother's flying. She's in an airplane, going places. For forty-five years the ground was good enough. Your mother's acceptance of things. The way she doesn't let anything faze her. Someday there'll be an announcement."

A blond stewardess who made some fine hushed stocking sounds as she walked gave pillows to Joseph and his mother. He had a fantasy in which he saw himself standing up in the aisle with a bomb in his hand, announcing he would drop it unless the stewardess took off her clothes and got into the small men's room with him. He saw himself democratically permitting five minutes of debate among the passengers before whisking her to the rear of the plane. Joseph's mother caught her wrist now and said, "Just in case you were getting any funny ideas, this is my son, not my lover."

"He is?" said the stewardess. "That's marvelous. I never would have guessed it."

"Yes, it's all very legitimate," she said, giving Joseph a pinch. "You girls are in some interesting work. I'll bet you meet fascinating people. Brilliant ones. Can't I tell by their faces?"

The stewardess smiled and swished off, returning with trays of food. "Mmmph," said Joseph's mother, biting into it. "They don't know how to get to you, do they, in case God forbid you want to return by train. I'd give a nickel to know how many

196

eggs went into these little rolls that you could die the way they melt into your mouth." She grabbed the stewardess and said, "Sweetheart, in my life I never tasted rolls like this." She pulled her close. "Do you think the plane would mind if you put three or four of them in a little bag for me that I could tear into at the hotel? And I'll give you something nice that I have in my purse."

The stewardess said she would see if she could arrange something. "She's sold on your mother's ways," said Joseph's mother. "Watch and you'll see she'll kill herself for me. She'll get herself fired and I'll have that on my conscience, too." The girl returned with a little bag which Joseph's mother put in her purse while he kept an eye out to make sure the jumper girl did not see the transaction. Although Joseph worried over his mother's minor thieveries, she herself was quite open in her technique. In full view of restaurant headwaiters, she would put salt shakers in her purse and tell them, "If you open your mouth, I'll bang you on the head." Now she took a pair of gloves from her purse and gave them to the stewardess. "Here, so help me God if I've worn them once. I'd have kept the price tag on if I'd known. I want you to keep them for being an angel. And you'll never know how much these rolls are going to mean to me."

The man in the seat next to Joseph's mother seemed to wake up then; he pulled out a goatskin flask, said, "To wash down," and then held it at arm's length, squirting a thin stream of liquid into his mouth.

"Well, your mother's in business," said Joseph's mother. "Have you ever seen anything so fascinating in your life? And you're going to college for culture. You should hang around a little bit with me if you want to run into wisdom. I'll bet you never saw anyone do that in your career."

The man was on the stocky side and seemed uncomfortable,

197

as though he wore his belt one notch too tight. "Turkish," he said. "It is a trick one must work on for many years. Most people get it in their ear when they try it first." He poured a little into a cup and offered it to Joseph's mother, saying, "I'm on my way to Kansas on a little business trip."

"Oh," she said. "You look as though you're in a fascinating line." Turning to Joseph, she said, "A little business trip. In two seconds we'll find out that very quietly he owns the whole Midwest. Them are the kind. The quiet ones."

"Motel design," he said, and she answered, "I thought so. You can tell when you meet people when they're in something brilliant. And you're Turkish. I'd like to know the stories you have to tell. I'm taking my son out to college. I said to him if he wants culture he could stick with his mother and forget lessons."

"One of my hobbies is anthropology," said the man. "I have actually lived among Pacific Islanders for months, leaving my wife behind. You can see many things in the faces of these simple people, the influence of many cultures, but one day I looked at three of them and saw that they were really Turks. Oh, I don't know, it was a little something around their noses, the way their faces are built. They're Turks, all right. On every last island. I'm getting it all ready to put into a book."

"What did I tell you?" Joseph's mother asked, poking him. "You wanted smartness. Did you ever hear anything so fascinating in your life? Your mother. She finds them. Ten more minutes and you can turn right around and look for a job, you've got a whole education, you don't have to take four years."

The man splashed some liquid into his mouth. "There is this thing they say about us Turks, that we are hot-tempered, you know, with scimitars, Arabian Nights. It is not true, and it is most irritating. We are quite peace-loving, I have my anthropology; when I am home I paint. This is very good for getting rid of what is inside of you. I sit and I put the paint on, and my son is in the living room playing the piano. Beautiful. My wife works her loom. My son brings his friends over, very nice. Sometimes, of course, they put papers on the carpeting, they make noise. When I see banana peels in the ashtrays and how my son tolerates it—it is after all his fault—I could cut his eyes out and pull his body apart." His face was very red and he sat forward to loosen his tie.

"Well, sure he's upset," said Joseph's mother. "The boy's got a decent home, do you think he ought to put banana peels all over the place?"

"Excuse me," said the Turk. "I am sometimes excitable. You will find that among my people.

"Here," he said, offering the flask to Joseph. "Perhaps you would like to try." Joseph lifted the flask; not knowing where the stream would go, he held it at arm's length and squirted it right into the back of his throat.

"No, you didn't do it good," the Turk said, snatching it from him. "It takes years."

"Well of course, he's a little upset," Joseph's mother whispered. "You had to top him. Someday your mother will teach you people."

The girl in the jumper was playing a banjo in the aisle now, several seats up. Joseph wondered what would happen if he told her he had been taken to see musical comedies from the age of five, and that when they were just getting started in a musical comedy called *Streets of Paris*, Abbott and Costello had given him a silver dollar apiece backstage for being "a swell kid." Not only could he sing the lyrics of old show tunes but also the obscure, chatty introductory parts before the refrains. Joseph's mother cocked her head, heard the music and said, "Look at the age on her and already she knows a beat. That's your youth today. They can't wait." She walked up the aisle and stood next to the girls, beginning to clap her hands, nod her head and say, "Na, na, na," in time to the music. She spun around slowly in the aisle, her eyes at the ceiling, tapping one foot and saying, "Listen to the talent in her fingers. Your mother found her on a plane. I could be anywhere and I'll seek out strains." Joseph followed her up the aisle and when the jumpered girl looked over at him, he smiled thinly and began to snap his fingers. A male steward told Joseph's mother she would have to stop dancing in the aisle and she said, "Just you dare," putting her fist in her mouth. "Just you start with me." Joseph took his mother's arm and led her back to her seat. "I just want to see him tell me to stop," she said. "I haven't run into his kind before. I don't care if I have to stop the goddamned plane."

After he had gotten her to sit down, a man in back of them with black, slicked-down hair leaned over the top of the seat and said, "I saw the whole thing, honey. You were in the right. Do you want me to break his legs? I do that kind of work out on the Coast."

"That's all right, doll," said Joseph's mother. "And I'll bet you could do it, too. I've seen your type." She patted his hand and Joseph smiled at the man, as though to thank him for the thought. Then Joseph's mother got up again, saying, "But once and for all I'm going to settle what kind of a plane this is and where I'm being flown. I want to see a pilot's face and I want to know why I was singled out. First of all, I wasn't even dancing, I was swaying, and there's no conveyance in the world that tells you you can't sway. I'm not finished yet. I want this plane's number."

He wrestled her down again and said they were almost there, getting her to take a cigarette. She turned to the man in back and said, "I think my nerves have had enough flying for a while. Next time I'll take vanilla."

"If you can stay away from these things you're better off," he said. "It figures sooner or later one of them's going to crap out."

Just as she dozed off, the pilot said they were coming in over Topeka for a landing. Joseph scanned about for the emergency hatches, wondering what his chances would be if they were to nose over and burst into flames on the runway.

After a forty-mile bus ride from the airport, Joseph and his mother reached the college town in the
early evening; she stepped out of the bus, took a deep breath
and said, "Well, your mother made it. She's in America. It took
a long time but she got around to that, too. Smell that air. Line
your stomach with a little. That's your country." Joseph noticed
that many of the streets around the bus terminal were named
Boone and quite a few of the stores had the name Boone in
them, too. The college was in Boone County and it seemed to
Joseph that many of the older men were calling each other by
that same name. Some of the people wore GI surplus clothing,
and others, the ones in Joseph's age bracket, took great, limber
steps and hollered out animal sounds to one another. "Hey,
boy," one would shout across the street, "soooooooeee," to which

the fellow being hailed would fold in half with laughter and shout back, "Kwee, kwee, kwee, kweep."

"That's what you're going to get," said Joseph's mother. "That's their humor. You were never tolerant. If you want to get along you've got to bend. God knows how your mother has bent in all her years of living with a crazy person."

Before tackling the reservation problem, Joseph and his mother decided they would get some dinner to sustain themselves. They entered a small restaurant near the terminal that specialized in patties. No matter what you ordered, veal, liver, hamburgers, even fruit salad, it was served up in patty form. "They've got a gold mine here," said Joseph's mother. "The man who thought this up must have a mint. That's when you have an idea and you have backing. Your mother always had the brains but you know what kind of encouragement she got at home? Crap."

"It doesn't look that busy to me," said Joseph. "There's hardly anyone in here."

"And you're worried about them?" she said. "Save your worrying for yourself. I'd like to have a tenth of what goes into that cash register on their worst day."

They took seats at the counter and when Joseph had ordered, his mother caught the slender aproned waiter by the wrist and said, "I want you to take an oath on something, all right?"

"Yes," said the waiter, giggling.

"I want you to cross your heart and swear to Christ that my son's patties aren't greasy."

"They're not," said the waiter. "They take off all the grease."

"All right," she said. "As long as you swear. Because I brought this fellow all the way from New York and he can't afford to get sick. Not with what he's got in store for him." When the waiter brought the food, she said, "Bend down, I want to whisper a little something in your ear." The waiter leaned forward and she said, "As God's your judge, tell the truth and hope to die, you thought I was buying him, didn't you? Did you for one second think this was on the up-and-up? Just for fun, I'd like to know."

"What gives you the idea I enjoy those?" asked Joseph.

"Why, it doesn't go on?" she said. "You could use a little college in you. I should have a good year for every time some-one with your kind of face was purchased."

After the dinner, she called over the waiter and said, "I was telling my son you've got quite an idea here. You know what I could do with a little place like this in New York, if I had a husband who would lend me the proper support? I could have a bonanza, that's all. Anyway, you do a brilliant job."

"Thank you, ma'am. It's not mine," said the waiter. "But glad you enjoyed your patties."

"And service," she said, as they were leaving. "Try to get this kind of solicitousness in New York. You'll croak first."

There was very little daylight remaining. Outside the restaurant Joseph and his mother took a cab to the Goatback Hotel. "How do you fellows like it in cabs out here?" she asked, and the driver said, "It's all right."

"When you get to New York, ask the cab drivers about Meg and how many times when she's had a little problem she's just hailed a cab and had him drive her around the park sixteen times while she poured her heart out to a strange hackie. Don't you worry. They didn't lose a nickel on the deal. Tell him about your mother's tipping policies, Joseph. This is my son."

"How do you do," said the driver, turning around to shake hands.

"Hi," said Joseph.

"I'd like to see some son of a bitch try to get a cab away from me on a rainy night, though," said Joseph's mother.

"People behave like animals. One woman tried, I'll never forget, and she won't ever try again with what I did to her with my brown purse.

"How do you fellows feel about a quarter tip on a fifty-cent fare?" she asked, when they had arrived.

"We like it," said the driver.

"Then that's what you're getting," she said.

"God," said Joseph's mother, taking in the packed lobby of the Goatback Hotel. "And you were worried nobody ever heard of your college. Princeton could take a back seat."

Most of the people were students and suspendered businessmen asking each other about highways. "Now, you go on out to where 25A cuts across the old ham house and then you take your first detour."

"Where are all the mothers?" asked Joseph. "You said the place would be packed with them."

"And you don't think these kids wouldn't give their eyeteeth to have their mothers with them?" she said. "I need your disposition now with the challenge I'm faced with." She smoothed her dress and looked over at the reception desk where a one-armed woman seemed to be in charge. "That's the one your mother has to buck," she said. "She must be a lovely person with the terrible frustration she has to face each day of her life. Don't worry. Your mother will tame her, too. She doesn't know what's in store for her. Wait. Jesus, I've never been so nervous. Is the dress all right? Do I have too much here?" she asked, touching her bosom.

"You look fine," said Joseph.

"Wish me luck, baby," she said. "This is going to take all of your mother's powers. If she muffs, we're out on the street."

Once she had told him that to avoid school, she used to

disappear some days, among the pushcarts on the lower East Side; as he watched her walk up to the desk now, it seemed to Joseph she had slipped back into her old, slightly bratty push-cart weave. An open-collared fellow in khaki pants, somewhat older than Joseph, asked him if he had come down to handle the bow and arrow concession on 25A. "I've got miniature golf on Route 12 and it brings in $325 a week. Your total investment is twelve thou."

"I've just come down to study," said Joseph. "I thought you might be a student."

"I am," said the boy, who seemed eager to hurry out to his concession. "But you've got to have something. You'd better line up archery. The only other things left are service stations and that's work. Is your mother going to help you operate?"

"No," said Joseph. "She's going right back."

The fellow dashed off, and Joseph saw that his mother, in what appeared to be record time, had the reservations clerk doubled over with laughter; the woman's one arm was draped across her chest as though her clothes might fall off if she really cut loose. Joseph's mother had passed a package across the counter to her, the woman calling over several other reservations people to look at its contents.

His mother waved him toward the desk and said, "Your mother's done it again. You were worried there wouldn't be people on the Mason-Dixon line. Well, I want you to meet Edna, your mother's new friend, and for swellness there isn't anyone in New York can touch her."

Joseph shook the woman's hand and his mother said, "Do you know what she's doing for us and your mother can't stop her? She's moving out of her own room."

"I can move in with Sarah Lee Johnson," said the woman, "and it'll hardly make any difference."

"Oh no," said Joseph's mother. "No difference at all. They'll just croak together in some little cubbyhole somewhere that I don't even want to see it. I'd like to get a look at Sarah Lee Johnson's face when she hears about this. But that's what your mother runs into, I don't care where she goes. It didn't take two seconds, did it, dear?" she said, grasping the woman's sleeveless arm. "But how much longer do you need to spot realness?"

"That's right, darling," said the woman. "Now, you just run along with your son."

"You know what I told her," said Joseph's mother, winking at the woman and putting her arm around his shoulder. "I said we were lovers and just had this one night together. Then tomorrow I had to get back to my old man so he shouldn't suspect anything. I think that's what did the trick, romance. Cross your heart and tell the truth."

"Now, you just get on with you," said the woman, ringing for the bellhop, then letting fly a delayed whoop and holding her clothes on. Joseph wondered what her stump looked like; it seemed to him it made her slightly more appealing than if she had been two-armed.

When she had disappeared into the mailroom, Joseph's mother said, "Christ, I was rattled there for a while. That's all I would have needed if she turned out to be a bitch. I thought I was going to have a heart attack. And you know what did it? It's amazing how that goddamned underwear will unlock a door. I don't care if you're in Moscow. I gave her a slip that I think I've had since your sister's high school graduation. It was never touched, but still, it's from the year one. She loved it. Well, it's not so hard to understand. What could she possibly see out here in this swamp? So she's moving out of her room. I think she'd give up her other arm, too, if I asked her. Your mother needed that filth from the Navy back in New York."

A Negro porter took their bags, and on the elevator Joseph said, "Are you going to stay now? I have to register tomorrow and then school starts the next day. When are you going to leave?"

"I just wanted to get you set," she said. "I can't leave knowing you're in an excited condition like this."

The following morning Joseph's mother whipped her legs out of bed, sending a great sweep of musty, early-morning nightgown smells toward him.

"Before you get any ideas," he said, getting dressed, "I'll tell you right now that I'm doing everything alone today. I really would like you to get rolling, Mom."

"So help me God if I had any other idea in mind," she said. "I just want to get some breakfast in your system and you'll see you won't know I'm alive. I'm not even getting into a girdle, so there's your test."

Downstairs they went into a restaurant that adjoined the Goatback and advertised ALL THE BREAKFAST YOU CAN EAT FOR 90 CENTS. Great platters of scrambled eggs, hot rolls, and hashed brown potatoes emerged from a steel mouth in the wall, traveling then along a circular counter. Guests sat on stools encircling the counter, the idea being to snatch at the platters as they rolled by. There were not many people on the stools, and Joseph noticed that the counter speeded up whenever the eggs paraded along, so that he and his mother could pry loose only single spoonfuls; the counter would then slow down for the next series, allowing them to get all they wanted of grits and hashed-browns.

"You could have a nervous breakdown trying to fill your plate," said Joseph's mother. "But I never tasted anything so delicious in my life."

Joseph kept snatching at the eggs until he felt he had gone past his ninety cents' worth; then he noticed a pair of eye slits in the steel wall from which the platters kept emerging. Every five minutes or so, a small cluster of dessert cups flashed by for a single rotation. When Joseph had finished his eggs, he timed their appearance and, using both hands, grabbed off three of them. The steel wall opened and a tiny woman ran out, snatching back two.

"It said all you can eat," said Joseph.

"Not desserts," cried the woman, disappearing behind the wall.

"Well sure," said Joseph's mother. "You had to prove you were smarter than they were. What did you expect?"

"I expected to be backed up." said Joseph. "Not to be told I'm wrong and they're right."

"I can't argue with a crazy head," said his mother. "I'm tickled to death I'm leaving."

On his way to the registrar's office, Joseph felt stretchy and free in the sun although in a certain sense it was as though he were being played out on the end of a fishing line and might at any second be reeled back. Blond girls of a sort he had never seen in Bensonhurst pranced along the campus streets wearing skirts and sweaters, some of them nodding pertly to him and saying, "H'ar yew," more in the nature of a sociological experiment, he felt, than a real greeting. The campus was made up of a wide arc of beige one-story barrackslike buildings in the center of which stood a great ceremonial heap of old ivy-covered Doric columns, sections of stained-glass windows and various pieces of antiquated debris. As Joseph was to learn, a fire had swept away the old and charming Kansas Land campus, leaving only these odd bits of rubble which the officials had gathered up and put into a pile. Their idea had been that sings and other ceremonies would be held in front of it, commemorating the college's past glories. While officials wrangled away on whether to patch the old campus together somehow or start fresh in a new style, the semicircle of barracks, from whose windows students could look out on the heap, had begun to grow. As Joseph walked along the campus, he noticed that many of the barracks were simply called TD-4 and TD-8, while others had taken on the names of the burned-out buildings such as Woodstock Hall and Heatherington House. A few of the structures had even gotten up some strands of ivy which crept feebly along their wooden walls. The registrar's barracks was two stories high, and as Joseph mounted the front steps, he passed a group of five blue-jeaned students who were singing a Kansas Land Grant pep song; Joseph recognized the melody as being a speeded-up version of the Columbia University Alma Mater and wondered whether his school had hit upon the tune first. On the words "Hail to thee, oh Kansas Land Grant Agricultural" the lyrics had to be rushed to keep the melody going smoothly. A boy in the thickest cashmere sweater he had ever seen processed Joseph's application. Joseph noticed that a fellow in line behind him kept spitting on the floor, and when one of the deliveries bounced up and caught him on the cuffs, Joseph whispered to the cashmered boy, "Why's he doing that?"

"That's Pleasant Gordell," said the boy. "He's on the basketball team and that's his trademark. He spits right on the court during games. Hey, Pleasant," he said, "soooooooooeee," to which the tall fellow bowed his head modestly and let another fly.

The cashmered fellow noticed that Joseph had put down the Goatback Hotel as his residence and asked if he would like to have dinner at his fraternity, to meet the members and, if it worked out, live there.

"I'd love that," said Joseph. "I can't see staying at the Goatback forever."

Returning to the hotel, Joseph found his mother sitting on her bed, talking to an embarrassingly thin-legged chambermaid. He had the feeling that if her limbs had been fleshed out a trifle more she would have been able to find more attractive work.

"My lover," said Joseph's mother. "How do you like who your mother picked to have a little discussion with? Her democracy. You'd be surprised, sometimes you can get more wisdom from a thing like this than you can from a real person. I was telling her not to get any funny ideas about the setup in this room, although now that she's seen your face I don't think she's so sure."

The woman told Joseph she loved Jews and that a Jewish family had once put a diamond ring on her finger. "And you always have Hollywood-type furniture in your houses. When I get around that kind of stuff, I ache to clean it." She spun around to leave then, her skirt whipping up above sharpened knees, and Joseph hoped that was the last such treat he was ever going to get.

"Don't think," his mother said, "that with those skinny feet she didn't find time to clip a drink on me when I was out of the room. Those are the kind you've got to watch like hawks."

Joseph told his mother about the dinner invitation and that afternoon took her for a walk to see the burned-out remains of the old Kansas Land campus. "Just your luck they had to have a fire," she said, staring at the great heap of wreckage. "And I like the way they arranged it, in case God forbid someone should want to forget about the goddamned thing. So, what do you care about a fire? You've got a good imagination. You'll pretend the college is still here." The campus seemed to fill suddenly with an army of young couples, strolling hand in hand, each of the sweatered girls wearing a pin at the geometrically centered tip of her right breast. "Oh, I love that," said Joseph's mother. "Where they picked for a little jewelry display. Tiffany's should try that and they'd double their business. Well, you can't miss seeing it, that's for sure. I'd like to try that around the house and watch your father's face." Joseph wondered whether he ever would get to march along at the side of a trinket-breasted girl and if there were any left who were not out on strolls. "But they're cute as church mice," said his mother. "Look at how they hold each other in case one should be too weak to walk and want to fall down. That's your young love today. They're not taking any chances. They're holding on to each other." She looked at Joseph and said, "And I don't know what's on my son's mind, either, do I? You're in a hurry to be right in with them. So look, take your mother around the waist, and from a distance we'll be a fast young couple."

"Let's just walk, Mother," said Joseph. "Don't fool around."

"Why, tell the truth, if you stood away a few steps your mother couldn't be eighteen with the way her figure's held up?"

"You could," said Joseph. "But I don't want to kid around."

At the edge of the campus, with daylight fading, they came to a church.

"Sure, churches they made sure there were plenty of," she said. "Don't worry about that. I'd like to know the last time they had a Jew in this town. But that never worried your mother. She always got respect from the worst kind of gentile

213

face." A sign on the bulletin board said that due to the slow pace of construction on the synagogue, Jewish holiday services were being held in a fenced-off section of the Baptist Church basketball court. They were taking place, for that matter, at that very moment. Joseph read the sign to his mother who said, "As God's your judge, swear to Christ you're telling the truth. You know I'm blind and can't see and if I find out you're playing with me, I'll tear your eyes out."

There was somethimg wrong with her eyes but she thought all eye ailments were the same and would use any eyeglasses that were handy, his father's or those of someone who was visiting. She had brought none along on the trip, figuring she would borrow someone's if she needed them.

"They're really having them in there," said Joseph. "We'd better hurry if you want to be in the thing."

"Don't run ahead of me," she said, blotting her eyes, "because I've got palpitations that I'll need oxygen in two seconds. Jewish services in a church. How do you like that? And you're worried because every once in a while a gentile looks at you. This is really one for the books. You want to know miracles and religion, you don't have to go any further. And *you* couldn't sleep because Harvard didn't send a letter. You picked some school when they let a thing like this go on. Brilliant."

Joseph led his mother into the church, the first step being just a little frightening to him since he had never been inside one before. He once had delivered an order of sweet cream to a parochial school, leaving it on the doorstep and racing off when a nun appeared, afraid she might put him under her robe. It smelled scrubbed and religious inside. "I'm an idiot," said Joseph's mother. "I'd completely forgotten about the holidays. It's lucky you saw that sign or that would have been the end of your mother's whole religion."

A notice posted at the end of a corridor said TEMPORARY

JEWISH SERVICES THIS WAY. Joseph and his mother followed it downstairs to a large basement, at the end of which a small area had been cordoned off for a group of twenty or so; they stood inside the ropes around a table eating square pieces of honeycake and drinking wine. Joseph's mother began to cry, saying, "Stay a second, I want to keep this picture in my mind. As long as I live, I'll never forget it. That right there, in a church that God forbid we should have to resort to this again, is your true Jewishness. They don't need a Torah, they don't need those old hypocrites with their donations. What you're looking at is your real religion."

Joseph pointed out the one he thought must be the rabbi, a tall pale fellow with an uncertain shave. "Look at the youth on him," said Joseph's mother. "That's what you get today. But you could see in his eyes your whole Ten Commandments. Come, I want to congratulate him on what he's been able to do, something I'd never heard of in all my born days."

She walked behind the ropes and, yanking the rabbi away from a middle-aged couple, introduced herself. "I want to tell you something, Rabbi, that they ought to pin a medal on you with the challenge you've been able to face here. My son and I are from New York where we've got enough synagogues to choke a horse. I don't have to tell you. But when I saw this, I said to myself, Meg, you don't need prayers, you don't need phonies with their beards that they'd cheat you out of a nickel two seconds after the holiday's over. This, what you're seeing now, in a Baptist Church that I hope we don't all get cursed for being here, this is your true beauty and this is your holiness."

"Vunderbar," said the rabbi. "Actually though, it was no snap. When you get down to it it's always funds that are in short supply. And I'm a real Mr. Clunk when it comes to that department."

"You don't need to apologize," said Joseph's mother. "If you were able to get a group like this together in a church out here in this place that I still don't even remember the name of it, they could make you king of the whole Jews. Beautiful."

The rabbi introduced Joseph and his mother to others in the group, pointing out a stout fellow in a vest at the end of the table. "That's Professor Dworkin," he said, "who teaches livestock."

"And he's a Jew, too," said Joseph's mother. "He must have some mind. And the face on him. Who in a million years would ever spot him? That's what you get when you go out of town. Everybody's a Jew these days."

The rabbi brought over a middle-aged couple, saying, "Dean Henderson and his wife attend all our functions. They're interested in Hebrew culture." Joseph's mother smiled at the pair, then turned to Joseph, whispering, "Them I could do without. I know the kind. They love Jewish culture. Take away the honeycake and you'll see how long they'll last."

Joseph spotted the jumpered girl from the airliner and waved at her. "I didn't know you were Jewish," he said, coming closer. "Oh yes," she said. "I've always been. Do you know Jim Folsom? They call him 'Sleepy,' but he's not. He's been dating me crazy since the second I got here. I don't think I've slept two hours straight. Is he *wild!*"

"I don't think I know him."

"How's your mother?" asked the girl.

"She's fine," said Joseph. "There she is."

Joseph went back to his mother who said, "I see your friend spotted you. She didn't waste any time. Boy, would she like to get at you, she could forget the whole services."

"I think you're wrong, Mom," said Joseph.

"Your mother's always wrong. That's why they made her your mother."

The rabbi said, "So when you get down to it, there are always those funds that you need. You think that this is Kansas and you'd get a break on supplies. But it doesn't work out that way."

"Rabbi," said Joseph's mother, taking his arm, "stop knocking yourself out. You're talking to someone who's a little grown up." She reached into her purse and took out some bills. "First of all," she said, handing him one of them, "comes a little something just on general principles." She gave him another, saying, "And here's for a little extra prayer I'd like you to throw in for my son's college because he's got some tough haul in front of him.

"And, Rabbi," she said, drawing him closer, "don't make a fuss, but take this and I want you to buy yourself a little something personal that has nothing to do with synagogues because God knows you need it to keep your strength up."

"You know, none of this was necessary," said the rabbi.

"Of course, darling," she said. "I haven't been around."

The rabbi shrugged, said, "Well . . ." and raised his arms to say the service was concluded. He led the group in a chorus of "Adonolum," Joseph's mother beginning to cry again. "They expect me to have a voice at a time like this," she wailed and then, turning to look at the silent, smiling Hendersons, said, "I'll bet you dollars to doughnuts they'd just as soon be back at the college now that the table's clear."

That night Joseph and his mother ate dinner at the cashmered boy's fraternity house. He met them at the door and led them into the parlor, where Joseph became aware of a great emphasis on garter-wearing. Each of the members sat with his legs crossed widely, displaying elaborate, complicated black ones over pale shins. Joseph's socks felt very hangy and he sat holding his trouser cuffs to his ankles so that his garterless calves would not show through. Every now and then, from behind his newspaper, a member would toss off the first line of a song; the others would join him in harmony, putting lyrics about how much they loved the fraternity to melodies from Irving Berlin shows. During the refrain of one of these, ten tough-looking fellows in team jackets marched in with fists clenched, their leader saying to the cashmered boy, "Your singing is loud and shitty. Ten of us are willing to take on your whole house and we'll mop you up." None of the gartered people stirred, although the tension seemed terribly thick to Joseph. The leader of the intruders walked slowly about the room, stopping to slap various athletic trophies lightly with the back of his hand; finally the cashmered boy, who appeared to be a high-ranking officer, arose and said, "We're not going to fight you, Beppis."

"I didn't think so," the leader said contemptuously. Walking up to him, Joseph's mother said, "I want to know something. Are you allowed to just walk in here like that in the middle of these grand boys? Does the school know what you're doing?" Joseph ran over and pulled his mother's arm, whispering, "For Christ's sake, Mother, you want to foul up everything?"

"All right, all right," she said, returning to her seat. "I said a word. I'd like to have ten minutes alone with that moron and you'd see how much good his toughness would do him."

"Sure there aren't any Humphrey Bogart types here?" asked the boy called Beppis. He emptied an ashtray on the carpeting and then backed out the door, the ten tough fellows close behind.

"They're from a house across the street that's been wanting to fight us," said the cashmered boy. "Our toughest guy, Flashberg, is upstairs with the flu."

"You're very smart not to fight," said Joseph's mother. "Not with dirt."

The episode had upset Joseph, getting a tempo started in his thinned-out arm; he wondered whether—as an invited guest— he would have been expected to participate had there been a free-for-all. The members seemed to have gone undisturbed by the visit and shortly thereafter broke into a song outside the housemother's room, beckoning her to come to dinner. She opened the door after several choruses, a handsome gray-haired woman in a shawl who might have been one of the jewelry-tipped campus girls grown beautifully old. Joseph wished for a moment his own mother looked like her. Every once in a while he had suggested to her that she let her hair get gray like the other mothers'. "If I did," she had answered, "you'd take a gun and kill yourself."

"You think a little job like she has is bad," she said now. "I could stand being romanced like that myself with the way my nerves have been."

Joseph and his mother had dinner at her table along with their host and a thin-nosed fellow who had on a seductive cologne and seemed to be president of the house. Also at the table was a stocky older boy who wore a strained and continual grin, explaining that he had had his face sheared off in the Ardennes campaign, *Life* carrying a picture of him swathed from head to toe in bandages. Apparently doubt had arisen at earlier campus residences of his as to whether he was really the one beneath all the surgical wrappings—and he had been forced to storm out of his lodgings in shows of protest.

"We believe him," said the thin-nosed man. "We don't think he'd lie."

"It's true I have no proof," said the grinning ex-GI, "but it was me under there, all right."

Two Negro houseboys came out with trays of *arroz con pollo*, setting one on each of the tables. When no one touched the food, Joseph's mother said, "It's a pity to just leave it lay there. It'll get cold and it looks delicious."

"They're waiting for our guests to begin," said the house-mother.

"Oh, I'll kill myself. An hour ago I was eating honeycake.

Well, I'll have to take a bite if I choke right on the spot. I can't break their hearts."

She took a forkful, and in unison the members plunged into the spicy Latin delicacy. The housemother appeared to be afraid of the heavily cologned president who made disgusted, lip-curling faces as he ate.

"How is it, Edmund?" she asked him.

"Slop," he said, shoving the exotic dish aside.

"Maybe if you put a little salt on it," said Joseph's mother. "Mine's delicious and this isn't the first place I've eaten."

"May I be excused, Mother Gibbons?" he said, his nose now waferlike in its thinness.

"Perhaps I could have Maybelle whip up some chile con carne?"

Taking his cue from the president, the ex-war hero got to his feet. "You get your tail shot up in a war, you want a decent meal."

The cashmered boy followed them out of the dining room and Joseph's mother said, "That's with all the serenading and the romancing and the standing outside her door. I saw the whole deal shaping up. They'll give her politness but then they'll cut her heart out. She's got some tough setup on her hands. I don't envy you one bit, baby."

"Where can I go?" said the housemother. "I've got three sons and last year they all suddenly went into wheelchairs. I try to get them the best dishes here."

"I think it's delicious," said Joseph's mother, taking another forkful. "Look at me. I'm eating like a horse."

Following dessert, the boys at the other tables struck up an after-dinner song, one whose lyrics indicated that the fraternity would survive whatever calamities it hit up against and go on to outlive its members.

"They've got gorgeous voices," said Joseph's mother, "yet two seconds later they'll show cruelty. So how can you figure them? Sometimes I want to give up on people."

"If they throw me out I'll really be in a fix," said the housemother.

"You'll come and live with me in New York and we'll make a lovely couple. I'm being thrown out, too."

One by one, the remaining boys trooped up to the housemother and said, "Begging to be excused, Mother Gibbons." When they had all gone into the parlor, Joseph's mother whispered something in the ear of a Negro houseboy.

"What did you pull?" asked Joseph.

"Can you think of once in your life when your mother let you flounder?"

In the parlor, where coffee was being served, the boy who had invited Joseph whispered, "I saw you and your girl over at the Jewish services. She's real cute. Did you know Sleepy Jim Folsom's been plowing her little tail around the clock? I saw him do it to her once on a fender and there've been at least twenty other times in his room. Doesn't that gripe your tail?"

"She's not my girl," said Joseph. "I just met her on the plane."

"I wouldn't like that if it was my girl. I'd squawk loud and hard."

A short elections meeting was held then at which a slender boy who had been enslaved for a year at Hitler death camps kept getting voted in as head of every committee, easily beating back all opposition. After each shoo-in victory, he stood up to take a bow and was applauded vigorously.

"They're trying to make it up to him," whispered Joseph's mother. "Don't I have the same thing with my delivery fellow? Yet how can they even start? It shows you how stupid people are. And he, like a jerk, accepts it."

After the meeting, the houseboy rang the doorbell and walked in with a giant grocery bag, saying, "From the New York lady."

He stood first in front of the president who reached in and took out a Dixie cup, examined it and with two fingers dropped it back in the bag. "My luck," said Joseph's mother. "They probably had ice cream the last ten nights in a row." The houseboy passed among the other members, each of whom looked inside the bag and then turned aside. The death camp victim fingered a strawberry-and-vanilla popsicle and then hurled it back in the bag with special vigor. "Well, him you have to discount," said Joseph's mother. "He's just showing off. I'm sure he saw a lot of nourishment where he came from.

"So," she said with resignation, "your mother did another wrong thing. I'll give it to the girls in the hotel and you'll see that they'll love it."

After coffee, the cashmered boy said, "Well, thanks for coming over. We'll call you after we have our blackball meeting."

Joseph shook hands with several of the members; on the street, walking by his mother's side, he said, "What'd you do that for? I don't think I'm in now."

"Shall I tell you the truth?" she said. "I don't want to be in a place like that. I saw what they did to that creature and I could get along very comfortably without the whole setup."

"But it's me," said Joseph. "I'm the one who would have to be in there. What the hell's wrong with you?"

"Your mouth," she said, glaring at him. "I don't want to be in an environment with garters and where they'll show cruelty to an old thing. And you'll see what good those garters'll do when they get out in the world."

"But you want me to go to school from a hotel room where I'm staying with my mother, is that it?"

"I don't want you to do anything," she said wearily. "In two seconds I'll leave you and you'll see how far you'll get."

The first day of school, Joseph awakened to a strong chill in the air; his slippers felt cold on his feet and so did his clothing, and he wondered how he was going to sponge up knowledge if he could not stop shivering. The cold got into his trimmed-down arm, and when he was dressed, he slipped back into bed for some last-second blanket warmth. His mother arose foggily and said, "No loves for your mother now that you're an official college fellow?" Joseph knelt beside her bed and kissed her neck, feeling great blasts of heat stealing up from beneath the covers. He remembered getting into bed with her years back on Sunday mornings, finding it black and stovelike and never being sure he wanted to be under there with her. "Don't try to be too smart in one day," his mother said now. "You've got all your life."

He walked toward the campus and began to see packs of

pretty girls in skirts and sweaters, carrying books against their breasts as though they were giving them hugs. He wondered how they could be oblivious to the cold that smacked against their bare legs and must certainly have been sweeping beneath their skirts to give them chilled behinds. Joseph's first class of the day was in pastoral literature; as he looked for his building in a sea of one-story barracks, he feared suddenly that he might never find it, might never find any of his classrooms and finally have to be taken to them by the police, a month behind everybody else. Shortly thereafter he walked into his classroom alongside a dwarflike boy with a great head who carried a stuffed briefcase and took a seat in the front row. Joseph was certain his massive head was crammed with information and was sorry he had gotten into a class with him. A girl with lovely knees was brought in then by a fellow in a team jacket, who knelt at her side and seemed to be warding off potential suitors. Joseph noticed he guarded her until the instant the lecture began, then left only to charge back to her side in an hour, timing his entrance to coincide with the instructor's last line. Other pretty girls began to take their seats, Joseph feeling certain that because of them he would be unable to get to his feet and answer questions with wit and brilliance. He had been to an all-boys' high school and could not imagine saying things in class, knowing that cute girls were there to hear possible boners. He wondered if it would be possible to have the girls troop outside during his recitations, then come back in for other people's. A young woman with spreading hips and great sopping rims around the armpit areas of her blouse came in then and headed for the front of the room. She turned out to be the teacher and Joseph, who had taken an aisle seat in the back row, was ashamed he had inhaled as she passed by. When the room was filled, she said, "I'm Miss Greco. To sum up all we know about Elizabethan customs and everyday practices, our New York fellow in the back. All stand at your seats while answering in class."

"Am I supposed to know that already?" Joseph asked, getting to his feet. "Are we supposed to come in here with that under our belts? They were superstitious."

"Jesus," said the dwarflike boy in the front row, slapping his great head in disgust and stamping his feet.

"*Bravissimo*," said the teacher, and Joseph was relieved to hear her go on as though his one-liner had given the class a leg up on the whole Elizabethan picture. She called then upon a muscular fellow in the rear who used the word "dichotomy" several times in his answer and kept kissing his wrist to make points now and then about Elizabethan sensitivity. At the end of his talk, the teacher kissed her own wrists to let him know he had gotten across to her. A middle-aged man who had taken down every word spoken thus far and seemed to have filled up several notebooks asked, "Are we all supposed to kiss our wrists while answering?" He turned out to be a Navy Commander on extended leave from submarine duty to take the course in pastoral literature. The classroom had been occupied one hour previously by home economics students; Joseph noticed that the desks converted into sinks and miniature electric ranges. There were some brownie crumbs left over on his seat from the last group and he found himself nibbling on them nervously in the hope he would not be called on again. There were four girls sitting in his row; midway through the lecture, he looked over to see a heavily ribbed, familiar-looking sweater heading his way, being passed along from girl to girl. "Hold it, class," said the teacher. Joseph turned to see his mother near the door. "I'm terribly sorry," she said. "I wouldn't have interrupted for the world. But he ran outside without anything on and you could die from the weather."

"All set?" asked the teacher, and when the sweater arrived at Joseph's desk, he held it aloft, saying, "I've got it now."

"He'll kill me for this," said Joseph's mother, turning to leave, "but what can I do? I'm one of those crazy mothers."

Joseph found that day and during the first several weeks that most of his courses had a heavy agricultural coloration, although he was assured by the dean of freshmen this was true only for the first-year students. After that, except for those who were going down the line in farming, the Kansas Land curriculum became "just like any other school's." Actually, there was only one all-out agricultural course in Joseph's program, a five-session-a-week series in basic livestock held late each day in a large indoor dirt pit on the outskirts of the campus. Students traveled to the class in an Ag School bus, those who could not squeeze aboard riding out on a thresher. Yet even in this course there was no actual contact with animal life. Once at the pit, students would change into farming overalls and then gather around on hay bales to hear lectures from nearby grange officials. It was understood that for those choosing to continue in the program, Guernsey cows would be herded into the pit the following year for close study. Joseph enjoyed the barnyard fragrance of the enclosure and from where he sat could hear animal moans from other pits nearby where advanced students were getting down to actual livestock problems. On the bale behind him, two boys joked continually during the lecture about a mutual friend who was having regular intercourse with calves. The more Joseph tried to press the image out of his mind, the more stubbornly it clung to him until finally he yielded and pictured himself stealing off behind a silo to seduce a young lamb.

A course Joseph did not enjoy very much was one in the history and principles of agriculture, a celebration, for the most part, of early agricultural heroes who had stubbornly kept after the government to revise its grain policies. Homework, for the first week, involved memorizing the names of editorial staff members who worked on courageous little turn-of-the-century farming weeklies. One lecture was thrown over entirely to the study of a journalist named Stenko who had called George

Washington a rascal in the public prints for blocking bean research. The first President had caught him by the collar one day and publicly caned him about the shoulders.

Another of Joseph's courses was one in feed chemistry, apparently a favorite among returning veterans. At his first session, Joseph saw before him a sea of open-shirted khaki uniforms, each student wearing myriad slide rules and measuring devices in his many-pocketed shirt. Joseph felt he had little chance against fellows who had actually thrown up bridges to hold advancing Allied armies. The instructor explained, during the first lecture, that students would be graded according to how they fared on a single project that was to range across the entire semester. Each class member would receive a lump of an unknown fertilizer, which he was to subject to a battery of tests, coming up with its identity by semester's end. The instructor called upon several assistants to pass along the aisles handing out white envelopes containing the mysterious lumps. Joseph opened his and saw that the specimen within was brown and flaky. The man in the next seat was already measuring his with engineering calipers. Joseph wondered if he would ever be able to break his own down and thought he might take it right over to a druggist for a fast analysis. Most likely, all surrounding pharmacies had been alerted not to take on any feed chemistry samples. He wondered if his mother knew anything about fertilizers. The professor looked at his watch, raised his arm, then lowered it and said, "Begin your breakdowns." In a panic, Joseph tore off a piece of his and smelled it. The man next to him said, "I think they gave you shit."

nce, without telling his mother, Joseph had gone to a basketball game at Madison Square Garden, only to look up at half time and spot her flying through the balcony in a bathrobe. After class each day, Joseph longed to join the other students at the Hog Trough, a favorite hangout, but was certain his mother would interrupt him in a robe. So he returned each day, dutifully, to the Goatback Hotel where his mother had taken to waiting for him in the cocktail lounge. "There's my kid now," she would say. "He must be exhausted. How's your smartness coming along, darling? Look, you wanted it. You could have stayed home and been a couch cutter like your father. He made a brilliant success of himself."

She would then order a drink for Joseph, ridiculing mothers who were afraid a single drink would corrupt their children.

"It's when you *don't* give them a drink that I've seen them turn into morons."

It irritated Joseph that his mother had not gone back to New York and he would say to her, "All I know is that I'm sitting here with my mother," pronouncing the final word with scorn. To which she would answer, "Name me one of them out there who wouldn't give his eyeteeth to be in your boots. You're really losing a lot on the deal."

Toward the end of the second week, he began to ridicule little ways of hers. She shouted to the bartender one evening, "Philly, give my son a bourbon over rock," and Joseph in irritation said, "Rocks, mother. There's more than one of them."

"And that's what you'll pick me up on?"

"I don't like to hear that," he said. "It may not seem important to you, but it makes me wince when I hear someone say rock over and over when it should be rocks. It's not charming to do it your way. It's terrible."

Another time, in a fury that took him by as much surprise as it did his mother, he whirled on his barstool and said, "Your teeth." She had irregular ones, some of them pointy, and had spent a lifetime writhing beneath dentist drills. She had to take careful, tentative bites of sandwiches, all over to one side of her mouth.

"What do you mean?" she asked.

"I don't know," he said. "The way they are. Can't you do anything about them? What do you want to have teeth like that for?" He plunged ahead, as though a railing had been removed and he was falling onto subway tracks. "Isn't there a way you can not have them that way?"

"I heard what you just said," she whispered, bringing her hand to her mouth.

"Well, of course," said Joseph. "I just said it to you." But then he leaned over and gave her a kiss, swiveling about to see if there was anyone who had agreed with his criticism so he could beat them up.

The college environment seemed to date her, and after drinks each night she would say old-fashioned things to him such as "The evening's yours to howl, baby" and "Shall we do the town?"

Once he said that they might as well go to the movies. The film was one that Joseph thought of as a "Please, Mr. Ackerman" type. A boy and girl from the Midwest move into a New York rooming house and try to crack show business. Discouraged quickly, they take temporary work as waiter and cigarette girl at a supper club and hear one night that a famous producer is at a side table. The boy drops his tray, runs up to the producer and pointing to the cigarette girl, says, "Please, Mr. Ackerman, you got to hear Angie sing."

"Sure," said Joseph's mother, "there's when a boy has an idea and he follows it through. You get ideas and you let them lay there." The theater was filled with hundreds of young couples; even before the lights dimmed, the fellow next to Joseph began to give deep, plunging kisses to his date, the girl groaning and trying to keep a strand of blond hair in place at the same time. "Would you hold your mother's hand?" Joseph's mother said a little sheepishly. "I would," he answered, "but what's the point?" In the darkness, the fellow next to Joseph seemed to rise above the girl, Joseph seeing him take the shape of a whaling captain, holding the tiller of a longboat and weaving back and forth in a stormy sea. In the middle of his passion, the fellow stopped, as though he had heard an alarm clock.

"Any objections?" he asked Joseph's mother.

"It's all right with me," she said. "I came to see a movie."

When he had gone back to his boat, she whispered, "Frankly, I think it's disgusting. I like where they picked for romance. Wait, in two seconds I'm calling the manager." All around Joseph, other couples seemed to be aboard their own boats and Joseph felt nauseated and told his mother he was going to the bathroom. A long line had formed in the men's room, leading to a single urinal, which was perched atop a dais. When a fellow took too long, there were hoots and catcalls such as "What's the matter, fella, can't you find it?" As his turn came near, Joseph began to get nervous. He stepped before the urinal finally, feeling as though he had marched out onto a stage. He stood there a few seconds, then zipped himself up and walked off. The man in back of him caught his arm in a vise and said, "You didn't go. I watched."

"Yes I did," said Joseph. "I only had a little."

All the movie couples seemed to head for an ice cream parlor nearby. Joseph's mother pressed her nose against the window, saying, "See, look at them. That's where they go. They have certain hangouts and you've got to know which ones. Otherwise you could perish. Would you want me to take you in there?"

"I could go in myself," said Joseph, "but I don't feel like it."

"You know what a little birdie just whispered to me that it never whispered before?"

"What's that?"

"That someone's ashamed of his mother."

He wanted badly for her to leave, yet there were times he felt that maybe she was right. That he would not be able to get along on his own. He would go hungry and not know what to say to people and wind up just standing in one place somewhere, finally having to be put in a large box with air holes and sent home to her. He came round finally to the idea that he would let her stay one semester and that was all. After that she would have to leave or he would go home and not go to college again, just staying indoors and listening to radio shows until he died at thirty-four. Once, at night, when she was standing near the hotel room window in her nightgown, he wondered what would happen if he shoved her out, whether she would flip end over end or drop, pancake style, to the pavement. He wondered what would happen legally if a son did that to his mother. The compulsion was so strong he began to perspire, and then for hours, just when he thought he was rid of it, the idea would file back into his mind. He would wonder how long it would take her to fall, was there a chance someone would catch her, was it mandatory that her face be smashed up or might it go relatively unmangled.

With it all, Joseph felt he had to demonstrate to his mother some of the things he was learning at school, to show he was getting his money's worth. One night, in the Goatback lounge, he pointed a finger toward the window and said, "Look at them all out there with their small wasted lives, none of them engaged in anything epic or worthwhile, not an immortal fellow among them."

"Gorgeous," his mother said, sipping a cordial. "The mouth on him."

"Sick," said a barboy, passing by.

"From a servant?" Joseph's mother glared.

"I just do this at night," he said. "I'm actually working toward a master's in business administration."

"And you'll succeed, too," she said. "General Motors is just waiting for your face.

"I can't get flustered by what comes out of youth today," she said to Joseph. "Meanwhile, if you think you've got troubles, take a look at my friend Philly over there. Drink him in. They took him on as a bartender and all of a sudden, quietly, they're slipping him soup bowls from the kitchen for him to do a little dishwashing in his spare time.

"Isn't that right, Philly?" she hollered. "Who did he say he worked for once? Some shah or something. He's an absolute crack bartender. He'll mix you a drink you never tasted in your life and they've got him working with suds.

"My son thinks he's got trouble, Philly," she shouted. "Tell him a few."

Stooped over a sink, elbow-deep in soapy water, the bartender flashed them a disgusted look.

"And you should very quietly try living on the tips they give you around here. They've got some very big spenders. Until it comes to parting with money. I give him a dollar at the end of the evening and you'd have thought I was the Virgin Mary the way he looked at me. He was ready to lick my feet."

Joseph wanted to tell his mother that he thought bartenders and chambermaids were fine, but he had never found the mechanics of their work as fascinating as she did. Some of it must have shown in his face. "Pardon me," she said. "My son's in college two weeks and he's giving looks. Meanwhile, it never cost your mother a dime to be nice to humans."

He could not quite trace the source of it for the moment, but something heavy and troubled had begun to crowd up behind him, catching him beneath the shoulder blades and making it difficult for him to breathe. It was as though he had been put into a vest many sizes too small while his attention was elsewhere. He became aware then of a man standing in the shadows at the far end of the bar and staring at his mother. Powerfully built, healthy, somewhat balding, he seemed a fraction too old for his youthful open-collared clothing. Joseph was reminded of bald boxers he had seen who had always been somehow feminine and embarrassing to watch, prompting announcers to say such things as "Although Johnny Dulio's hairline gives you the impression he's a much older boy, the gamester is only twenty-seven." Such fighters always seemed a little tougher than others to Joseph, as though they were infuriated by their state and out to avenge themselves against heavily pompadoured opponents.

The man wore the collar of his plaid shirt over his sports jacket lapels, a spray of hair appearing at the V of his neck that might have been traveling upward from a black water fountain beneath his shirt. His trousers were too short, his sparse hair wetted back in the style of reluctant railroad workers who have had to dress for church. With it all, he gave off an impression of great vigor, as though he had just taken a brisk workout and shower. In his mind Joseph somehow connected the man with law enforcement.

Joseph tried to cut across the fellow's gaze, but the man continued to smile at his mother, paying no attention to Joseph, finally lifting his glass slightly in a silent toast. He put one hand to his middle then, raised the other above his head, and as though he were holding a partner, did a little samba step in his place. His eyes were partly closed in dance-floor ecstasy.

Joseph's mother said, "Oh, you saw him? Don't worry, I spotted him ten minutes ago. The day something gets past your mother.

"Ooooh," she said, biting her lower lip. "Leave me alone. Did you see his mean face. I get a shiver when I look at him. That's Murder Incorporated if you ask me.

"And you're worried again, is that it?" she said. "You saw him looking at your mother and you're fainting. Your mother can't handle a little chaos."

"I just don't like people to stare that way," said Joseph. "I think it's bad manners."

"Hey, Philly," said the fellow, slapping his glass down on the bar, continuing to grin at Joseph's mother. He had a high-rumped inverted pelvis which to Joseph meant bad sports jacket fits for life, but great staying power in athletic events. "Where's the action in this graveyard? What ever happened to this place?"

"I could have told you that," Joseph's mother whispered, returning the man's stare. "I knew in two seconds he wasn't here to talk geometry. And your mother doesn't know what kind of action he means, does she? She hasn't the faintest idea."

"Let's leave," said Joseph. "Let's go up to the room."

"I knew it," she said. "I knew there'd be fear. You'll still let things get the best of you. All right, I won't fight your willpower. Let me put down something for Philly so the night won't be a total loss for him. The place is full of heavy spenders."

"Hurry," said Joseph, his body chilled. When she had gotten her wrap, he let her leave first, then backed out the door, covering their retreat like a Western gunslinger.

While his mother was at the desk getting cigarettes, Joseph asked the Negro attendant about the man in the bar.

"Oh, that Wirt," said the porter. "He used to play defense back for the football team. They ain't nobody in the world move him from the place he want to stand. He smash up everybody, I don't care who they got. Now he just hang around. He up to something though, you can be sure of that."

It never occurred to Joseph to doubt old Negroes when they made such pronouncements. Whenever Winnie, the cleaning woman at home, issued statements on foreign policy, such as "France, they goin' to fox Roosevelt next week, you wait and see. First time he turn round," Joseph accepted them as gospel, as though she alone of all the nation's citizenry had been given access to secret international position papers. He felt the information called for a tip, but wasn't sure of the amount, finally deciding on twelve cents.

The Negro took the money, which seemed to spur him on. "That Wirt," he continued, "I mean the way he just hang around, you just know he fixin' to do something. Otherwise, you tell me, why he do what he do? You follow me? That man take it into his head to do something, he goin' to do it, I don't care what you try to run up against him. I mean you a tractor, he ain't goin' to pay you no mind."

235

Joseph took stock of what he had to send against the bar man and could come up with nothing formidable. He tossed the Negro porter another eight cents, making it an even twenty, and went upstairs with his mother. In the room he still felt bunched up and imprisoned; on an impulse he opened the door, scanning the hallway on both sides and then shut it, bolting it tight.

"I can't wait to get out of this brassiere," his mother said. "Someday I want to meet the lovely angel who thought them up."

She laid her blouse on the bed and said, "And you're still sensitive . . ."

"I'm not worried about him," said Joseph. "He had no right to keep staring though, after he knew I didn't want him to."

"I never worried about a stare," she said. "Those I can fluff right off."

All through the next day, Joseph kept up a watch for the man, in the Goatback lobby and on the campus, but by dinnertime had seen no trace of him. One of Joseph's courses, conducted daily at the Kansas Land gymnasium, was in sports fly casting. The procedure was for students to stand in a row and heave lines out at imaginary fish, then haul them back while the instructor trotted along behind them, correcting their casting form. Joseph had never actually seen the instructor and for a moment that afternoon sensed it might be the Goatback man. He wanted to wheel about and confront him, but held off, thinking it might embarrass them both. He kept his eyes straight ahead, making hunched and tense casts throughout the session. That night, the third Friday after their arrival at Kansas Land, Joseph and his mother took a cab to a highly recommended restaurant on the outskirts of the college town. They found it rather elegant, warmly lighted and quietly decorated; aside from table lamps in the shape of Western saddles, it was largely free of the gimmickry that seemed to characterize the other local eating places.

After the dessert course, a barboy brought over two tiny clear-colored cordials, saying, "Compliments of the young gentleman at table 12."

"Well, how do you like that," said Joseph's mother, lifting her glass and waving it with a smile toward their benefactor. He was a stocky boy in a pinstripe suit whose glasses were misted over with steam. His hair had a smashed look to it, and inside his sleeves his arms were ballooned up as though they had been worked on with a bicycle pump. He puffed grandly on a cigar. The boy's jacket was open and he wore his belt low, giving his stomach the appearance of being presented, as though he were offering it for sale, like a choice section of beef. Opposite him sat a slender green-complexioned boy with a crew cut that seemed to have been measured scientifically for horizontal perfection. The latter boy's body was wasted, reminding Joseph of a thin and disheveled biology frog that had once been passed to him in junior high school for dissection. (Afraid of what might happen if he cut into it, Joseph had turned it back for a plump and vigorous one.) Now and then the biological fellow would let his eyes go wide and his head fall over on his shoulder, smiling with moronic innocence and allowing a small quarter of his tongue to protrude. Joseph heard the heavier boy say, "You try another of those crazy routines, Feldman-Forsythe, and I'm tossing you out of a window."

The pinstriped boy approached then, bowing a little and saying, "Compliments of Gatesy, a cute little guy on a one-man crusade to teach these agricultural cornballs around here some class."

He said he had spotted Joseph and his mother aboard the airliner and they had reminded him of New Yorkers. "I saw you doing that Havana Madrid wiggle in the aisle with your son snapping his fingers like one of those slick Latin gigolo types and I said to myself here's an East Coast team." Despite his comic mannerisms, the boy had a turbinelike power to him which Joseph found threatening. He could not relax entirely and felt somehow that he should be on guard lest his mother get hurt. The boy said that he had come to Kansas Land from Philadelphia, where his mother and father were in the children's ready-to-wear business. He had been telling girls that he was a fabulous garment tycoon. "But actually," he said, "I've got a Davie and a Bessie slaving away in a little store to see that Gatesy gets an education. Incidentally, back me up with broads on that tycoon yarn. They eat it up."

"I saw the way you sent over those drinks and your folks have nothing to worry about," said Joseph's mother. "If my son could do that I'd go home on the next train."

"Your son is one of those humble yet brilliant East Side guys fighting his way from the steaming underprivileged streets of Bensonhurst to academic glory and stardom," said the boy. "My hat goes off to the kid."

"From your mouth in God's ears," said Joseph's mother.

"Is your mother insulting me?" asked the boy.

"Of course not," said Joseph.

"Ten years from now, when Gatesy is hauling down six big ones a week, people will be sorry they crossed the cute little guy from Philly off their list."

"Why don't you introduce your friend?" asked Joseph's mother. "He looks as though he could use a good meal."

"Feldman-Forsythe," said the boy, snapping his fingers and yanking his arm. "Center stage." The second fellow approached, holding his wrists limp and fetuslike near his chest, his head lolling freely on one shoulder. "Help me, please," he said. "You're laughing, I'm dying."

"Is that tragic," said Joseph's mother, clucking her tongue.

"I'll give you one last chance to cut out that crazy stuff," said Gates. The boy quickly returned to a normal pose.

"How do you do," he said to Joseph's mother.

"Meet Feldman-Forsythe," said the stocky boy, "who unsuccessfully tried to change his name from Feldman to Forsythe so he could get into medical school. He's from that same torrid Bensonhurst jungle as you are, but he hasn't got your class."

"So why do you treat him so nasty?" said Joseph's mother.

"Because he tried to turn his back on his heritage," said Gates. "He should be proud of those teeming streets which have produced eminent judges, filmdom personalities and Tammany politicians who've all made it the hard way.

"Dismiss, Feldman-Forsythe," said Gates, giving the air a powerful little punch. "Back to the salt mines." The second boy raised his arms before him horizontally; with his eyes in slits, he began a shuffling walk to his table, saying, "You who have eyes, give to those who cannot see."

"You can't tell me that's normal behavior," said Joseph's mother. "Not on your life."

"He'll drive me out of my head with those routines," said Gates.

The thin boy sat down and began clutching at his throat, gasping, "I can't breathe, it's too tight, let me out of here." When Gates got halfway out of his chair, the boy broke into a grin and sipped his coffee normally.

Joseph asked where Gates lived and whether he had been able to get a room. "Some Navy guy in New York fouled us up and we've had to live at the Goatback Hotel."

Gates took six hunched steps, then whirled sourly and made a mournful sheeplike sound. "Maaaah," he said, "I've never been so insulted in my life. Why don't you take Gates into your confidence?" He said he and the other boy were roommates at a place called the Ben Boone Rooming House. "I'll throw another sack right in there, for Christ's sake. . . . Hey!" He beamed. "Wouldn't it be something if Gates yet realized his dream of having an all-New York room! We'll run those agricultural cockers off the court. If necessary, I'll heave that little worm Feldman-Forsythe right out of a window with his crazy routines."

"I'd certainly like to see the place," said Joseph, getting excited.

"For Christ's sake," said Gates with a yanking gesture as though he were pulling a trolley car string. "Would Gates steer another New York guy wrong?"

"I thought he was supposed to be from Philadelphia," said Joseph's mother.

The boy swiveled his head back and forth disgustedly a few times and then said to Joseph, "Look, uh, that stuff may be all right for the Havana Madrid, but your mother has got to stop dropping turds on me."

"She's not doing anything," said Joseph. "And don't use that kind of language when she's around. You *are* from Philadelphia."

The boy bared his teeth a little and then seemed to come to a decision. "You win, Boss," he said. He grinned then and got to his feet, punching the air and saying, "Goddammit, I'm proposing a toast. To a great new team. Gatesy and the Boss. Ten years from now, when we're tipping the cup of nostalgia at a smart East Side *boîte*, we'll look back in fondness on this night when the Boss and Gatesy joined forces in one of the great New York combos of all time."

"It's all right with me," said Joseph's mother. "This is exactly what I traveled 1,500 miles to find."

Outside the restaurant, Joseph stood near a lamppost with his mother and asked her if he could go back with his new acquaintance to look over the Ben Boone Rooming House.

"And he's going to be your new friend?" she asked.

"Well, why not? Wouldn't it be great if I had a place to stay and you could go back to New York?"

"And what am I supposed to be doing while I know you're living with that thing? He looks about forty-two. I think you could forget about everything and have him for a delightful father. And that's what goes to college today."

"Well, just let me go there and see what it's like," said Joseph.

"Go. Have I stood in your way yet? Just remember not to let any ideas rub off on you. I can just about imagine what goes on in that moron's mind."

"Are you sure you'll be all right?" asked Joseph.

"Your mother's had to rely on a lot of help all her life, hasn't she? Do you know the legions she could have at her toes if she wanted to snap her pinkie?"

"I don't want to know about them," said Joseph. "That's the wrong kind of last thing to tell me."

"Excuse me," she said. "Again your mother spoke too much. Go join your friend and maybe his brilliant ideas will relax you."

The boy named Feldman-Forsythe had gone ahead to the rooming house. Joseph found Gates waiting for him with tears pouring down his cheeks. His thick rimless glasses had steamed up and he was wiping them with a cloth, his eyes tiny mosaic pieces, the skin around them puffed and battered as though he had been in a long, bruising fight. "Maaaah," he wailed, "Gatesy's eyes are getting worse. I'll be checked in at the Lighthouse before I'm forty." He put the glasses on and suddenly cheered up. "Hey, can you see Gates approaching broads in horn-rims? He'd have an entirely different head. But I can't compete with you, though. I'll never forget the way you approached those broads on that plane with that little lob of hair falling down over your eyes, a New York operator zeroing in for the kill. I wanted to run over and congratulate you. And the way you walked over here just now while Gatesy was working on his poor eyes, that same lob hanging down. You look wild, Boss. If I were a broad, I have to admit I'd be after your pecker. You don't mind if I call you Boss, do you?"

"I don't see that it makes any difference."

The boy got hysterical and said, "Great, really great. You just threw a load of turds at Gates and made it seem like a compliment."

He pulled Joseph's suit lapel and whispered, "Excellent ax job, Boss."

They began to walk toward the campus now, the shorter boy stepping along at a brisk, powerful clip, Joseph, despite his longer legs, having a little difficulty keeping up. The boy explained that he had always had a "Boss." For years, in Philadelphia, it had been a great basketball player named Zubrow who had allowed him to carry his gym clothing satchel into tournament games and sit on the bench alongside him during the halves. "Those other peasants would see me next to Zubie and they'd cream right there on the court."

Joseph asked the boy if he would slow down a bit, and Gates sweetly and considerately said, "Why, of course, Boss. Would you like me to fly Ash Gerstein, rubber *extraordinaire* of the Philly Y, down here to get you in shape? One of Ash's back jobs and you'll be heaving in set shots from forty feet out."

"You wouldn't really do that, so what are you saying it for?" said Joseph. He was a little afraid of the boy's reaction and averted his eyes as he spoke.

"Antic," said Gates. "Excellent comeback. You're one of those antic New York guys, slaving away in the wilds of New York's famed Catskills, ready to tear off his busboy jacket and fill in for an ailing M.C. Tell the truth, Boss, you've done a turn in the Catskills, haven't you?"

"I never worked up there," said Joseph.

"Neat cover-up," said the boy. "Never admit you've worked the Borscht Circuit to a class broad."

Their talk had a breezy texture to it, and Joseph knew he should have been enjoying it but was not at all sure it was working out that way. He was still shaken by the collision between the boy and his mother; one purpose behind his taking the walk, it seemed to him, was to get the boy farther from her so that she would be safe.

The boy's walking pace was much too brisk and it was impossible for Joseph to appear casual as he struggled to keep up. He could not see any reason for the rush, and the boy's way of stopping short and furiously whirling about before he spoke was unsettling. Then, too, he never really talked to Joseph but made little speeches instead, lifting his fist to his mouth and announcing things into it as though he were doing television documentaries. Joseph wished he could hurry up and room with the boy for four years, somehow getting it all over quickly so that he would not have to speculate on whether he had made the right decision.

"What the hell's the hurry?" said Joseph, tearing across the campus at Gates's heels. The boy lifted his fist and announced, "The Boss and Gates. Gatesy and the Boss. The most unstoppable team in the history of the rich, verdant, world-renowned Kansas-Missouri farm belt."

He stopped and wheeled suddenly, poking a finger in Joseph's face and saying, "I'm scheduling an early charge over to Windsor College for broads. You'll lead it, Boss, with Gatesy debonairly bringing up the rear. I'm guaranteeing full wire coverage. Feldman-Forsythe gets left behind in the trenches where that classless cocker belongs. Remind me to have him throw a little Chanel Number Five on his feet. Take a memo on that, Boss."

Once across the campus, they came to a row of sorority houses, Gates making a low, sweeping bow in front of the first and saying, more to himself than to anyone else, "Girls, Gates invites you to an all-night hocking session with Gatesy lined up and ready to hock the eyes out of your agricultural heads."

A trio of blondes came out of one house, their browned knees in a froth, a quilt of summer perfume moving along in front of them.

Gates stuck his cigar in his mouth, then, frozen-lipped, ventriloquist-style, said, "Girls, meet Gates, known throughout the Catskills as the legendary little guy who once ripped off six turns in a single all-night hocking session."

He turned to Joseph and said aloud, "See Matzoh Abramowitz, the fleet-footed crooning bellhop at Farber's Cottages for a sworn keyhole report."

"Have you gotten to meet many girls since you've been down here?" asked Joseph. "I've been hung up with my mother and haven't been able to do anything."

Gates stopped and began to waggle his tongue through cracked and ruined teeth. "Hey, Boss," he said, "Gatesy working on a pair of size forties. What do you think?"

"Very nice," said Joseph, who decided it was one of the worst sights he had ever witnessed. It occurred to him that they were talking as though they had known each other since childhood and he wondered how the other boy had managed it that way. Yet it seemed pointless to say, "Hold on a second, let's be a little more distant."

In front of them now, fogged and bleary in the darkness, Joseph saw the blinking marquee of the Ben Boone Rooming House and wondered whether he had not carried things a little too far and ought to return to his mother's until he got a real place to stay. He could not imagine doing a single night's studying in a place that had a marquee like that.

The boy stopped for a moment, locked his wrists behind his back and, head down, began to pace back and forth as though dictating a memo. "Let's face it, Boss, Gatesy is a very hot little guy. Are you hot? I've never queried you on that. Hey, I found out where I get my heat. From my old man. Just before I left for school, Davie gave me the complete scoop. 'I love your mother,' he says to me. He's the cutest little guy. But it turns out he's been hocking *schvartze* cleaning ladies in the back while Bessie's upstairs plucking chickens.

244

"What about your old man?" he asked, in a spirit of scholarly research. "Does he do any free-lance hocking?"

"He'd never talk about anything like that. I don't want to talk about it either."

"I can see the Boss, senior, now, one of those meticulously dressed Seventh Avenue guys stepping into a fitting room with one of those long-stemmed New York garment center beauties, slipping her a few wholesale brassieres to keep her mouth shut."

The picture made Joseph feel shaky and he said, "I don't like to discuss sex. I just like to do it."

"Shrewd reverse con," said the boy.

He suddenly bulled his way out to the center of the street. "Goddammit," he said, "I'm not letting a New York guy move around without a cab."

"We're only twenty steps away," said Joseph. "What's the point?"

The boy stood paralyzed in his tracks, then ran toward Joseph, his fist in a ball, saying, "I've taken enough, Boss. Gatesy's handing in his resignation." Joseph got set for him, watched him gather speed like a locomotive, then stop.

"Only kidding," he said. "Gatesy would never throw a punch at his Boss. Why, the Boss has given Gatesy everything he owns."

"Well then, don't fool around like that," said Joseph.

"Hey," he said, switching moods, "one of those wild New York cabbies giving you a lecture on politics. Those bastards'll walk right into the State Legislature and argue down an amendment. Never turn your back on New York, Boss."

"I haven't," said Joseph. "And we're here now."

"Hey, that's right," said the boy. He took a minute to straighten his tie and smooth down his lapels. "Everything straight?" he asked.

"You look fine," said Joseph.

Then the boy hollered up the stairs, "All right, agricultural shitpickers, clear the decks. Make way for Gatesy and his new Boss."

The room was small and bleakly lit, with a double-decker bed against one wall and underwear scattered in every direction as though a bundle of it had been blown in by a fan. It lacked a scholarly atmosphere and Joseph was unable to imagine himself sitting in the room, soaking up great ideas of the Western world. Gates stood at the door, his arms stretched out before him. "Aaaah, it's New York," he said. "Gatesy makes his return to the hustle and bustle of fabulous Gothamtown. It's New York at night, and if you can't take the pressure, grab the next train out of town. We've got a parking problem anyway."

In slightly yellowed underwear, the boy named Feldman-Forsythe lay on the top tier of the bed, eyes abulge, smiling blandly and staring at the ceiling. In a sweet, whispered voice, he said, "Oh yes, I love it here. I won't try to go home again. They put things on my head and make a boom-boom. I don't bite the men any more. In the morning we make wallets. We eat jello, too. It is good. I am trying to be nice and not make peepee a lot."

"He's at it again," said Gates exasperatedly. "Get your net ready, Boss. I may go out a window if he keeps up these crazy routines.

"Feldman-Forsythe," he said, in a mild scolding voice. "Can't you see we have guests? Will you please get your skinny ass out of the rack and start cleaning up the place? Goddammit, the Boss is here."

"Excuse me," said the thin boy, vaulting down from the bed and beginning to sweep the room with mock servitude.

"He just started to call me that 'Boss' thing," said Joseph, a little embarrassed. "It makes him feel good."

The thin boy seemed to have a seizure and said, "Awwwrrrf," suddenly tearing at his feet and scratching them through a pair of green socks. "I'm not kidding around now," he said. "They itch like hell."

"Feldman-Forsythe," said Gates, as though making a supreme effort to be patient. "Really now, you've got to do something about your feet. For Christ's sakes, you're a New York guy. Will you please begin to act like one."

"What am I supposed to do?" said the boy, on the floor now, clawing at his toes in genuine agony. "You don't know what it feels like."

"Does it help if you put them in water?" asked Joseph. He picked up an anatomy textbook and began to thumb through it, hoping to see pictures of women's breasts that were not too badly diseased. He wondered if he would be able to borrow the book and thought of places he could hide it in his mother's hotel room. "Ah, education," said Gates. "Jesus, are you brilliant, Boss. Word has gotten back to Gatesy of your classroom performance. Hey, can you see Gates in cap and gown skipping down the aisle for a sheepskin with that cute little guy Davie on hand for the festivities?"

He turned then to the boy on the floor, the spell broken, and said, "Goddammit, I'm checking out. I can't take it any longer. When I get back will you please have your feet under control?

"I'll go round up some of the fabulous Ben Boone crowd," he said to Joseph. "They're all New York guys at heart."

Whatever had flown into the thin boy's feet seemed to pass on now, giving way to a pleasurable sensation. He stroked his once inflamed toes and said, "Aaah, that's much better." It seemed to Joseph that he was actually quite handsome, although his body was on the wretched side and did not really match his face. It was as though someone had worked very hard on him above the neck, then lost interest, finishing him off quickly with the torso of a Ganges River thief. He got to his feet now and smiling handsomely said, "Crazy guy, isn't he?"

247

"I don't know," said Joseph. "I haven't had time to figure out what he is. I've just sort of fallen in with all that Boss stuff. I can't stay too long. I've got my mother waiting over at the hotel."

"Gates is all right," he said. "Hey, here's one. Guy in the next room is dying of cancer and the relatives are all grouped outside when the grandfather begins to speak." He hunched himself up and let one lip rope over to the side, contorting his face so that he really did look like an old man. "Oh, terrible, terrible," he said. "I don't want to say from my mouth what that poor boy is suffering from. A boy so young, with such a beautiful face."

"Very good," said Joseph. "I've seen that deal myself. But why do you do all those depressing imitations?"

The boy explained that when he was a child his guardian aunt had been shipped off regularly to institutions for shock treatment and that during his visits he had gotten to observe the inmates at her various rest homes. The treatments had left her very sweet and passive but had stolen away her hearing. Then, too, just before he had left to begin college, he had been called down to lower Broadway by police to identify his older brother who had been found sealed up overnight in a blind newsdealer's wooden stall. "You who have eyes," he said, stretching his arms out in front of him and doing a blind man's walk. "Get it now?" That had been years back. He had not been sure at all he would be able to go off to college until a check had arrived from a mysterious man named "Goldie" for his first year's tuition, enabling him to start his premed course at Kansas Land. Expense checks kept coming in every few months from the same fellow.

The boy turned on a phonograph now, and began whirling romantically in his underdrawers and yellowed T shirt, spinning and finger-clicking to a Doris Day record. He was quite graceful and Joseph envied him for his romantic way of twirling about. He explained that he had had to take his first year of premed three times because of romantic entanglements with three separate girls named Cathy. Each was small, blond and blue-eyed. He would meet one at the beginning of each school year, starting up a love affair that would last until the Christmas break. The girl would then return to school and explain that it was all over, that she had decided to get engaged to a fellow back home. His anatomical dissections would then go completely to pot and he would finish out the school year in a twirling romantic fog until the following September, when he would start up the process once again. He took a billfold out of his yellowed shorts and showed pictures of the three girls to Joseph. Not at all sure he wanted to touch the underwear pictures, Joseph nevertheless held them at the corners and found the girls most appealing, easily worth a year each of squandered premed studies. He was jealous of the boy, wiry thieflike body and all, for his hopeless love affairs with the three golden-haired charmers.

Gates returned with two other boys, one a tall, scowling unshaven radical fellow Joseph remembered from his history and principles of agriculture class. The fellow was always furious over minor historical events and would get to his feet quaking with rage, and say to the teacher, "Why *did* Grainger decide to shake up his *Farming Tides* staff in 1912 and replace Fredson as executive ed? I'd like to have that cleared up, if you please."

"Meet Georgie Elias," said Gates. "One of the most pissed-off guys who ever worked his way West from the charming stucco-lined streets of Staten Island. He's your kind of guy, Boss."

The boy scowlingly shook Joseph's hand and Gates said, "No one can figure out why he's so pissed off. And he won't tell anyone either."

The boy bitterly kicked at the floorboards while Gates introduced the second fellow, a balding boy with loose breasts joggling beneath his undershirt. "Say hello to Boils Buffkins. He just stays in his room all day taking care of those boils of his.

Fire one for the Boss, Boils." The boy lifted his hand as though to fix an overhead light bulb, and a small white pellet slipped out of his armpit, hitting the wall mirror with a *ping*.

"Can't you have anything done about that?" asked Joseph.

"It's not really that bad," said the boy. Gates told Joseph that he had better be nice to Buffkins, since he was in charge of the commissary, keeping all the Ben Boone food supplies in his room.

"Hey, Boils," he said, "make sure I don't find one of those torpedoes in the white bread, okay, kid?"

"Sure thing," said the afflicted fellow, leaving the room, the scowling boy close at his heels.

"Just two of the fabulous New York-type guys you'll find on hand to entertain you nightly at the notorious Ben Boone Rooming House," said Gates. "Wait a minute," he said, beginning to inhale deeply through his broad nose. "What's that? Has that little bastard been at it again?"

He rooted about the room like a dog, finally plunging his hand beneath Feldman-Forsythe's mattress, pulling out a cloth bundle of the sort slung over the shoulders of hoboes.

"Goddammit, I knew I'd catch you," he said to Feldman-Forsythe. "The bastard's been cutting up cats again."

"Leave it alone," said the thin boy in terror. "That's a month's work in there."

"I've had enough of your routines, Feldman," he said, flinging the cat bag out of the window. "I'll teach you some class yet."

"You didn't have to do that," said the thin boy, holding back tears and then running barefoot out of the room to retrieve his specimen.

"I agree with him," said Joseph, worried how it would look for the boy to appear in the street wearing underwear. "That was really a lousy trick."

"Uh, Boss," said Gates, sitting down behind a desk and toying with a pencil. He took some time, as though gathering his thoughts, and then continued. "Uh, let me tell you something. Uh, your mother wears a lot of makeup. She's a New York woman and that's all right for a turn at the Havana Madrid, but you really ought to tone her down a little for out here."

"That's none of your goddamned business," said Joseph. "What about *your* mother? I don't see you talking about her. What does she wear on *her* face?"

"Oh," said the boy, playing with the pencil and smiling calmly with unusual composure. "Maybe you'd like to play the Dozens . . ."

Joseph had never heard of the game before, yet there was something about the boy's total self-composure as he pronounced its name that frightened him and made his hands flutter involuntarily. Joseph knew it was the one game on earth he did not want to play.

"I'm not playing any games," he said, getting to his feet. "I've got to go now."

"Okay, Boss," said the boy, and Joseph realized he had dropped the "Boss" salutation a moment before. "Be on hand tomorrow night to lead a charge on the notorious broad-packed campus of Windsor College, known for attracting the daughters of cattle barons and cowshit tycoons who couldn't get into the swank, sophisticated halls of Bennington."

"I'm not so sure I'll be there," said Joseph. "I'll see."

Joseph ate breakfast alone the next morning and then stood outside the Goatback, watching a float pass in front of the hotel. Two girls in short skirts stood in its cab carrying a banner that invited one and all to attend an open house that night at Windsor College for Women. The girls did not seem to be float girls; they were scholarly in appearance, each with pale, mottled legs. The float had gotten entangled in heavy bus and truck traffic and Joseph felt sorry for the girls as they gave festive little kicks at the few passersby, their legs chilled in the October wind. "You be sure to be there, hear?" one cried out to Joseph, giving him a bluish, bent-legged half kick. "Wouldn't miss it," said Joseph. But the float remained jammed in its place and he felt obligated to keep up an innocuous conversation with the girl so that she would have something to do. He wondered whether he should not run inside and then race back in a disguise so that she would have a second fellow to do her invitation kicks at.

Joseph knew little about Windsor College other than that the desirable campus fellows felt it a chore to go out to it, preferring the more convenient Kansas Land girls; it was generally the awkward, leftover boys who traveled out to the all-girls' school where the sledding was much easier. Even so, floats had to be sent out now and then to ensure some male attendance at Windsor get-togethers. Chief among the school's attractions, Joseph had heard, was that a famed Hollywood makeup man sent his daughters there and they were often visited by filmdom dignitaries. In addition, a certain great lady of the American stage had come to Windsor as a dramatics teacher after her retirement. She had turned out to be terribly shy, spending most of her time in a sealed-off cottage, sitting at her window with a pair of field glasses. It was said that whenever she spotted a Windsor College girl doing something graceful she would charge down upon her to pay the girl a compliment. One such girl reported that on a summer day she had thrown up her arm to block out the sun's rays, when the celebrated thespian suddenly appeared at her side with the word "Lovely." Joseph knew, too, that Windsor girls were not allowed ever to ride in cars: the college employed a squad of elderly Windsor Watchers whose job it was to peer into passing vehicles and make sure there were no girls squatting in them.

That night, preparing for dinner, Joseph's mother said to him, "Tell me which dress you want. Whichever one is your heart's desire is the one I'll wear." She stood before the closet mirror in her slip, waggling a stockinged foot out to the side in a style she might have used decades back at a grammer school recital. Joseph had slept uneasily the night before, unable to decide whether he had really enjoyed the stocky boy's company and whether he wanted to return to the Ben Boone and perhaps live there. The people who did fascinated him in the same way as the overcoated stompers of the Koke Kanteen, yet he could not imagine himself living at the Boone and making any headway with logarithm tables. Then, too, all through the night the threatened game had boiled in his stomach.

Yet during the day he had felt an obligation to the pathetic Windsor float-kicker. Then too, the scented air that poured in through the hotel window now was unsettling and made him think of dormitories filled with girls, all crammed together like bags of flour in a New England pantry.

"There's an open house tonight," he said to his mother. "The new fellows I just met are going to it. What would happen if I went along?"

"Two nights in a row you'd just walk off and ditch your mother," she said. "It's all right with me. I'm not saying a word."

"Well then, I don't have to go," said Joseph. "I can stay right here. I'm not that crazy about the new guys, anyway."

"Now, don't be silly," she said. "Are you out of your mind? You still don't know a pleasantry. I was only teasing. You go right ahead and don't you worry about your mother. She'll be right here when you need her."

He dressed in great haste, not bothering to shower. On the way out he said, "Are you really sure? It's no big deal."

"Have a good time," she said. "Only be careful who you associate with. You've got all your life to be crazy."

A special airport bus was the only way out to Windsor College. He had decided to go alone but then felt it might be embarrassing to meet Gates at the open house and headed for the Ben Boone instead. The farther he got from his mother the more chilled and mysterious he felt. For no particular reason he began to run and to take in deep, drunken swallows of the night air. At the Ben Boone he saw Feldman-Forsythe in the hallway, wearing what appeared to be the previous day's shorts and making a phone call. In a telephone operator's voice he said, "Hello, is this Mary Jane Robley of Hotchkiss Hall? Hold on for long-distance, pleeyizz."

"I certainly shall," came a high-pitched voice at the other end.

"All right," said Feldman-Forsythe, continuing in his phone operator's voice. "Come in, Chicago. I have your party."

He made some teletype sounds into the phone, then dropped his voice several octaves and spoke with the exaggerated charm and excitement of a television announcer.

"Hello there, do I have the honor of speaking to Miss Mary Jane Robley of Hotchkiss Hall way out there in distant Windsor College?"

"Yes indeed," came the excited squeal.

"Well, this is Bert Fedders, of the one-hour coast-to-coast Hit-It-Big video show. Let me be the first to congratulate you on winning our annual September Queen Giveaway Award." He cupped his hands and blew into the receiver to simulate a crowd sound. "Hooooowaaaahhh."

Apparently the girl had brought over some of her roommates, and Joseph heard what sounded like a series of gasps and fainting sounds at her end.

"Are you ready to stand by for your list of exquisite gifts, Mary Jane Robley?"

"Oh, of course," said the girl.

He held his nose and gave a perfect imitation of a trumpet blast. Then he covered the receiver with his T shirt for still another, even deeper, voice and said, "An all-silk Ling-Beddoes Bridal Ensemble," quickly blowing in some crowd applause.

"A silver-blue let-out horizontal mink stole by Finatzo of Milan."

He continued to reel off half a dozen other prizes, punctuating them with trumpet blasts and crowd sounds, then let the master of ceremonies take over. "Are you a happy girl at the other end there? I'm sure you are. All right now, Mary Jane

Robley, stand by for your delivery date. Your Hit-It-Big gifts will be delivered, listen closely now, in front of the Bengal Flower Shop on Ninth and Elm *this very evening* at midnight. How about that, fans?"

"Hooooowaaaaahhh," Feldman-Forsythe blew into the phone.

"So there you are, lucky Mary Jane Robley of Hotchkiss Hall. This is Bert Fedders of Hit-It-Big in Chicago wishing you good night and happy sheep-counting."

Feldman-Forsythe followed with a few additional teletype signals, then dropped the phone.

"Hey, that was great," said Joseph, marveling at the production. "Who was the girl?"

"I don't know," he said. "I just took one out of the directory with a cute name."

With that, he pointed his forefingers, as though he were shooting off pistols, and went spinning crazily down the hall, hollering, "Free Puerto Rico, bang, bang."

He practically ran into the arms of Gates, who had just left the hall bathroom with his shaving equipment. "Feldman-Forsythe," he said with sweetness and great forbearance, "I don't want to have to dump you on your ass. Will you please try to class yourself up?"

"I defend my cawntry to ze last breath," said the boy, spitting at the wall and then doing an arrogant foot-stamping flamenco step into the bathroom.

"I'll cut that little bugger's schvonce off," said Gates, leading Joseph into his room. "Hey, Boss, you know what Gatesy heard about today? Queer guys. Can you imagine? Guys playing with each other's peckers. You think a thing like that goes on?"

"I've heard of it," said Joseph.

"Jesus, are you informed. I'm signing up for a six-month Freudian course with you, Boss. You're one of those Freudian New York guys who knows how to handle a broad.

"Hey, what do you think of Gatesy's body?" He was standing

in front of a mirror in undershorts and black patent leather evening shoes, his shorts low so that his bushel-like belly was able to pour forth in a grand and splendid manner. "Gatesy's always had a great body and a terrible head. Would you believe it though? Gatesy has a beautiful mother. If I had Bessie's head, I'd have broads crawling all over me.

"Hey," he said. "This is going to be one of the all-time great New York charges. Goddammit, broads will be discussing this night long after they've rapped out three kids and are mowing lawns in suburbia. The night two humble operators from the pavements of New York swept in and captured the hearts of Windsor College's cute and sophisticated young debutante types."

He lathered up his face and said, "Do you have any shaving tips, Boss? Each time Gatesy shaves he has to check in at the Clinic for an emergency stitch job."

"I think it comes out smoother when you shave twice, once up and once down," said Joseph.

"Jesus," said the boy. "Are you a knowledgeable guy. Those stories of your brilliance all check out, Boss."

The flattery was so obvious it made Joseph wince, and yet, for some reason, he could not find it in himself to tell the boy he did not like it and would he please stop. When Gates was finished dressing, he said to Joseph, "What do you think of the cut, Boss? Can you see having dinner with Gates in this outfit, the top dinner man on the Eastern Seaboard?"

On the way down the hall, Gates stopped at several rooms, commenting on the different Ben Boone people who lived inside them. He pointed to a bushy-haired boy who was ironing slacks. "That's Jack Pollackson, a humble operator from the playgrounds of the Bronx, out to nail a rich broad. He'll live with a pig as long as she's got money, right, Jack?"

The boy looked up and said, "What the hell do I care what they look like."

"Meet Turkey Goddard, his roommate, son of the famed Midwestern gynecologist, whose pecker has never been gazed upon by mortal man, although some have claimed to spot him in the shower taking a late jack. Hey, Turkey, give us a look at it."

The thin boy sitting on a sofa blushed and covered his legs with his bathrobe.

"No one can get a peek at that little bastard's pecker," said Gates.

In another room he pointed out the fabulous Rod Myerberg, "A wealthy guy who turned his back on fraternities to hole up at the colorful Ben Boone. His father's one of the top hardware tycoons in the Missouri Valley, yet he craps on Greeks.

"Actually, it's because of his stomach, Boss," said Gates, dropping his voice to a whisper. "All he can eat is soft-boiled eggs, and Boils Buffkins is the only one he'll trust to whip them up. Boils has also promised not to slip any of those armpit torpedoes in there, although frankly, I think he's tossing in a few.

"Still and all," he said, raising his voice, "he's Rod Myerberg who drops turds on fraternities and has hung up a home-sweet-home sign at the fabulous out-of-the-way Ben Boone Rooming House."

The husky blond boy inside the room waved a weak arm and said, "Cut it out, will you? I got cramps."

On the way down the steps they passed a bottom-heavy fellow who seemed in a great rush. "Boodle Bodinsky," said Gates, "whose old man has been filing corpses in Denver for the last twenty-five years. Boodle is classily pretending he's a history major, yet everyone knows he'll be working the slabs with his old man the second he pulls out of here."

The boy looked back angrily from the top of the stairs, and Gates said, "Hey, Boodle, will you file Gatesy someday when he takes the final ten count?"

At the bottom of the stairs, in master-of-ceremonies style,

Gates said, "Some of the lovable types who've decided to log their golden college years at the celebrated Ben Boone for wild guys."

"Do you think I could get a room somewhere in there?" asked Joseph.

"Boss," said Gates, "when will you learn that Gatesy's on your team? Goddammit, don't you realize I'm backing you to the hilt?"

He had not really answered the question, but Joseph decided not to press it. Outside, Gates grinned and said quietly, "It's a New York night, Boss. Can you picture it? The houselights dimming for a ten-rounder at the Garden. Sashaying through Central Park with a class broad on your arm. The cherry cheese at Lindy's and then two on the aisle for a Mike Todd musical extravaganza. One of those New York cabbies crowding you over to the side and almost tearing off an arm." He threw out his hands beseechingly and continued: "New York's fabulous East Side with its smart *bistros* and $100-a-night hookers. Garment-Center guys with six-foot Copa dolls on their arms. Bronx girls trying to pass as Vassar queens and quickly unmasked by anyone who's been around. A stroll through Washington Square with one of those Village tomatoes feeding you a little Tolstoi. It's all part of the blazing Empire City panorama, Boss, it's New York, the world's most fabulous burg.

"And you've turned your back on it," he said disgustedly. He rapped Joseph's shoulder with the back of his hand and said, "For Christ's sakes what are you trying to hide?"

"Nothing," said Joseph. "I never once tried to hide anything."

"Goddammit, that's the way I like to hear you talk," said Gates. "It shows that down deep you're still a New York guy at heart."

■ ■

They found the Windsor bus on the flight line of the terminal, illuminated every few seconds by a rotating slice of light from the control tower. Sliding into a seat, Joseph thought for a moment the bus might be about to take off like a plane. "Jesus," said Gates, getting in beside him and shivering with glee, "this is turning into one of the great all-time charges. Can you see us discussing it ten years from now—Gatesy, totally bald by then, a cute little guy coining at least six big ones a week; the Boss, a distinguished guy with a full head of gray lobs, just married to one of those cute little Sarah Lawrence broads, running home for lunchtime hocking sessions. Gatesy will be the old, loyal family retainer, Uncle Gatesy, visiting the Boss for strolls down Memory Lane and reminding him of that historical charge on Windsor College."

"We haven't even done anything yet," said Joseph. "Wait till we get there."

As they approached the girls' campus, Gates sat forward abruptly and said, "I can smell those palpitating cute little debutantes now. Goddammit, sometimes I think I belong in the hocking business. I could hock all week long." Just before they got off the bus, Gates raised his chin and said, "All right, final head check. Could I pass on a dark night?"

"Stop worrying about yourself," said Joseph.

"Jesus, are you on to Gatesy, Boss," said the boy. "You're one of those guys who knows about head complexes."

The girls were gathered out on the terraces of their resident cottages, sipping soft drinks; their sheer number dazzled Joseph, who saw only a dizzying pattern of sheath dresses and white rabbity knees, which he was unable, somehow, to break down into individual girls. It was only later he learned it was because he was nearsighted and needed glasses.

"All right, Boss, check your ammo and get ready for the charge. Jesus, is this great. Gatesy will do some light reconnaissance and you come on quickly with the first wave. Wish me luck, Boss."

He approached a group of four girls who were sitting along the railing of the first cottage and began pacing back and forth in front of them, taking deep puffs of his cigar, as though he were about to address a jury. He stopped finally and said, "Uh, do you know anything about Mount Holyoke girls? I've got one of them lined up and could use some tips on how to handle her."

The girls looked at him peculiarly and he said, "Girls, I'd like you to meet one of those fabulous New York Freudian operators. Meet the Boss," he said, gesturing grandly as though he were ushering an act out on stage.

Feeling ridiculous, Joseph nevertheless came forward in a little run and said, "Hi, he's kind of flamboyant, isn't he?"

The girls nodded, slightly mystified, and then turned toward a pair of rangy boys in blue jeans and plaid shirts.

"Shitpickers," Gates whispered to Joseph. "Cut their water, Boss."

"What do I do?" asked Joseph.

"Goddammit, let's pull out of here," said Gates, stamping on his cigar butt. Before walking off, he turned to the quartet of girls and said, "Uh, you girls should really get to know your way around."

He grabbed Joseph's arm and stormed back onto a path that threaded its way through the row of cottages. Then he became hysterical, howling with laughter until he could not catch his breath. "Oh Jesus, is this great, Boss. We'll be talking about this charge for years. The way you walked over there with that little Borscht Belt trot and slipped them that 'flamboyant' line. They must have pissed when they heard that. And how about Gatesy giving them a few instructions on how to handle themselves? I'm giving Winchell an inside on this immediately."

261

Joseph felt a little frustrated and said, "I don't think it was that great. We never really got started."

"Jesus, Boss," said the boy in a horrible, broken-mouthed grin. "What an operator. Gatesy's proud to be signed up for your course in broad-handling."

They walked toward another cottage, Joseph growing panicky, imagining somehow this was his last chance ever to be with the Windsor girls. He pictured himself flying from cottage to cottage, unable to get rolling with any of them, finally having to be carried kicking through the gate.

"All right," said Gates, as they neared the next cottage, a coach now, sending in a backfield replacement. "Take a solo on this one, Boss. Gatesy will be waiting in the wings, polishing his material."

Joseph walked up to the terrace and was a little disappointed at the girl who headed him off at the stairs. She had a pretty figure and there was evidence she had gone to great pains to make her bosom seem smaller and more demure than it was. When she came closer, Joseph saw that her skin was coarse and began to look around for other possibilities. Yet her face was open and aglow and she talked with animation as though years back she had learned to be doubly pleasing as a way of balancing off her complexion.

"What's a married man like you doing in a place like this?" she asked. The joke agreed with Joseph and when she offered him a sip of her drink he decided he would stay and get to know her. Glancing back at the path, he saw Gates doubled over with laughter, punching the air and saying what appeared to be "Great, Boss, great."

"Where's your wife?" asked the girl, continuing along the same line and lowering her eyes with mock shyness. "I'm not sure I ought to be sitting out here with a married man." Joseph squinted so that he could not see the ridges of her skin. He decided she was quite lovely and tried to imagine a little jeweled pin on the tip of one of her suppressed bosoms.

They talked a while, Joseph asking her why she bit her nails. "Why do all seventeen-year-old girls bite their nails?" she asked softly. Delighted by the innuendo, Joseph decided he would stay right there and forget the droves of other girls. After some minutes, she leaned back on the terrace railing, closed her eyes and asked, "What's it like being in love?"

As he was framing his reply, he saw his friend make an angry, waist-high thumb-jerking motion. "Excuse me a second," said Joseph, going out to the path.

"Let's cut out of here, Boss," said the boy. "We're wasting our time."

"Why?" asked Joseph. "It isn't so bad."

"For Christ's sake," said the boy, looking at Joseph with incredulity. "Don't you understand that Gatesy's a veteran of many coed wars? I've cased the place. There's nothing here. Can't you see that Gatesy's not at home unless he's got one of those thin-lipped cultural Vassar types backed against a wall, discussing a little Picasso?"

"They looked all right to me," said Joseph.

"Boss," said the boy, half closing his eyes, as though trying to get through to a child, "you're in the Big Leagues now. If it ever got out Gatesy was fooling around with nothings, he'd be the laughingstock of the Philly Y."

Joseph waved a feeble goodby to the girl on the terrace and they began to walk back to the bus. He took a final look then, and saw a tall boy in a windbreaker streak up the steps and stop in front of his new friend.

"That's Sleepy Jim Folsom, the notorious fender-hocker, teaming up with one of your rejects, Boss. You could leave that manure spreader in the dust. All he can do is hock girls on fenders. Get him away from a set of fenders and he's lost.

"Goddammit," he said, coming to a halt and stamping his foot. "I'd rather throw a private jack in my room than horse around with one of those manure tycoon's daughters."

"I didn't even get her number," said Joseph as they got back on the bus.

"Boss, you've got to be careful who you're seen with. You show up with too many pigs and you're a dead man."

But when the bus started off, the boy said, "Jesus, did we operate. Those broads won't see anything like this if they live to be a hundred. Jeez, did we knock them on their charming little agricultural tails. This has been one of the Pulitzer Prize-winning charges of modern times."

"I thought they were supposed to be so awful," said Joseph, looking back at the college.

"They'll never forget you, Boss," said Gates.

Back at the campus, they decided to get a bite at the patty restaurant. Once inside, Gates put his feet up on a chair and said, "Hey, two of those slick Madison Avenue types congregating at the notorious State Delicatessen for a playback on the evening's hocking activities."

"I really didn't have that great a time," said Joseph.

"Boss," said the boy, "be reasonable. These are the shortest, gladdest years of life." Gates began to announce into his fist. "And now, as the sun sinks slowly into the west, we bring to a close one of those fabulous New York-type evenings."

"It's so early," said Joseph. "Everyone's still out."

Gates shook his head slowly. "You're one of those tough guys to please. Have some New York food."

A crap game was going on in the lobby of the Ben Boone. "Throw five in there, Boss," said Gates. Joseph followed instructions and when he had lost on one roll, the other boy whispered, "Let's get out of here. The dice are loaded. Gatesy just donated five to stay on their good side. Those are the roughest guys on the campus. They'll cut your pecker off."

"But it was *my* five," said Joseph. "I really needed it."

"You're a close guy with a buck," said the boy. "Gatesy's always known that. You could come to me for a grand if I had it and I'd turn it right over to you. Yet Gatesy could never go to the Boss for money. Advice yes, cash never."

He began undressing as he walked up the steps, and by the time he got to his room, he was wearing only his dress shirt, shoes and underwear. He flipped on the light, and surprisingly, it was many seconds before he noticed the huddled mass in his bed.

"Goddammit," he said, clasping the top of his head. "He's got those stinking feet in Gatesy's rack. That did it." He yanked back the covers to reveal a nude and shocked Feldman-Forsythe. The boy jumped to his feet and Gates punched him in the stomach, spearing him in midair with perfect timing. Feldman-Forsythe crumpled to the floor and a slender girl in brassiere and panties flew out of the sheets to kneel at his side.

"And he's got one of those goddamned Cathys in there with him, too," said the stocky boy. "In Gatesy's pure rack."

"You didn't have to hit him," said the girl, helping the doubled-over boy to his feet. Her body was wiry, too, much in the Feldman-Forsythe style, yet Joseph found it most appealing.

"There was no point in doing that," Joseph agreed.

"Uh, you're really one of those sophisticated Radcliffe types," Gates said to the girl as she led Feldman-Forsythe into the hallway bathroom. "I'm sure you know a lot about Mondrian."

"I like that kid," said Joseph when they were alone. "He's a very nice boy. Didn't he tell you about his brother being sealed up in a newsstand? Your hitting him makes me sick."

The boy seemed flustered and began to scratch at his belly, beneath his undershorts. He took a long time to sit down, his hand on his lower back as though he were very old. After thinking a moment, he began to speak with great calm and deliberation. "Uh, Boss, I think it's time we played the Dozens."

"No," said Joseph, in terror. "I don't want to."

"Oh yes," Gates said, and then, leaning back grandly, with his hands supporting his head, he puffed on a cigar and said, "Gatesy will serve first. Your mother was screwed by an eagle and forced to hatch the Boss on a bloodstained rock at high tide. Your turn."

"I don't want to," said Joseph. "Your mother is an ugly pig."

"Your father is an infected pimple deep in the ass of suffering humanity," said Gates, sucking richly on his cigar. "Take it."

He continued for half a dozen more, Joseph skipping most of his turns, the few rejoinders he did make weak and halfhearted. When the boy had done one involving Joseph's grandmother and a batch of sanitary napkins, he lowered his feet and said, "Had enough, Boss, or do we continue playing the fabulous Dozens game, conceived between halves at a Catskills basketball tournament by Abe Fishberg and several other bored hoop stars?"

"No more for me," said Joseph, and he ran down the stairs.

Once, alone in his mother's apartment, Joseph had opened the door for an hysterical next-door neighbor who said that a great bird had flown into her living room and was in the drapes. Handing him a broom, she shoved him into her apartment and closed the door. Joseph tiptoed over to the drapes, tapped them three times with the broom and then ran out into the hall. Later he learned that police had identified the bird as a monster chicken hawk, the first ever seen in Bensonhurst. Now, as he crossed the campus, the game still clung to Joseph, as though the old drapery hawk, hoary, vindictive, toughened with age, had caught up with him in Kansas to ride his shoulders. A light rain peppered Joseph's forehead, refreshing him somewhat after the socks and underwear of the Boone. The couples parading across

266

the campus seemed to be just starting out on their dates. He wondered if the Windsor College girl had gone off to lie on a fender somewhere. He could not get the image of Feldman-Forsythe impaled on a fist out of his mind, and yet he envied the boy for having been able to get such a pretty girl into the double-decker bed with him, a great triumph considering the condition of his feet. Swinging into the lobby of the Goatback, he noticed the powerfully built man who had stared at his mother, kneeling now beside a spittoon and tapping out a melody with a pair of swizzle sticks. Joseph looked fearlessly at the man, passing right beside him on his way to the elevator, aware that he had just been through a small cloud of perfume.

Upstairs in the room, his mother was freshening her makeup before a mirror, her lips folded into her mouth as though she were trying to swallow them. She wore a slip and high heels, reminding Joseph of a time, at dawn, years back, when he had waited all night in bed for his sister to come home for an undressing, only to have his mother slip in through the door instead. Unwilling to let the long vigil go down the drain, he had watched her get out of some loose-fitting step-ins, not really sure he was enjoying the spectacle.

"There's the gorgeous lover," she said. "You must be starved after your good time. Go look what's doing on the table. Philly let me sneak some canapés up from the bar, fat little good things that you love and that only your mother could commandeer. Go gorge yourself. I had to fight two other mothers down there to pry them away."

"I'm not hungry," he said, sitting on the bed. "And what ever gave you the idea that I loved canapés? I was never that crazy about them. They won't solve anything."

"All right, forget I breathed a word and I'll tell you right now there isn't going to be any conversation because I can see you've been poisoned. I can just about imagine what was poured into you by those morons. I sent you out with a head that was scrubbed clean and now you're back and I've got some job cut out for me."

"Nobody poisoned anyone," he said, lying back on the bed and screwing his head into the pillow. "I just feel lousy."

"What happened, darling?" she asked, sympathetic now, sitting beside him. "Girls didn't devour you? Give them time to spot your kind and what's behind a boy like you and you'll see that you'll need a stick to keep them in line. What's the matter, your mother didn't have a period there as a young girl when she wasn't hailed? It really stifled her. Oh yeah. Go downstairs right this second in the lobby that I just arrived here and nobody's supposed to know I'm alive—and you'll see what's waiting for your mother if she gave a snap. Frankly, I think you'd be better off without an entourage of morons."

"I'm not worried about girls," said Joseph. "I had a bad time. Something happened there at the end I can't tell you."

"Your life took a tiny wrong turn and you can't stand it, is that it? You're ready to faint? Wait, darling," she said, chuckling. "Take a breath. Wait till you really have to say hello to life. Have you got some surprises coming. You think this is something? You'll want to run right back and laugh in your own face for getting excited over nothing. This baby's been there and could tell you a few. Take a look over your shoulder when you get a minute and you'll really see what's coming."

In the pillow, Joseph pictured tornadoes wiping out his home, the slow death of loved ones by Bright's disease, yet he had the feeling his mother's promised horrors were to be much more terrifying.

"In the meanwhile," she said, "while you're passing out, come over here and give me a love and I'll soothe you. Come," she said, taking his head, "I just made a lap. You know your mother could always provide you with a fast good time where no one else could. He's worried about girls. I showed a woman in the bar your picture and she was amazed I could just sit there calmly, like a normal person, not making a fuss, with a son that looks like that. Come over here fast and I'll be your social life."

"That isn't what I'm after," said Joseph, getting to his feet. "You think that's how I want to wind up the evening?"

"I can cope with the King's horses if I have to," she said exasperatedly, walking toward the sink and pouring out some Scotch, "but I could never take on a twisted head." The drink she tossed down now seemed to push her over a ledge. She swayed a little, and when she spoke, her words floated, collided as though she were talking through an ocean wave.

"You detected something and you're ready to call me on that, too. This is one for the books. All your life . . . You want to hear clarity I'll give it to you that you'll think you're tuned in to the Secretary of State. I'll give you the Yalta proceedings if you want to test me. Do you know where I'd be if I didn't take a sip? With what I've had and who I've had to prop up? Thank your powers it's only liquor. I pity your home, with the way it's always been like a pin, if I couldn't seek release. What was it, a drop, a speck, that you couldn't measure with your fingernail. Just you worry about this cookie and you'll see how far it gets you in life."

Joseph walked over to say he was sorry for his disapproving look, but then she collapsed in a little-girl squat, as though she were about to play jacks, sending off a light, alcoholic breeze and patting a place on the rug beside her.

"I'm not getting down there with you," he said. Once, a short, tense friend, bitter at being diminutive, had skimmed a garbage can lid at Joseph, catching him on the nose, causing it to hump up and giving him a forever hawkish and Indianlike profile. Now, nine years later, Joseph found himself recalling the episode, using it to lash out at his mother. "How come you never took me to get my nose set?" he asked bitterly. "It was swollen for weeks and people on the block noticed it. There was plenty of time to do something, but you let it pass, and now I just have to go around like this." Dredging up the story made him feel comfortable for the first time that night; it seemed a fine idea now to rattle off a long series of injustices he had suffered at his mother's hands; he snapped and flailed them at her as though they were chains. He reminded her of the time she had made him wear an out-of-style fingertip-length coat to a dinner in honor of muscular dystrophy victims at one of the Caruso chain restaurants. Humiliated, he had settled into a crouch on the subway, to make the coat seem full-length. Once, a heavily powdered English teacher had torn up Joseph's composition paper and sent him home early for using the phrase "black clouds of Nazi oppression," saying he had copied it from a book somewhere. "I really made that line up," he told her now, reciting the episode, "and you didn't believe me." He brought up all the times she had snatched him from deep midnight sleeps to sing "Prisoner of Love" for living room company.

"Who were those people that they were so important?" he asked her now. "How do you think I felt singing at those hours, a little boy?"

He reminded her of the long, gray afternoons she had forced him to spend in corsetieres' anterooms while she climbed in and out of Merry Widows; the winter he had chicken pox and she had whisked him along anyway on her St. Petersburg vacation, hiding him in lower berths whenever conductors strolled by. "What's the kid got on him?" asked one, who finally spotted Joseph's contagious body. "Just hives," she had hollered back.

His mother listened with a little chuckle, an appreciative sheen on her forehead, swaying slightly and saying, "I'll kill myself. And the son of a bitch remembered. Who knew it would come back? Who knew it would develop such a mouth?"

Joseph told the stories with increasing relish and confidence, a performer finding his rhythm and timing after a nervous start. He amazed himself with his recall and felt he had all the poise he lacked during the Dozens game. Somehow, though, the stories seemed more nostalgic than enraged and he tried to reach for others that had more cut to them.

"How about when you made me take a mound of kasha varnishkas to Mrs. O'Connor at the end of the fourth grade for being nice to me? How do you think it made me feel when she unwrapped it and read my name to the class?"

"Mmmmph," she said, weaving in her place, as though she had tasted a gourmet food. "His creativity."

He strained some more, bringing up the champagne dance contests she had forced him to enter each summer as her lindy-hop partner at Hirsch's Seaside Cottages. "Fling me out," she would wail when the judges passed by. "Do intricate things and they'll pass out."

"I'm not forgetting those," he said. "They were among the worst—a boy, the only one in the social hall, dancing with his mother."

"All right, now," she said, as though her patience were exhausted. "I let you recite, you had fun, now come over here fast, because if I don't get a kiss I'll tear your face off from your cuteness. Who knew about such a mouth? Get down here with your lips or there'll be all-out war."

It frustrated him that the anecdotes had come out sounding so benign and he was infuriated suddenly by her loving reaction to them. The idea flew into his head then like a small spear and would not leave.

"Say," he said, "was that guy downstairs up here tonight? While I was gone? You know, the lilac fellow from the bar last night?"

"What are you talking about?" she asked.

"You know who I mean. He was, wasn't he?"

"Are you out of your mind?" she said. "That's what you want to discuss? What am I, crazy? You think all of a sudden I forgot my mission here?" She filled her glass again and with her back to him said, "Someone visited . . . for two seconds . . . and you're carrying on. You saw a whole Chicago Fire. I can just imagine how those morons must have upset you. Didn't I just hear your mouth? That's when you don't select and you go around with cattle."

"What did he do," said Joseph, "stick his hand in your pants?"

"I don't believe what I just heard."

"Did he get you on the bed and get your boobs out? I'm sorry, I didn't mean that one."

"And that's what you were saving for me, darling?" she said, lifting her eyes to him, sweetly, horrifyingly sober.

"I wasn't saving it," said Joseph. "It just came out. You know I don't say things like that. Look, maybe I really ought to move into that place, the Boone. It doesn't have to be with the guys you met. There are other people there. I really do think it would be best."

"I'll tell you what, sweetheart," she said now, getting to her feet and wiping her mascara. "As long as you're capable of having a new kind of mouth that I'd give a nickel to know who supplied you with it, tomorrow morning I'll quietly pack my bag and buy a ticket and you won't even know I'm gone. How's that, fast enough for you? And we'll see how far your new mouth will get you."

"It doesn't have to be tomorrow morning. That isn't what I was getting at. But you know there isn't a single mother in the whole place."

"I'll pay my bill like a lady and I'll have a fast breakfast. Wait a second. I'll go you one better, I won't even *stop* for breakfast. I'll have my bags picked up, the porter will get me a cab—he knows the way I tip and I think he'd hand over his head if I asked him—and I'll be gone before you can say Jack Robinson, and you'll forget there was even a mother here. You want action, you want speed, I'll give it to you in spades. Okay, darling? Now get a Kleenex and wipe your face."

272

"I didn't say one word about tomorrow," said Joseph, a guilty tingle curling through him. "You're missing the whole point."

But the next morning he awoke to find her looming above him, stale and bedraggled in a bathrobe, eyes still sealed with sleep, a cigarette bouncing on her bottom lip. She held an armload of clothing and said, "All right, slip into these. They're nice and fresh. I want to see how pretty you'll look. Don't ask what time I was up doing a little ironing. That's just your mother's kind of work."

"I thought you said you were going," said Joseph.

"I can't be accountable for what was said when people were flaring. There was a little excitement—it's a wonder I didn't go out of my mind with the snares that were placed in my path. You think it's easy tackling a strange farmland that who even knew it existed six months ago? They ought to put up statues for the way your mother's conducted herself like a rock. So if there was a little venom you'll have to fluff it right off. It's the only healthy way."

"I'm not fluffing anything off. Not when a person says they're clearing out and then they don't. Now I'm really sore. I can't believe what's happening. This is like some disease that I wake up every morning and still have."

After class that day, Joseph for the first time bypassed his mother entirely and went straight to the Boone, flinging open his books and telling Feldman-Forsythe, "This is really great. I can absorb things here. You can't do that with a mother around." The other boy backed against the radiator, twisted his neck and shot his eyes toward the ceiling. "A guy in an institution at midnight," he said to Joseph. "He's gone to the latrine and on his way back to his bed he suddenly gets panicky." Then, in a tortured croak, Feldman-Forsythe addressed himself to imaginary ward patients: "Help me, please. Help me, please. You're laughing, I'm dying."

Joseph's mother took his first absence casually. "You want to test your mother's nerves?" she said when he returned late at night to the Goatback. "See who bites the dust first?" But each day thereafter, he stayed away a little longer, clenching the sides of Feldman-Forsythe's desk, ducking into the pages and holding his breath, a swimmer trying for a new underwater record. Her behavior then became scattered; one night she greeted him at the hotel door with a bag of litchi nuts. "What's the deal?" he asked, cracking a few.

"You used to love them from the Chinese laundry when you were a pup. A little bag would shut you up for a week. Don't ask the channels I had to go through to get them into this Godforsaken place. In case you think your mother's brain hasn't been active."

At one point she began to feel that college was bad for Joseph and was throwing poison on the feeling they had for one another; she spoke then of golden opportunities in theatrical public relations, a field in which college training was scoffed at. "Say the word 'college' to them and they'll throw you right out on your ear," she said. "But don't kid yourself. They make some living. I'd like to tell you a few stories about the cute little $80,000 summer homes those boys have been able to buy because they're supposed to be starving." For some mysterious reason, when Joseph was ten, she had become fascinated by the theatrical public relations game and decided to spare no effort in seeing to it that he became a Broadway agent; one day she whipped him downtown to see one of the great ones, a man who had handled thirty straight Katherine Cornell farces. Joseph did not know what to say to the fabled pressman and finally asked, "How do I become one?"

"It blows hot and cold. What do you need it for?" the man said and then wheeled around to check billboards for the new Cornell.

"And you don't think he'd remember you?" Joseph's mother said to him now. "With the way he admired your head even when you were an embryo? I only hope to Christ he's alive and he'd be tickled to death to move you right in with him. Then you know where you can put your college."

"That's the last thing I want to be," said Joseph. "A theatrical press agent. You become one, it's your idea."

"Continue to fight me," she answered. "But if you listened to your mother you'd be on velvet. How many boys would prostrate themselves to have your connections in the theater?"

One night she called to him from the Goatback cocktail lounge. "Come in and look at the godsend your mother corralled." A heavily pockmarked stalk of a man sat beside her. "Take a look at him," she said, "the wrath of the gods, right? And yet would you believe on your life that this used to sing with Pupi Campo? We had some laughs together at Pechter's Hillview. Don't get your mother started on the grace in his body, what he does quietly with his hips when nobody's looking. He was just passing through and God knows what kind of ditch he'll wind up in, but if I never live another day I want him to hear your voice."

"I could tell on a couple of bars," said the man.

"You're starting that again?" said Joseph. "All the way out here at college? I'm not singing in any lounge. You think I'm crazy?"

"And he was always ashamed, too, with that voice and how it tore my heart out. Tell him, Ruby, what professional singers would do to have real vocal cords. Aren't you being silly? If he hears one note that he likes he'll get you right next to Campo, Noras Morales, he knows them all. You want Cugat, he can touch him, too. You'd let that voice and what it's capable of doing to me just lay there?"

"Make your ma happy, kid. Give me a little in my ear."

"You won't be able to tell anything that way," said Joseph. He sang a few notes and then said, "Jesus, that's all I'm doing."

"It's hard to tell, Meg," said the man. "He might have something, he might not. With his kind of tone you got to hear more."

"The cockeyed son of a bitch," she said. "So who asked him in the first place? He's so coked up he doesn't know what day of the week it is. Don't worry, you insist on Cugat, I'll get you in to see him myself. What is he suddenly, the Prime Minister? I was never afraid to face anybody in my life, a doctor, anyone. I really need this bargain here. He was no damned good when I met him and he's a worse mess now."

And then one day, like Marshal Joffre retiring to a new defense line, she accepted quite gracefully the idea that Joseph could not stay at the Goatback forever; it was important only to keep him from the wilds of the Boone. She learned of a mother-and-daughter team of sociology teachers with a room to rent and arranged for Joseph and herself to meet them at the Goatback lounge. When he got there, both mother and daughter were at the bar, their hair in Russian buns, the daughter fingering a sparse mustache above her lip.

"I took one look at the daughter and I know the whole setup," his mother said, heading off Joseph at the door. "A brilliant mind, but wait till you see what's going on above her lip. A whole jungle. The mother had her hidden away in Israel for two years, but she's back now and God forbid what she's going to be able to do with her. A room? I think she'd give up fourteen houses if she knew she could palm off that creature. Still, what do you care? You'll have clean sheets, I'll get them to throw in a breakfast, and if you're asked to give the daughter a little charm you'll croak but you'll swallow your pride and you'll do that, too. And your mother won't have to worry that you're with degenerates in a hotel. The old lady's another story. She has an authoritative air I can't stand, but I baffle her and she'd give her life to be able to penetrate me."

"A clash of the matriarchs," the daughter said to Joseph after the introductions.

"Ummmph, a mind on it," said Joseph's mother. "I'd like to know where they get such brilliance these days. Don't worry, my son will give her back some. Go ahead, Joseph."

"I don't know sociology," he said. The daughter smiled, her teeth still filmed with earthy kibbutz delicacies.

"Lomi does not yet have many nice young friends on the campus," said the older woman.

Joseph's mother took her arm and said, "So she'll have my son, and believe me, sweetheart, when I tell you she won't need anyone else."

An appointment was made for Joseph and his mother to inspect the room; in the early evening they took a cab to the outskirts of town, parking in the driveway. The porch lights suddenly blinked out and when they rang the doorbell there was silence.

"That's when you have Israel and that's when you have too much smartness and I didn't like those severe little buns either. Your mother could handle anything in life but she could never cope with fanaticism. Wait till she tries to palm that daughter off on someone else. She's going to have some picnic on her hands. Come, I'll get you a dozen rooms once I get started."

"The Boone's not so bad," said Joseph.

That night Feldman-Forsythe arranged a date for Joseph with a slow-witted farm girl who reportedly forked over her plump backwoods body seconds after introductory handshakes. To keep her as pure as possible, her sorority roommates had trussed her up from knee to shoulder with intricately webbed, circulation-pinching foundation garments, then wheeled her out to the lawn like Lancelot before a joust. Joseph picked her up at dark and carted her along to the rear of the stadium where he tried for hours to fight through her network of heavy, powerfully seamed contraptions. "How are you coming?" she asked from time to time as though he were a mechanic fixing her sports car. "It's a bitch," he would answer, hacking and prying at her metallic dainties. When night was nearly gone, he hauled her back to the sorority house, totally unsuccessful but for one dull sliver of upper back he had jimmied loose in the final hour. As they got to the porch, she told him not to be dismayed. "I wear skirts and sweaters on second dates."

"There'll be none," he hollered and then hurried back to the Goatback.

As he stepped beneath the front awning of the hotel, a patrol car pulled up at the sidewalk, carrying his mother, nightgowned and chain-smoking in the front seat.

"All right, let me sit here a second, officer," she said. "Thank God I saw a whole body and I saw breathing. Right now, I'll settle for that. Because I swear on my life if I ever thought I'd lay eyes on that child again."

The doors of the car were stuck and the two patrolmen inside said they would have to ease Joseph's mother through the driver's seat window.

"And I'll survive this, too," she said, as she was being passed along to the sidewalk. "And I'll end up bigger and more powerful than ever."

She yanked down her nightgown and asked Joseph, "All right, where were you that I wasn't allowed to hear a voice on a telephone? That it wasn't important enough that I be contacted? And how I always trained you to use a dial."

"I was out with a girl," said Joseph. "I don't see that it was a police emergency."

"Don't sass your mom," said the driver, who had slipped through the window after Joseph's mother.

"That's all right, officer, I'm used to it. I found out that I have a very smart son in college who suddenly developed public speaking. I don't have a boy any more, I have Winston Churchill."

"Instead of showing freshness," she said to Joseph, "go over to those officers and lick their feet because if it wasn't for their support you'd be without a mother. Those are some grand guys, I don't care where in the hell they're from. Not that they're going to lose anything on the deal when they see the little packages I have in mind for their wives."

Joseph thanked the officers, adding "But it really wasn't necessary."

"That mouth," his mother said, biting her fist, letting out a silent scream and sweeping him into the hotel.

"Did you see the face on the one who was driving?" she asked, unlocking the door of the room. "The grooming of his hair when he took off his cap? And he didn't know it either, did he? I'll bet he's very faithful, too, in his lovely marriage. Until he gets across the street. I think he would have enjoyed sliding me through that goddamned window a few more times. They have some gorgeous sons of bitches out here. And that's with the farming and the innocence and that they're not supposed to know they're alive. Meanwhile, I think that very quietly New York faces can take a back seat to what's doing right around this hotel.

"All right," she said, sinking into the bed, "what kind of a girl was it?" Her stockings had been torn in the patrol car evacuation and the flesh came through at the knees in scuffed and domelike blisters. "I can just about imagine if you had her out till all hours. To tell the truth, it isn't a very pleasant thing to hear. You don't need that while you're getting settled. You can talk to me. Just because I can't give you sex, is that what you're worried about?"

On the way to the room he felt as though he had been carrying the vision of her in the patrol car strapped securely to his side in a small, highly volatile glycerine capsule; now it seemed to slip down his leg and ignite, scalding the length of him. When he spoke, his voice climbed a ladder, getting louder on each rung. "Cancel out anything else I may have said. But now I'm really saying it to you. When you start in with cops and patrol cars you've got to get the hell out of here. What if somebody saw that production? I really want you to get the hell home and leave me alone."

She ignored his words as though they were bad cards she had drawn in an important poker hand; she needed more time to fiddle before picking them up and accepting them.

"I needed to bail out of a car to round out the picture," she said. "To test my nerves a little. You know how it's been for me out here? Did you ever have something rub you that no matter how swell it was it went against your grain? Your Aunt Hester's like that with her saintliness, and that's how this college has been to me, too."

She poured a drink with hands that seemed befuddled and then she was ready to pick up the cards.

"I don't believe what you just said because if you wanted me to go you would have said so before. If you'd uttered one sound I would have been on the next train. You think it's been a picnic for me out here? I don't have your father waiting that if I'm not there to guide him he's like a helpless imbecile? I don't have an apartment to paint that I'd be ashamed to bring the worst derelict in the neighborhood in to see it? And your sister to contend with that if she insists on that thing in the overcoat that's what she'll get? And I'll make a wedding for her anyway and I'll stand up proud with my chest out to here and I'll withstand that, too. Your mother has nothing to do in the city? I don't have organizations waiting for me that if I wanted to condescend and become that type there aren't women who'd give their right arms to have me on their side? There aren't charities that are passing out right now for your mother's interest? Real poor ones, my kind, on the lower East Side, that could break your heart? That when I go to them quietly with fat bundles when nobody's looking I don't have to insert an ad in the paper telling everyone to look what I did? There isn't a job waiting for me as a receptionist in my millinery shop for sixty-five dollars a week that Polly knows good and well she would get it back, times ten, with the trade your mother's charm would lure into the store? There isn't a judge—we'll forget what's on his mind for the moment—who wants to set me up in politics that if I let him you'd never see me standing in supermarkets like Mrs. Saltzman, the very important district attorney's wife, to save three cents on a can of string beans? It's so becoming. There aren't forty-two positions on Broadway that I could step into with how I forgot more about the theater than J. J. Shubert ever knew? With how I spotted Ethel Merman when nobody knew she was alive and said, 'That girl's going places'? How I picked Van Johnson out of a lowly chorus line on the end and said, 'He's not kicking that high for nothing'? And when I raved about Gene Kelly and they said I was nuts? You're afraid your mother will be idle? That she'll wilt? I don't have fourteen offers a day to sit like a madonna and play mah-jongg if I wanted to be the kind that doesn't care if their families croak as long as they've got their pleasure? And if their husbands get a hard-boiled egg for dinner that night, that's all right, too? Sometimes I wonder who's better off, the other kind that sits and is smug and says to the world, 'All right, entertain me' or your mother with the way she's constructed and how she could love that it's not even healthy.

"All right, I'm leaving tomorrow. And if you'd opened up your mouth just once, if there'd been a peep, one syllable, a nuance, I'd have been out of here a month ago. What am I supposed to do, read your mind?"

The following morning she awakened early and stormed into the day, healthy, exuberant, brown-armed, humming to herself, stuffing clothes into her valise with great-breasted vigor. When Joseph woke up and got his toothbrush, she said, "Oh, you're coming with me? I wasn't going to wake you. There's a check that'll carry you for the first month on the sink. And you'll receive others, right on the dot, so put your mind at ease."

"I'll skip my first class," said Joseph. "It isn't important." It was a course in beginning French, which Joseph felt for a while was going to be his only nonagricultural area of study. Not until the second week did he notice a heavy emphasis on names of leafy vegetables. (It turned out later that the accent being taught was that of a small group of embittered shepherds who had broken with metropolitan France, sealing themselves off in the northern provinces to develop their own mode of speech, their own embittered customs.)

He could not remember his mother ever looking more robust, and for the first time it occurred to him that she must be of hardy stock and that he himself might live to get into his seventies. She gave not the slightest sign there had been any trouble between them the previous night; in the lobby she stopped off to kiss the lady hotel clerks goodby, handing each of them slender tissued packages. She made a great fuss over the clerks, and Joseph just naturally took it for granted that each was a special person. He wondered, if he had been on his own and just run into one of them, whether he would have known she was of such Olympian importance. His mother returned to Joseph and said, "As long as they live, they'll never forget Meg. You should know what I slipped each of them that I ought to get my head examined. They never saw stuff like that from the Pope."

Joseph had hoped for a bleak day to fit his mood, but the early sun was bright and cool, catching him upon the forehead and spinning him around in a nauseated circle. His mother's mouth was mint-fresh, her hair combed in a subdued style. Tapping her foot on the pavement, as they waited for a cab, she hummed quietly and said, "Dad will faint when he sees me. He'll think I had an accident." The cabdriver was a petulant, womanish fellow who wore an apron. He put the valises in the trunk and when Joseph and his mother had gotten in and closed the door, he said, "Hey, easy on that, will you? You want to break it?"

"Pardon me," said Joseph's mother. "Don't look now, but we just stepped into Buckingham Palace." There were signs posted on the cab's interior saying, "Would you do *that* in your own home?" and "I do not have a brother in the carpeting business.

Ashes in the ashtray, please." Joseph's mother read them and said, "Listen, what do you do if you want to breathe in here? I hailed a cab and I'm in the Smithsonian Institute." He scowled back as he drove, but she teased him along the way, telling him he ought to relax a little, that he wasn't a bad-looking fellow and that she bet he could have plenty of nice women if he took off the apron and behaved like a human being. By the time they reached the station, the fellow was chuckling to himself, and when she paid the fare and gave him a half-dollar tip, he wheeled about and pressed the cash back in her hand.

"Please, miss, you keep this. Please, you're a wonderful woman."

"Keep the goddamned thing," she said impatiently. "What is it to me?"

"No, I'd like for you to have it," he said, toothless, unshaven. His smile seemed to call upon muscles that had long gone unused. "In Jewish, we have an expression for it. We call it *mazzel*. Luck. Keep this for *mazzel*."

Joseph's mother kept the coin this time and began to cry as she opened the door. "I can have something like this happen to me," she said, turning to Joseph, "and you want me to worry about being put away on a train."

"Stay another few days," said Joseph. It went quickly after that. Without realizing it they had almost missed the train. It was in the station, on the single track, hot and smoking. Joseph saw his mother to her seat, kissed her hair and then walked back onto the platform. Involuntarily he leaped back on the first step of the passenger car, then got off, repeating this action several times in what might have been a new leg exercise for soldiers in transfer. He had to stop when the train began to move and then he trotted alongside it until he came to the end of the platform. Stopping there, he began to holler things after his mother, first softly, then at the top of his lungs, anything

285

he wanted to: "What was the rush?" and "You're not great at all."

"I never enjoyed one second with you," he shouted, and kept on, fairly much in the same manner, until the shriek of the engine no longer covered his words.